"I've been enjoyi... workshopped with him back in 1996. In the ensuing years, he's gone on to win Aurora Awards for his fiction and more Aurora Awards as an organizer of literary events. He's a wonderfully gifted fantasist with a light comedic touch. After a high-tech career, he's recently transitioned to full-time writing... and the worlds of fantastic fiction and of Canadian literature will be the richer for it. I was one of Randy's first fans— but you can be his latest. Read this book, then seek out everything else he's written; you'll be glad you did."
—Robert J. Sawyer,
Hugo Award-winning author of *Red Planet Blues*

"McCharles uses a wry sense of humor..."
—Kris Rudin, *goodreads*

"...well done."
—Rich Horton, *Locus*

Awards and Recognition

Winner: *Anansi Press* Seven Day Ghost Story Contest
Winner: Aurora Award ("The Saint")
Winner: Aurora Award ("Ringing in the Changes in Okotoks")

THE NECROMANCER CANDLE

And Two Additional Tales of Contemporary Fantasy

Randy McCHARLES

EDGE
EDGE SCIENCE FICTION AND FANTASY PUBLISHING
AN IMPRINT OF HADES PUBLICATIONS, INC.
CALGARY

The Necromancer Candle:
And Two Additional Tales of Contemporary Fantasy
Copyright © 2014 by Randy McCharles

This is a work of fiction. Names, characters, places, and incidents are the products of the author's imagination or are used fictitiously and are not to be construed as real. Any resemblance to actual events, locales, organizations, or persons, living or dead, is entirely coincidental.

EDGE

Edge Science Fiction and Fantasy Publishing
An Imprint of Hades Publications Inc.
P.O. Box 1714, Calgary, Alberta, T2P 2L7, Canada

Editing by Anita Hades
Interior design by Janice Blaine
Cover Illustration & Design by Neil Jackson

ISBN: 978-1-77053-066-9

All rights reserved. No part of this book may be reproduced, scanned, or distributed in any printed or electronic form without written permission. Please do not participate in or encourage piracy of copyrighted materials in violation of the author's rights. Purchase only authorized editions.

EDGE Science Fiction and Fantasy Publishing and Hades Publications, Inc. acknowledges the ongoing support of the Alberta Foundation for the Arts and the Canada Council for the Arts for our publishing programme.

Alberta   Canada Council   Conseil des arts
                 for the Arts   du Canada

Library and Archives Canada Cataloguing in Publication

McCharles, Randy, author
The necromancer candle : and two additional tales of contemporary fantasy / Randy McCharles. -- First edition.

ISBN: 978-1-77053-066-9
(e-book ISBN: 978-1-77053-067-6)

I. Title.
PS8625.C43N43 2014   C813'.6   C2014-903413-X
                                    C2014-903414-8

FIRST EDITION
(G-20140625)
Printed in Canada
www.edgewebsite.com

TABLE OF CONTENTS

The Necromancer Candle 1

Full House 83

Merlin's Silver 163

DEDICATION

This book is dedicated to the members of the Imaginative Fiction Writers Association (IFWA), many of whom provided feedback on various drafts, for their support of Calgary, Alberta's writing community.

THE NECROMANCER CANDLE

PROLOGUE

Near Prague, 1161 A.D.

The wind outside the bone house howled with the agony of whole herds of pigs being slaughtered, their moist flesh thrown onto the coals, the bones, skin and fat tied together to be brought to Master Dupek and then boiled and separated, the tallow gleaned for the dipping of candles. Yet Jiri knew it was not pigs he heard in the wind. The pigs had been slaughtered hours earlier. What howled now was something else.

Master Dupek shouted from the doorway. "Is the cauldron ready?" The old boneman leaned heavily against the open door, his skeletal hands clutching at the wooden beam as though to keep his lean frame from being blown out into the storm.

"The water begins to steam," Jiri answered from where he stood hunched over the vast cauldron, waiting for the heat of the flames and warming water to seep beneath his skin and thaw his numb hands.

If Jiri was cold, the old boneman must be half frozen. If only he would close the door and trap the escaping warmth inside.

On most winter nights the bone house was a source of boundless heat, but shortly after nightfall Master Dupek had returned unexpected and ordered Jiri to empty and clean the cauldron.

"But the rendering has only just begun," Jiri complained. He gestured to the huge vat where the fat and bones from the slaughtered pigs had scarce begun to boil. It was Jiri's task to attend the boiling and rendering which took all the hours of night. With the rising sun he would collect the white fat from the surface of the cauldron into a tall, narrow kettle in which Master Dupek would dip the wicks, later to sell the candles to the townsfolk.

"We'll have new fat," Master Dupek had said. "Bishop Straka brings rendering to be made into candles. And," the old boneman smiled rapaciously, "he'll pay richer coin than the dirty pennies of the townsfolk."

"Have the Church bonemen died then?" asked Jiri, for he could see no reason for the Church with its copper kettles and perfumed beeswax to seek tallow candles from the town.

"Don't be a fool!" spat Master Dupek. "When the Church offers to pay good silver, you don't ask why."

And so Jiri had cooled the fires and dumped the cauldron into the trench, scraped the metal clean, poured in fresh water and added new wood. And as he did, the storm had risen and the sky grown cold, and the heat from the newly stoked fire was not sufficient to warm him.

Outside the open doorway, lightning broke the sky much like the fingers of leading in the stained glass of the tall church on the hill above the town. Time was, after long nights tending the cauldron, Jiri had enjoyed going to morning mass. Old Bishop Dagar had never spoken with a loud voice or acted condescending when Jiri didn't have a penny for the plate. But when the old Bishop had died, the town died with him.

The arrival of Bishop Straka had failed to resurrect the town. If anything, the town had died anew. The new Bishop never smiled, nor had a good word for anyone. And from the pulpit he preached brimstone and damnation. Jiri had not once heard the words *love* or *forgiveness* leave the new Bishop's lips.

Jiri had ceased attending mass, as had others. Neither was he fool enough, despite Master Dupek's frequent calling him such, not to notice how some of the townsfolk flocked to Bishop Straka. Townsfolk who had sneered at old Bishop Dagar.

The sky outside the bone house blossomed again with lightning, illuminating Master Dupek's gaunt face. Master Dupek was one of those who had sneered.

The wind, if it were possible, increased its wailing. Jiri smelled smoke, or thought he did. There was too much wind for fire to burn. Too much icy damp in the air.

The lightning raged a third time and Jiri knew the storm was not natural. It seemed a battle cry. Or a cry of bitter wounding. Or both. Evil imbued the night.

Jiri knew what evil was. Not the stench of raw flesh boiling in a cauldron, though the townsfolk said the stink was the worst evil there was, almost as bad as the tallow candles Master Dupek sold them. Jiri knew real evil. Tiny children laid out in pine boxes.

Wars that took the town's strong men and killed them, with no benefit to the town that Jiri could see. Disease wasting young and old alike. Theft, and murder, and hate. All these were evil. Then there was the secret evil Bishop Dagar had claimed was in the world. The Serpent's Lie, more subtle and dangerous than any wrong devised by mortal Man.

The evil in the wind and the lightning was of that sort. The kind that crept into one's soul and made a man shudder for no reason he could put his finger on. Jiri could warn Master Dupek that the lightning was evil, but the old boneman would just call him a fool. "Lightning is lightning," he would say. "It just is. Now get back to work."

Jiri could hear screaming in the wind. Not the wail of gusting air through the houses and trees, but the death cries of a soul being rent.

The lightning flashed a final time and Jiri knew that would be the end of it. The battle was over, the outcome decided, and not to the good he was sure.

Master Dupek cursed in the doorway and Jiri could see that it had begun to rain. The wind was dying and, except for the hammering of raindrops against the bone house roof and the hard earth outside, the night had grown silent.

"I see him," said Master Dupek.

Despite the heavy fall of rain, Jiri could hear movement outside, the tread of many men slogging across ground grown suddenly muddy. Through the open doorway he looked past the boneman to see the new Bishop, tall and imposing in his scarlet cape, kicking up mud as he stamped toward the shelter of the bone house.

Bishop Straka pushed through the doorway with a fury of animal triumph and flying water. His mitre, rochet, and cape were sopping. Water coursed down his face and beard. Master Dupek fell back as the Bishop brushed past him and stood examining the iron cauldron and its accompanying implements. The Bishop's deep, coal eyes were sharp and fierce as he took in the rough metal and the smoking branches of the fire. "It will have to do," he said. The Bishop did not see Jiri standing beyond the cauldron. Jiri was beneath the Bishop's notice.

A half-dozen men followed the Bishop into the bone house. They were dressed in the scarlet and black of the Church garrison. Soldiers of Christ. Bishop Dagar had not required any of the townsfolk to serve the Church in this fashion. Bishop Straka, on the other hand, had made himself a small army.

Between them, Straka's Church Dogs dragged a man, broken and stripped of most of his clothing, and threw him onto the ground before the cauldron. Blood leaked darkly from several wounds.

"Your Eminence?" Master Dupek asked in a strained voice. "Where... where is the vegetable oil and beeswax?"

Jiri knew his master had made a mistake even before the Bishop cast him his barbed gaze. Straka said nothing, but turned his cold eyes to the man on the ground.

Master Dupek's face paled, and then he squinted at the beaten man's face. The old boneman trembled. "The necromancer," he whispered.

Bishop Straka's lips parted in a feral grin. "Yes. The sorcerer himself. Milos Radimir. Old Dagar would not raise a finger against him, but I am unafraid. God is on my side."

As are the Church Dogs, thought Jiri. With their strong arms and swords. Jiri had recognized poor Milos when the Dogs first threw his beaten body to the earthen floor.

Old Bishop Dagar, too, had called Milos a sorcerer, a necromancer, for the small magics he was rumored to practice in his house by the river. Some few went to Milos for simple healings and advice, and no one was ever hurt. Bishop Dagar had seen no cause to make trouble.

Bishop Straka, however, delighted in trouble. He beckoned to one of his Dogs who produced a sack filled with silver moulds. Jiri had seen candle moulds before, used only by the Church and the wealthiest of townsfolk for the making of ornamental candles, candles that look pretty on a table or shelf, but that burned poorly or inefficiently. The Bishop's moulds, however, were unlike any Jiri had ever seen. They stood six inches high and four inches across, with a delicate hinge along one side that allowed them to snap open after the tallow had hardened. From the flickering light of the cauldron fire, Jiri saw the suggestion of etchings on the inner surface of the moulds.

"You will make twelve candles," Bishop Straka told Master Dupek. "Fill the moulds to an even height so that none is taller than the others. You must use all the renderings. Throw none away. Add nothing to contaminate the tallow. Fail me in this," the Bishop glared at Master Dupek, "and you will pay with your soul."

Master Dupek looked again at the man lying beaten on the ground. Jiri watched in silence as the boneman made his second mistake. "But, your Eminence, he isn't dead."

That Master Dupek made no complaint of rendering a human body led Jiri to believe that he had done this before. How many rich folk, Jiri wondered, even now display trophies on their shelves— candles made from the fat of their enemies?

Bishop Straka scowled at Milos Radimir. "He is a necromancer. Cold steel will not kill him. But no man, not even a sorcerer, can survive the cauldron. He'll be dead when he is in your pot an hour." The Bishop nodded to one of his Dogs. "Stay here and see to it the boneman does as he's told." Then he led the others out into the rain.

When the door was closed, Master Dupek cursed and yelled at Jiri to remove the necromancer's remaining garments.

Jiri did as he was told. He did not know whose wrath he feared more, Master Dupek's or Bishop Straka's. The Bishop's Watchdog, scowling near the door, would make a detailed report.

The necromancer did not resist Jiri's ministrations. He was badly beaten, stabbed repeatedly, and bled from at least a dozen wounds that should have been fatal. The dirt where he lay was fast becoming thick with black mud. Only the slow rise and fall of the man's chest convinced Jiri that he was alive. Perhaps the Bishop's words were true, that Milos Radimir could not be killed by the sword.

Jiri prodded the necromancer's trousers and smallclothes into the flames beneath the cauldron. There was a ring on the middle finger of the right hand that Jiri removed and slipped into his pocket before Master Dupek's greedy eye could see it. The Bishop's Dog did not seem to care.

Milos opened his eyes and looked at Jiri, but there was no anger there. No hatred. Only sadness, making Jiri feel all the worse for being party to this evil.

"Let's get him into the pot," Master Dupek muttered, gripping the necromancer beneath the arms. Jiri quickly took the feet and together they lifted the still-living man into the cauldron.

The water was hot, though not yet boiling. Milos did not resist, nor did he breathe a sound as his flesh was lowered into the scalding bath. The necromancer was very light, Jiri thought, like smoke, though his flesh felt warm and solid. As his head slipped beneath the water, Jiri prayed that Milos did not have the strength to raise it up again. Drowning would be a quicker, easier death than boiling.

When they were finished, Straka's Dog snorted and glared at them like they were about the devil's work, which Jiri believed was true despite it being the Bishop's bidding.

Master Dupek slouched to a far corner and sat on a crate, where he stared at the cauldron without seeming to see it.

Jiri alone stood by the steaming cauldron, more for penance than a desire to thaw his frozen bones, which still could not seem to get warm. Within the pot, the water steamed and swirled, like smoke in a troubled breeze. He expected at any moment for the scalded man to leap up screaming from the cauldron and run naked into the icy rains outside; but within the clouded water there was no movement.

Jiri had heard gossip of Milos Radimir, that the man was a self-made healer who had learned to tap into the forces of nature. Widow Novosad claimed he had raised her youngest son from the dead, thus earning him the title necromancer. Milos had denied the praise and denied also that he consorted with demons. Old Bishop Dagar had agreed. "God made nature. If Milos has learned in some small way to use one of God's tools, what evil is there? So long as his heart is good."

Bishop Straka did not share his Church-brother's view. "Radimir is a sorcerer and a heretic, and must be destroyed." And this night Straka's will had won out. What, Jiri could not help but wonder, would Bishop Straka do with the ungodly candles?

A small bubble broke the surface of the water, followed by another, and soon the water was well to boiling. Necromancer or no, surely the man was now dead.

"Fool," Master Dupek muttered bitterly from his cold corner of the bone house. "The fire needs wood. Can you not perform the simplest of tasks?"

Jiri quickly began feeding branches and hewn bark to the embers beneath the cauldron. How long had he been staring into the waters? Straka's Dog, he saw, was leaning against the bone house wall, his sword sheathed and his eyes half-closed. Master Dupek had not moved, but now wore a blanket about his shoulders. The cauldron emanated heat like an oven, but the boneman would not come near it.

Jiri found he was no longer cold. Sweat rolled down his face and soaked his clothes, but it was not a comfortable warmth; he had preferred feeling numb.

The water in the cauldron had become a roiling soup. Jiri could not help but envision Milos lying in its depth, the dead man's flesh softening with the heat and coming free of the bones.

The burning wood beneath the cauldron filled the bone house with a familiar smoke. Even so, Jiri imagined he could smell tallow smoke, the acrid aroma of burning candles. The necromancer had used candles in his magic, he remembered suddenly. Not the beeswax candles from the Church or the tallow candles Master Dupek made, but candles of his own devising. Milos Radimir had been a man of moderate means, and kept his own kettle and cloth and candle moulds.

"Stir," the old boneman said angrily from his crate.

It was too soon to stir, but Jiri did as he was told. The wooden paddle was stout as a boat oar, though shorter. It slid into the boiling water along the side of the cauldron and moved freely along the bottom. Jiri felt the necromancer's body shift as the oar scraped along the cauldron wall. In no place had flesh stuck to the hot metal. It was too soon. Jiri pulled the paddle out of the water.

"Must I do everything!" Master Dupek screamed as he stamped across the bone house and wrenched the paddle from Jiri's hands. The oar broke the water with a violent splash that threatened to spill over the cauldron's sides. The old boneman stirred vigorously. His eyes were wild, and within them Jiri could see the shame of a murderer.

Straka's Dog came awake at Master Dupek's agitation, and eyed the boneman.

Tiring quickly, Master Dupek thrust the paddle back into Jiri's hands. "You know what to do. I shall return before sunrise." Without another word the old boneman stamped out into the rain.

Through the open door, Jiri watched him go. The bone house had grown hot so there was now no need to close it. A shadowed figure slouched after Master Dupek, another of Straka's dogs.

Jiri removed the paddle from the cauldron and set himself to waiting, which was what most of his job entailed. The water settled into a steady boil, and the stench of smoke was stronger than ever. Straka's Dog moved further away from the cauldron, but remained alert after his earlier doze.

The hours of night passed, with Jiri feeding just enough wood to the flames to keep the cauldron at a boil. He stirred the contents regularly to prevent the renderings from sticking to the hot metal. Slowly, the bubbles of oil on the water's surface thickened into an oily film.

Shortly before dawn Jiri let the flames die down and the bone house began to cool. Straka's Dog, instead of approaching the cauldron for warmth, shut the door and took up Master Dupek's blanket.

Jiri stirred the vat, expertly freeing up pockets of oil from the flesh and bones in the depth of the pot. When further stirring threatened to contaminate the congealing tallow on the surface, he set Master Dupek's brass dipping kettle over a smaller fire, poured in two inches of clear water, and tied a loosely woven cloth across the top.

With a shallow ladle, Jiri scooped the rendered fat off the surface of the cauldron and poured it onto the taut cloth. The tallow remained liquid enough to leak through the loose weave, which collected tiny bits of bone, flesh, and other impurities like fish in a net.

Jiri had performed this task so often that he could forget the tallow came from a man and not a pig or a sheep. It was a long, onerous task, requiring waiting for the cloth to drain before adding more tallow.

During this time the rain ceased to fall and Master Dupek returned, though the roughness about his eyes and in his voice suggested that he had slept little. The old boneman stared into the cauldron and complained that Jiri had not done as the Bishop had instructed and harvested all the tallow.

Jiri said nothing, but repeatedly scraped his ladle across the surface water, scooping up tiny globules of oily tallow and pouring them onto the cloth.

When at last Master Dupek was satisfied, Jiri removed the filthy screen from the kettle and stirred the creamy white liquid with a clean metal spoon. Since the boneman had kept him overlong with the cauldron, gleaning for fat, the tallow and water mixture in the dipping kettle had become too thick. Soon it would burn and blacken. Jiri quickly added additional water beneath Dupek's scowling gaze and stirred the tallow to an even thickness.

"Now it is too thin," grumbled the boneman. But without further castigation he went to his work table and set out a wide board upon which he placed the Bishop's moulds. With bony fingers he snapped the hinged edges together: twelve silver cups with no bottoms. Jiri derided himself for not examining the unusual moulds during the long night.

Master Dupek's usual morning task was to dip lengths of twisted flax into the narrow kettle, repeating his efforts until tall, thin candles hardened about them. In the afternoon he would sell the results of his labor to the townsfolk.

Candle moulds were more difficult. One mould at a time, Master Dupek held twisted flax through the center of the mould while Jiri lifted the hot kettle and poured the steaming tallow.

"Spill that and Bishop Straka will have *you* in the cauldron next," said the Soldier of God.

"Fool," Master Dupek muttered, though Jiri was not certain whether the boneman meant him or Straka's Dog.

Jiri poured until each mould was almost filled before moving onto the next. He remembered the Bishop's words that the candles were to be of the same height, and knew he would be told to melt the candles down and start again if Straka was not satisfied.

When the twelve moulds were done, Jiri set the kettle back over the flames to loosen the remaining tallow and then quickly added a spoonful more to each of the moulds. Master Dupek grunted and cursed as he cut the wicks and smoothed the surface of the candles with practiced fingers.

"Is it done?" boomed an acid voice from the doorway.

Jiri looked up to see Bishop Straka and his contingent of Dogs.

"The moulds need to cool," said Master Dupek. "But not too long or the candles will break when they are opened."

Bishop Straka sniffed at the now lukewarm cauldron. Chunks of flesh and bone floated on the surface and the smell was insufferable. The Bishop seemed not to mind. His gaze searched for unharvested tallow but seem satisfied there was none.

He pointed to two of his Dogs. "Bring it," he said and turned to go. The Soldiers of God lifted the board with the twelve candle moulds and followed the Bishop outside. The rest, including the Dog who had stayed with Jiri through night, followed.

Master Dupek watched them go in silence and apparent relief, then remembered that he had not been paid.

"Clean this up!" he snapped at Jiri before racing out the door after the Bishop.

Jiri waited only a moment before piling wood onto the embers beneath the cauldron and waving a piece of board to stoke the flames. He then rebuilt the small fire and placed on it a pot

THE NECROMANCER CANDLE

with a little water. The straining cloth from the dipping kettle he stuffed into the water, and then he picked up the paddle and stirred the cauldron.

Sour meat and bone roiled to the surface then plummeted again as Jiri stirred the soupy mixture. The water in the cauldron was still warm and did not take long to resume boiling. Jiri stirred continuously, then stopped and broke up the fire when he grew worried that Master Dupek might return and see what he was doing. The old boneman would have gotten his thirty pieces of silver by now, but would likely lurk about the Church hoping to see what Straka would do with his candles.

The small pot was steaming, so Jiri added more water and then rinsed the gore and fat out of the straining cloth. He added a small amount of water to the dipping kettle and restretched the cloth over its mouth. Then he poured the steaming contents of the pot onto the cloth, harvesting the tallow that had clung to the threads.

With the ladle, he quickly skimmed new bubbles of fat from the surface of the cauldron. There was always more fat to be harvested if you stirred long enough. With pig fat it was never worth the effort, but Bishop Straka had been adamant. "You must use all the renderings. Throw none away." Jiri knew there must be good reason. He ladled the congealing fat onto the cloth and eventually acquired a good quantity of milky tallow.

The Bishop had taken the silver moulds, but Master Dupek had a few ancient copper moulds stored in a chest. Jiri selected one that was similar to the Bishop's, though perhaps slightly narrower and taller. It was round and hollow, with no etchings, and no delicate hinge that allowed it to pop open. Jiri held a flaxen wick in place with his teeth while using both hands to pour his collected tallow from the heated kettle.

The tallow came near to filling the mould. The resulting candle would be taller than those Dupek had made for the Bishop, which satisfied Jiri. Straka was adamant that the candles all be of the same height. Why, Jiri did not know. But he did know that he would do everything in his power to frustrate the Bishop's plans.

He remembered then the ring from the necromancer's finger and pressed it deep into the still soft tallow, being careful not to disturb the wick.

When the candle had hardened sufficiently, Jiri plunged the mould into water he had heated in the pot. The hot water scalded his fingers but he did not care. Master Dupek would be returning, and Jiri feared the Dogs would be close behind. The heated water softened the tallow sufficiently for Jiri to push the candle free of the mould.

While the thirteenth candle made from the murdered necromancer hardened on the table, Jiri poured out the cauldron into the trench and cleaned all the implements. He took care to return Master Dupek's mould to its place, and then peered out the bone house door.

Master Dupek was coming down the path from the Church. There was a smile on the old boneman's face, a smile that would disappear when he turned to see the Church Dogs following behind him.

Jiri knew then that his fears were justified. If Bishop Straka was not above murdering Milos Radimir for necromancy, doing away with his accomplices in murder was only prudent. Master Dupek would not live out the day, and neither would Jiri if he stayed.

After wrapping the necromancer candle in soft cloth and stuffing it into a sack, he began his long escape. He could not leave by the door without the boneman and Straka's Dogs seeing him, so he went out by way of the trench, little caring that he could not avoid smearing his clothes with rendered gore.

It was a terrible thing the Bishop had done to Milos Radimir, though perhaps less terrible than the evil Straka would enact with candles rendered from a man with true magic.

Bishop Dagar had once said that great evils might be thwarted by small, goodly acts. Jiri only hoped that this night he had wrought such an act, in rendering a thirteenth candle.

· δ ·

Los Angeles, Today

A mound of fresh-turned earth stood next to the open grave, the dark soil peppered with sand, mold and the bone-white corpses of decaying roots. The coffin, suspended in a cradle of worn leather and tough nylon rope, descended with agonizing slowness toward a cold, sunless resting place.

Cassidy watched the pinewood box inch steadily downward, unable to escape the uncanny sensation that it was her own spent body being lowered into the uncaring ground. Almost, she could feel the dark earth close around her, the icy touch of sand and clay and gravel rasping against the pale frailty of her flesh, the feeble light from above blotted out as yet more earth was shoveled on top of her. She wanted to scream.

But she did not scream. The pulleys squealed as the coffin descended ever deeper. And somewhere in a nearby stand of trees, a magpie squawked. Yet Cassidy kept her silence.

Over the past year she had screamed often, and long, all to no avail. A month ago, on her sixteenth birthday, she had given up on screaming. Screaming was a fool's complaint. Better to be silent. To take what life gives you and to choose your battles wisely. It was a hard lesson to learn at sixteen.

Perhaps a dozen others stood with her at the graveside. Friends and acquaintances of her mother. They stood with heads bowed and hands clasped, shrouded in dark suits and long, drab skirts. The women wore cheerless hats, some with dark lace covering their eyes. Cassidy wore no hat, no lace to cover her eyes. She didn't care what others might read there.

To her left stood Emily Sanderson, her mother's best friend and assistant, a handkerchief crushed to her ruddy face. Somber Dr. Kinman stood at Cassidy's right, a comforting hand feather-light on her shoulder. At the head of the grave a white and scarlet-clad priest waved his hands and mumbled words Cassidy couldn't make out.

It wasn't fair.

For almost a year Cassidy had prepared for death. They all had. Dr. Kinman, after a long series of uncomfortable and often painful tests, spoke with them at the hospital. He used long, clinical words: Medulloblastoma, malignancy, metastasized tumors. Then translated them: Brain cancer, untreatable, incurable. Only it was Cassidy who had been diagnosed, not her mother. Mother wasn't supposed to die.

Cassidy was in the hospital when it happened, on one of her increasingly frequent overnight visits. Mother was late coming to take her home. Then Dr. Kinman sat beside her and told what had happened. That evening, the story appeared on the six o'clock news:

Carolyn Faith, 35, was found dead this morning in her Garden Grove home, victim of a break and enter turned violent. Police have no leads.

That was all. They left out that Carolyn Faith was a loving wife and mother, whose husband had run out on her when their fifteen year old daughter was diagnosed with terminal cancer, that she was a businesswoman and a leader in the community, and that today she would be sealed in a box and hidden beneath the ground. Locked away. Forgotten.

The coffin settled into the grave and the pulleys lapsed into silence. Attendants worked the leather straps out from under their heavy burden and pulled them from the grave with practiced efficiency. The priest let out a heavy sigh, mumbled "Amen", and then, with empty eyes, nodded to Cassidy.

Cassidy nearly collapsed with panic. Why is he looking at me? Am I supposed to say something? Is there something I'm supposed to do?

Dr. Kinman must have sensed her anxiety through his gentle touch. He leaned down and whispered in her ear. "It's all right."

Then, to the surprise of everyone, Emily stepped forward. Timid Emily, who had worked in Mother's shop for as long as Cassidy could remember. Shy, introverted, the last person in the world to assert herself, Emily Sanderson stepped forward, reached down, picked up a handful of dirt, and tossed it into the grave. "Goodbye, Carolyn," she whispered, half choking on the words. "We miss you dearly." Then she stepped back.

There was a brief pause, then everyone looked at Cassidy.

Awkwardly, Cassidy bent down and clutched a handful of dirt, then prized her fingers open so the grains would fall into the grave. The dry dirt rattled as it scattered and bounced across the pine cabinet of the coffin. What does this mean? she asked. It's difficult enough seeing you put in the ground. Must I help bury you, too? "Goodbye, mother," she said. "I'll see you soon."

Her words startled the priest, who likely knew nothing of Cassidy's illness apart from her sickly appearance. His disquieted look settled slowly into a frown.

Dr. Kinman stepped forward next. He said a good deal over Cassidy's mother's grave. Since the diagnosis he had become a staunch friend to both Carolyn and Cassidy, in many ways standing in for Cassidy's father who had not even come to the hospital to say goodbye. Carolyn Faith had been very brave, holding Cassidy's hand at her bedside, saying again and again that it was not Cassidy's fault William had gone. Dr. Kinman said much the same, insisting that William Faith's departure was a lack of character, not a lack of love for Cassidy. Cassidy, caught up in the revelation of her illness, the shock of her father's leaving,

THE NECROMANCER CANDLE

and in awe of her mother's strength in the face of adversity, had not known what to think.

As Dr. Kinman spoke, Cassidy caught bits and pieces of what he said, how he knew how much Carolyn loved her daughter, and that leaving was the last thing in the world she would want, especially now. That it wasn't her fault, and she shouldn't blame herself, that he'd take care of Cassidy as best he could. Cassidy thought she could hear Dr. Kinman crying.

Others around the grave shuffled past Dr. Kinman and tossed their handfuls of dirt onto the casket and muttered their words, and still Dr. Kinman stood by the grave. Minutes went by and the priest looked as if he were becoming impatient. One of the grave workers backed away toward a stand of trees and lit a cigarette.

It was all too much for Cassidy. Her ears began to ring and the world to spin. Nausea swept up from her stomach and her whole body felt on fire. Her legs and arms turned to rubber and her eyes burned. As always, when she had a fainting spell, the world twisted, parts of it going dark and hazy, other parts coming into sharp focus. She saw Emily's tear-reddened eyes widen with distress, saw the priest frown, the worker drop his cigarette. Further down among the tombstones she saw a rumpled man watching, his face waxen, hair like bleached straw. His eyes were a fierce blue and they bore into her like coffin nails. Cassidy felt uncomfortably vulnerable and forced herself to look away. The sky reeled and the last thing she saw was Dr. Kinman turning away from the grave to look at her, the smooth, olive skin of his face wet with tears.

· δ ·

Candles & Things

The letters etched into the sign above the door were slender, with soft, winding curves and short, tapered serifs: *Faith's Candles & Things*. Cassidy's mother had opened the shop before Cassidy learned to walk. The family business sold candles and soaps and taught courses on how to make them at home.

The day after the funeral, the shop was busy with many of Carolyn Faith's friends and customers dropping by to pay their respects.

"I'm so sorry about your mother," said Mrs. Goodhouse as Cassidy saw her to the door. It was nine p.m. and time to close up.

"It's kind of you to say," Cassidy answered mechanically. The steady barrage of her mother's consoling customers had worn her out; Mrs. Goodhouse no less than the earlier procession of well-intentioned visitors.

Outside, the darkening summer sky had grown overcast, the sour scent of ozone foretelling a pending storm. The leaves of the orange trees outside the shop swayed and fluttered with agitation in the rising winds.

Mrs. Goodhouse glanced sharply at the sky, and then turned her hawk gaze on Cassidy. Cassidy thought the old woman was going to say something that was none of her business, something along the lines of how a sickly young girl can't manage without a mother — she had been hearing that and similar unwanted counsel throughout the day — but in the end the woman's eyes softened and she shuffled down the street.

Cassidy closed the door against the wind and listened to the soothing tinkle of the chimes before sliding the deadbolt.

"You should have stayed home today," Emily said from behind the counter where she was doing the day's books. "I can handle the shop on my own. There's no need for you to wear yourself out."

"I need to be here," Cassidy answered. She looked around at the shelves of bright candles and exotic soaps, taking in the scents of lavender and vanilla and a dozen other familiar smells. "I grew up in this shop. Being here I feel closer to Mother."

Emily put down her pen and a smile worked its way across her lips. "Of course, dear, and I'm glad for your company. But all those people today.... I just worry about you."

"I'm all right." Cassidy forced herself to stand a little straighter, putting on a show of strength. "Nothing to worry about."

Emily snorted a mouse laugh, her way of showing that she wasn't fooled. Cassidy knew she put on a good act, had perfected it over the past months. But those who knew her best — Mother, Emily, Dr. Kinman — knew her too well. Emily sighed and returned her attention to the books.

Cassidy resumed her accustomed slumped posture — the mere effort to sit and stand straight exhausted her these days — and double-checked the door bolt. She then began arranging a shelf of candles that had been disturbed by customers. She remembered her mother teaching her as a child to fill in the holes where product had been sold: "Customers want a full shelf to choose from."

Too young to know better, Cassidy had spent hours rearranging candles and soaps and cards and music chests, driving her mother near to madness when everything moved about the shop from day to day. But Father was there to give Mother hugs. "If it makes Cassie happy," she remembered him saying.

It was a vivid memory, and Cassidy was glad for it. Since her illness she had trouble remembering things. Dr. Kinman couldn't say for sure if it was the cancer, an effect of the treatment, or something else entirely. There were holes in her memory, complete episodes of her life— gone. What she had trouble remembering most, though, was her father. Since he'd walked out of her life, memories of him had begun walking out of her mind.

Cassidy stepped further along the aisle and almost lost her balance. She caught herself against a shelf and leaned against it, keeping absolutely still until her equilibrium returned. Then she glanced at the sales counter. If Emily saw her sudden dizziness, it would worry her. But Emily was no longer behind the counter. Cassidy could hear her moving around in the back room. When had Emily gone into the back room?

In recent weeks Dr. Kinman had begun suggesting that Cassidy stay at the hospital on a permanent basis. Her dizzy spells were growing worse, and she had begun vomiting more frequently. "It's not that the treatment is no longer working," she overheard him explain to Mother. "Cassidy's time is simply running out. Her cells are deteriorating more rapidly."

"Do you *want* to go back in the hospital?" Mother had asked her.

"No," Cassidy answered honestly. "I want to stay in the shop with you."

That was enough for Carolyn Faith. She and Cassidy both had been through a lot, and no amount of urging from Dr. Kinman would make her put Cassidy back in the cancer ward.

That was before Mother died. Over the past week Dr. Kinman had resumed his requests that Cassidy return to the hospital. After her fainting spell at the graveside yesterday, he asked yet again.

"It was just stress," she told him, "from seeing Mother's coffin in the ground. Besides, there's nothing for me to do in the hospital, except wait to die."

Those last words always worked with Dr. Kinman. They were his Achilles heel. Sometimes, when Cassidy used them, she regretted it afterward because of the sadness it brought to his eyes. But that didn't stop the words from being true. The last thing in the world she wanted was to sit in a hospital bed waiting to die.

If not for Emily telling Dr. Kinman that Cassidy was in good hands, and taking her home with her from the hospital, Cassidy would still be there. Emily was a good friend, and had opened her home to Cassidy since the break-in. Of course, even out of the hospital, Cassidy was still just waiting to die, but at least she was waiting on her own terms.

Cassidy flinched as the phone on the counter rang. She waited for it to ring a second time before sitting on a stool behind the counter and answering, just to make sure it was real and not her cancer-riddled imagination.

"Hello. Faith's Candles & Things."

"This is Estelle Walker," said a businesslike voice. "I'm with Child Welfare Services and I'm looking for a Cassidy-Ann Faith."

Dr. Kinman had warned her that these people would call. If she didn't return to the hospital, Child Welfare would place her somewhere she could receive *proper care*. A sixteen year old could not live on her own without a legal guardian, especially not a sixteen year old who was ill.

"I'm sorry," Cassidy told the woman, "Cassidy isn't here. Have you tried her home?"

"Of course I tried her home," the voice answered, with more than a hint of irritation. "There is no answer."

"Maybe she's asleep," suggested Cassidy. "She's ill and may not answer the phone."

"Do you know where I might find her?" insisted the voice.

"No, I'm sorry," said Cassidy. She hung up.

"Who was that, dear?" Emily stood in the back room doorway, an inventory book in her hand.

"Someone for Mother," Cassidy lied. "I couldn't tell them...."

"It's all right, dear," said Emily. She came behind the counter and put an arm around Cassidy's shoulders. "It's not important. It's time we went home, anyway."

"Actually," said Cassidy. She had been fretting all day on how to broach the subject, and had failed to come up with a plan. So she just blurted it out. "I really would like to go home. My home. I miss my room."

Emily's forehead creased and her lips trembled. "Oh, Cassidy dear," she said. "That's really not a good idea."

"But I haven't been home since...." Cassidy did not have to finish. Except to pick up some of her things to take to Emily's house where she had been staying, she hadn't been home since her mother's death."

Emily wrung her hands together. "I promised Dr. Kinman that I'd take care of you. Your mother wouldn't...."

But she would, thought Cassidy, and knew that Emily was thinking it too. Carolyn Faith had been very mindful of her daughter's needs and wants since her illness, not spoiling Cassidy, certainly, but always very accommodating.

"Very well," said Emily. Her face took on a decisive look. "I'll get some things from home and we'll both stay at your house. We'll make hot chocolate. It'll be fun."

"No," said Cassidy, and instantly regretted it as the smile drained from Emily's face. "I mean," she added hastily. "I need to say goodbye. On my own. It won't work if you are there."

"Oh," said Emily. "Oh. Oh." Clearly this was something Emily couldn't handle.

"I'll be fine," Cassidy continued. "It's my home. I've lived there all my life."

"But Cassidy," insisted Emily, "are you sure? You'll be alone."

"Sometimes I need to be alone," Cassidy told her.

Emily shook with the weight of the decision, but in the end she relented, as Cassidy knew she would.

"Just this once," said Emily, her voice still rife with worry. "I'll drive you."

"It's just a five minute walk," Cassidy told her. "I miss walking home from the shop." If Emily drove her home, Cassidy feared she would sit outside all night in her car, worrying. Cassidy didn't want that.

Emily frowned. "I don't know. You're sure you'll be all right?"

Cassidy nodded.

Truth was, the short walks home exhausted her. But they also kept her from seeing herself as an invalid. The day she couldn't walk six blocks between her home and the shop was the day she would reconsider Dr. Kinman's request she return to the hospital. What scared her was that she felt that day was fast approaching.

Emily fretted and frowned all the way to the door.

"I'll lock up in a minute," Cassidy told her. "I just want to have the shop to myself for a moment."

"Please be careful," Emily cautioned. "I don't know what I'd do if anything happened to you."

"Nothing is going to happen," Cassidy insisted. "I just want to feel the places I'm familiar with. I've done it a thousand times before. You do understand, don't you?"

Emily bit her lower lip and nodded. Cassidy didn't know if she really did understand, or if she was just saying so for Cassidy's sake. But Emily did step outside into the rising wind and, clutching at the collar of her jacket, strode off down the sidewalk toward her car.

Cassidy rebolted the door and sagged into a sitting position on the floor. It was done. Convincing Emily had taken more out of her than she had thought it would. Emily had a good heart, but was a pushover when Cassidy wanted something. This time she had put up a fight. Still, it was worth it.

This past year had been filled with her constantly being watched. Doctors and nurses poking and prodding. Mother and Emily ever at her elbow. And then this past week she had not been allowed to be alone for a single moment. Sometime this afternoon, as the umpteenth caller offered their condolences and suggested how alone she must feel, it struck Cassidy that she was not alone. Just the opposite: she had lost any illusion of independence that she may have had. She missed her independence.

Well, now she had won it back, if only for one night.

· δ ·

The Disheveled Man

When she felt rested enough, Cassidy climbed to her feet and prowled about the shop, as she used to do as a young girl when the shelves were taller and more mysterious. Here and there she found memories: a porcelain boy with a flute leading a lost sheep back to the flock, an old favorite of Mother's; a frosted glass angel that Cassidy admired for the serenity in its face and humility of its hands folded in prayer; a music box with a dancing ballerina that her father used to open, and he would take Cassidy's hands and they would dance in the aisle. He would twirl her around and laugh and tell her she was his beautiful princess.

She remembered William Faith as a tall man, clean-shaven with sandy hair and a smiling face. He was forever on a stool or a stepladder, bringing down or taking up stock from the higher shelves. He had a passion for reading. It was rare to find him without a book in hand. He had loved her mother and, until he ran away when she took ill, Cassidy thought he loved her, too.

Sometimes she wondered if it wasn't so much her illness that let go her memories of him, but the trauma of his leaving.

Cassidy raised a hand to her cheek and was surprised to pull her fingers away wet. She felt a rush of sadness and quickly pushed it away. Since first becoming ill she had asked so many times *Why me?* without receiving an answer, that she was sick of the question. The time for self-pity was past. Cassidy now accepted what was to come, but she *would* face the short time that remained with what little dignity she could muster.

Without meaning to, she found herself in the back room where boxes of wax and soap were kept and the candle-making classes were held. In the center of the room a dozen chairs huddled around a long cedar trestle table. An array of plate-warmers, beeswax rolls, jars of vegetable wax and perfumes crowded the tabletop. The room smelled of smoke and old wax. The familiarity put a smile on Cassidy's lips.

Carolyn Faith had lived for her candle-making classes, warming beeswax and then rolling and carving the most beautiful candles with apparent ease. The ladies and occasional gentleman student would *ooh* and *ahh* and then proceed to produce such utter monstrosities that Mother would chuckle and show them again how it was done.

Cassidy knelt down and opened a lower cupboard from which she took a hideous, smelly, dark yellow candle that mother always brought out when her students began feeling sorry for themselves.

"This is one of *my* early attempts," she would tell them, and then hold the horrid thing under their eyes and noses. Once they got past the acrid smell, they would note how rough and uneven the surface was, and how the white wax carried harsh shades of yellow and brown and even dark red. The idea that Carolyn Faith could make so abhorrent a candle revived the students' spirits and they would try again.

"Did you really make that candle?" Cassidy remembered asking as a little girl. It was unthinkable that her mother could make so ugly a candle. Mother laughed and mock-whispered: "No, honey. Your father made it."

"Very funny," her father said, putting on a wry face before resuming his characteristic smile.

Cassidy concluded that neither of them had made it, which begged the question: who did?

Slowly, she turned the old candle in her hands. She was used to the horrible smell, and sometimes found the varying yellows and browns attractive. The candle had always been like that, attracting and repelling her at the same time.

There were times when she imagined that she herself had made it. Either so long ago that she couldn't remember, or the memory was simply gone, like so many other memories her cancer had taken. But if that were true her mother would never use it that way, as a bad example. If Cassidy had made the candle, her mother would love it no matter how awful it was.

Another memory of her father that hadn't quite disappeared washed across her mind: William Faith asking her mother to leave the candle alone in its cupboard, and her mother shaking her head and telling him there was no harm done.

They argued about the candle, Cassidy now realized. Her parents, who had rarely argued about anything. An ugly old candle pushed them apart; that and a daughter's illness.

Cassidy felt a sudden urge to throw the candle into the trash, or better yet, set it on one of the hotplates and melt it into slag. She stood from kneeling to do just that, and found herself some time later still standing there, the candle warm in her hands.

"What was I doing?" she asked out loud to the empty room. She was going to do something with the candle, she remembered. Put it away?

The room smelled suddenly of burnt candles, of wax left too long on a hotplate. None of the hotplates were plugged in, of course. None had been since Mother's death. Still, the air carried an acrid scent: sulfur, and smoke, and dead things. Cassidy looked over her shoulder with the uncomfortable sense that someone was watching her. She was, of course, alone inside the locked shop.

Shaking her head, she knelt again by the open cupboard to put the candle away, then instead stood up and closed the cupboard. Irrationally, she decided to take the candle home. Maybe put it on the coffee table in the living room. There was so little at home that reminded Cassidy of Mother, who'd spent most her waking hours in the candle shop.

Above the cupboard stood a roll of packing paper. Cassidy wrapped the candle to protect it, then stowed it away in her Medi-Pack backpack. It was a small backpack, bright blue with the words, *Fountain Valley Hospital* printed on the front in large white letters. Dr. Kinman had given it to her so she could carry her medication with her. There was a small pocket in the front that contained her health information and numbers to call in an emergency. So far, she hadn't needed anyone to call the numbers for her. How much longer would that last?

Cassidy stared at the Medi-Pack's contents: a dozen plastic bottles of pills, the sandwich she had forgotten to eat for lunch, a half-full bottle of mineral water, and now a bundle of brown paper that contained the world's ugliest candle. Could she be any more pathetic?

She sighed and walked out into the shop. Featured in the storefront window was a large book on candle-making that was her mother's favorite. Cassidy decided to take that home, too. She would read from it tonight, and afterward dream about Mother.

The front of the shop accommodated the customer entrance and a wide bay window. Cassidy leaned through the shelves and signs and some of the better books and knickknacks that *Faith's Candles and Things* had to offer, and retrieved the heavy book.

Outside, the sky was already dark. Wind rattled the leaves in the trees along the street, and raindrops splattered against the glass of the storefront. Cassidy had no idea it had grown so late. How long since Emily had left?

There was a thumping sound, a tree branch banging against the outside wall. Cassidy peered past the shelves and saw that it wasn't the wind. It was a man banging on the door.

Rainwater washed across straw hair, runneling down a face swollen like melting wax. The man turned and looked at her with flashing blue eyes. It was the scarecrow from the tombstones.

After her fainting spell in the graveyard, Cassidy had forgotten all about the rumpled man. What could he be but a homeless man, wandering through the graveyard for whatever reason the homeless wander anywhere. But why would he be here? Now? Outside mother's shop?

The man hammered again, his blue eyes glaring at her — a demand to be let in.

Cassidy had the sudden, irrational fear that this was her father, unrecognizable after a year's absence, her cancer-ravaged memories of him more unreliable than she had thought. That would explain his being at mother's funeral. And now here. But it couldn't be. Cassidy didn't want it to be. The few memories she retained of her father were nothing like this creature outside the door.

"We're closed!" Cassidy mouthed at the man through the glass.

Cassidy ran to the door and drew down the window shade. Then she switched off the light and fled through the darkness into the back room and out the delivery door. Running down back alleys and through neighbors' yards, she made it home in a record three minutes, despite the wind and the rain and the darkness. Her body still pumped adrenalin when she collapsed into the leather chair in the darkened living room of the empty house.

Not Father, she told herself. The man looked nothing like her father. It's one of the Child Welfare people, tracking me down.

The red light on the answering machine flashed, but Cassidy was too dazed and tired to hit the play button. More Child Welfare. And mother's friends offering condolences. And possibly... her father, disheveled and decaying in a phone booth. "Cassie, let me in. I love you baby."

Cassidy cried until she fell asleep in the chair.

· δ ·

Extra Patrols

The man in the raincoat rattled the locked door. When the door refused to give, he tried the side window. It, too, was securely latched, as was the rear door to the shop. He returned to where his rented Chevrolet Impala was parked by the sidewalk, and stood in the rain. The street was empty of traffic as he watched for movement through the darkened shop window.

The rain was cool on his skin and he was content to simply stand and wait. Neither did he mind the wind blasting against his face. It was invigorating. There was power in storms, and it almost seemed as if he could draw from that power simply by standing in its path. Perhaps one day he would be inclined to pursue that mystery. Today he had other business.

More than a week had passed since the murder. Half that time he had spent in his hotel room, watching for news of the manhunt on television. The remaining time he spent watching the empty house and the occasional activity of the shop. It amazed him that the manhunt was going nowhere. With all the advances in forensics in the past fifty years, one would think they could uncover some clues. But his fears had been for nothing; the local police were next to useless and the investigation had stalled. Even the extra patrols near the shop and house had ceased.

As this observation passed through his thoughts, a police cruiser rolled by, slowing as it went past a pub where the door opened and music and a gaggle of patrons poured out into the street. A spotlight appeared at the passenger-side window, angling light into the dark corridors between the buildings. The disheveled man covered his eyes with his hand as the light played across his face. Then he climbed into the Impala and drove away.

Well, perhaps not all the extra patrols. But he had grown tired of waiting. Later tonight he would come back. A crowbar was all he would need to get in through the back door. If the girl was still there, she would be less trouble than her mother.

· δ ·

Three Tragedies

Cassidy awoke feeling the urgent need to vomit. When she was done, she leaned against the vanity counter and studied her reflection in the mirror. Her hands shook and her skin was pale. Her short-cropped hair, once long and a rich auburn like her mother's, was thin and lifeless. It hung from her head like the leaves of a dead plant.

She remembered a year ago in the hospital, when the doctors battling her cancer tried radiation treatments and chemotherapy, sessions that left her weak and tired, sometimes even unconscious. At the time she often thought that death would be a comfort. But Mother was there, so hopeful and supportive. Cassidy couldn't disappoint her by giving up.

The worst part was the way her friends from school looked at her when they came to visit. No matter how the doctors or their parents prepared them, the horror in their eyes when they saw her was almost unbearable. Of course, Cassidy didn't blame them. Her hair had mostly fallen out and she had lost weight. She looked like a zombie in a cheap movie.

In time her friends stopped coming to visit, and in many ways it was a relief. Cassidy did not want them to watch her wasting away. When Dr. Kinman admitted that the chemotherapy was not working, that it was only a matter of time, Cassidy decided not to return to school. What was the point?

Since then her treatment was a simple one. It consisted of a regimen of vitamins, antioxidants, and a host of other pills meant to retard the cancer's growth. "This is not a cure," Dr. Kinman had made her painfully aware. "The best we can hope for is to slow the cancer down and help your body function on a day to day basis." He also insisted she eat five solid meals a day, "to keep your strength up."

For a time it had worked. Cassidy was released from the hospital after about a month. She remembered how good she felt, how strong, after the initial treatments had left her so drained. Her weekly visits were enough to satisfy Dr. Kinman. Sometimes he would draw blood and occasionally put her inside the MRI machine for "a closer look".

Her hair began to grow back, but never as thick and lustrous, so she kept it short. It was a reminder that Cassidy was still sick, and growing sicker. Mother's forced smiles and Dr. Kinman's vague assurances that she was "doing well, all things considered", were a clear signal that there was no miracle in sight. And month by month, week by week, and now day by day, she felt herself growing weaker, her life slipping away. The cancer was winning.

It was only a month ago, on her sixteenth birthday — most probably her last birthday — that Cassidy accepted the loss. She had celebrated the day in the hospital, feverish, weak, unable to hold down food. Dr. Kinman came to check on her every hour, taking blood, adjusting medication. The next day he let Mother take her home, her Medi-Pack bulging with more and different pills for her to take.

She could tell by the look on Mother's face, and on Dr. Kinman's, that they were worried. Mother said everything was fine, that the new drugs would put her back on course. But it wasn't true. It was a white lie. The truth was too frightening to admit.

It was then that she resigned herself to dying. Really resigned herself, though she had known it all along. Instead of railing against her fate she concentrated on how to make the most of the time remaining. And what she decided was to spend it by being with the things she loved: Mother and the shop.

Then, just as her life regained a semblance of happiness, Mother was taken from her. A blind chance of fate. A tragedy that happens to someone else, not you. Cassidy had received three such tragedies in the space of a year. Her illness, her father leaving, and her mother killed. There were times when Cassidy thought herself the most unlucky person in the world.

Well, it would be over soon. Soon she would see Mother again and no more tragedies would be able to touch her. In many ways, she found that prospect comforting. When it came, Cassidy would go without regret. Until then....

Cassidy hauled herself into the kitchen and cracked an egg into a frying pan, sunny-side up. From the fridge she poured a tall glass of whole milk to wash down a fistful of drugs and vitamins from her Medi-Pack. The milk was past its expiration date, but Cassidy didn't notice whether or not it was sour. She didn't taste food anymore.

Finally, she forced herself to eat half the egg. It was all she could manage. Eating was supposed to keep her strength up. Lately, Cassidy found that eating just exhausted her.

For several minutes she sat in the living room chair where she had fallen asleep and slept through the night, bracing herself for the six block walk to the shop. On the stand beside the sofa, the answering machine still blinked, less urgent now than in the darkened room the night before. Cassidy left the house without checking the messages. There was nothing there she wanted to hear.

· δ ·

Trampled Lives

Emily was waiting for her on the sidewalk outside the shop. Parked near Emily on the street was a police car, its lights flashing.

"Oh, Cassidy!" Emily cried when she saw her. "We've had burglars!"

Cassidy froze, her mind thrown back several days. She was in the hospital recovering from a particularly bad attack, watching TV but not really paying attention. Mother was late coming to pick her up and she was worried.

There were soft voices in the hall and then Dr. Kinman came in and sat in the chair beside her hospital bed. He rested his hands on his knees and his expression carried that forlorn look he got whenever he lost a patient. Cassidy feared it must be one of her friends in the terminal ward at the other end of the corridor.

"Cassidy, I..." he began, then stopped. "I don't know how to tell you this." He took a kerchief from his lab coat pocket and wiped his forehead. Cassidy watched him pull the kerchief lower across his eyes and cheeks before he crumpled it his hand. "Something's happened," he said. "Burglars broke into your home. Your mother must have surprised them. They... they...."

Cassidy felt her throat go dry, her eyes begin to well with tears. "Is she hurt? Is mother going to be okay?"

Dr. Kinman's lips began to tremble and he shook his head. He hunched forward in the chair and buried his face in his hands. "I'm sorry. I'm so sorry."

"I'm sorry, dear. I'm so sorry." Emily's voice dragged Cassidy back to the present. She folded Cassidy in a hug and cradled her like a child. "What was I thinking? It's nothing really. Only a little damage. No one was hurt."

A policeman in a brown suit stepped out from the shop. He was thirtyish, with short black hair and thick brows. His face was serious and there was an open notepad in his hand. He waited for the two of them to separate before he approached.

"Is this Cassidy?" he asked.

Emily nodded.

The policeman smiled through taut lips. "I'm Detective Donald Savoy, Cassidy. I'm sorry you've had this trouble, especially after...." His voice trailed off.

Cassidy gave him the blank expression she used when people became too embarrassed to talk about her troubles.

Digging into his shirt pocket, the policeman pulled out a blue and white card and handed it to her. "This is the number for my precinct. If you ever need help, for anything, you call. Day or night. Ok?"

Cassidy nodded, and tucked it away in a pocket of her Medi-Pack,

Detective Savoy turned back to Emily. "There's still money in the cash box, and nothing looks to be missing, though there is a lot of damage. Has anyone made threats against the shop? Disgruntled customers?"

"No, of course not," said Emily. "Everyone loves the shop."

"And Mrs. Faith had no enemies?" the detective asked, and then glanced quickly at Cassidy.

Emily shook her head. "No." Then she, too, looked at Cassidy. Her eyes held a lost expression. "Why don't you go inside, dear? See if you can find anything missing."

Cassidy nodded and walked toward the shop entrance. Since her illness she had learned all the cues, codes for, "Please go away so we can discuss you." They were always polite and well-intentioned. She had learned to accept them.

The shop looked like a scene from a bad movie. There wasn't a single book, candle, or soap bead left on the shelves. Everything had been knocked onto the floor and trampled on. Cassidy reached into the tumbled mess on the floor and found the music box, the one she and her father had danced to, back when she was his princess. Its sides were bent and crumpled. When she opened it, the dancer limped around her pedestal. Five notes of music squeaked out brokenly before stopping altogether. A tear fell from Cassidy's cheek onto the box as she returned it in its place on the shelf.

She could hear movement in the back room, police looking for clues they weren't likely to find. They had done the same at her home after the break-in, and had found nothing, just a jumbled mess for her and Emily to clean up. A mess almost as bad as this one.

Cassidy inched back toward the shop entrance and listened.

"It's too big a coincidence," Detective Savoy said to Emily. "First the house. Now the shop. They were searching for something."

"It's just a gift shop," Emily said. There were tears on her face. "Candles and soap. Nothing valuable."

A large, black car pulled up to the curb and a heavyset woman with starched white hair climbed out. She took in the *Faith's Candles & Things* sign and the police car, and then marched up to Emily and the detective.

"My name is Estelle Walker," she said, handing each of them a card from her jacket pocket. "I'm with Child Welfare Services and I'm looking for Cassidy-Ann Faith."

The detective examined the card and then looked at her, saying nothing. Emily turned the card over and stuffed it in her pocket. "Cassidy isn't here," she said. "I believe she's in school today." Emily glanced at the detective and brushed at the tears on her face.

"Cassidy hasn't been in school for over a year," the woman said. "And they don't expect her back."

"Really?" said Emily. "You do realize the poor child's mother just died?"

"That's why I'm here," the woman said. "Cassidy no longer has a guardian and requires proper care."

"I'm taking care of her," Emily said.

The woman frowned. "And that's why you believe she's in school?"

Emily stuttered for something to say, but the woman waved her off. "If you wish to become Cassidy's guardian you will have to come down to the Child Welfare office for evaluation."

"Oh," said Emily. Her face brightened. "That's wonderful."

Detective Savoy spoke up. "I understand evaluation usually takes several months to complete."

The woman nodded. "There are background checks. And board approvals. And home inspections."

"During which time," added the detective, "Cassidy will be placed in a group home."

"Yes," said the woman.

"But Cassidy isn't well," said Emily. "She needs special care."

"Then she should be in the hospital," said the woman. "In the absence of a guardian, she belongs in one of our service homes. We have nurses on staff."

"That isn't fair," said Emily.

"It's in the best interest of the child," said the woman. "Do you still insist that you don't know where she is?"

Emily glanced at the detective. "She's likely at Fountain Valley Hospital," she said. "Under Dr. Robert Kinman's care."

"I've already spoken to her doctor," the woman said curtly. Then she climbed back into her car and drove off.

"Thank you," Emily said to Detective Savoy, "for not turning Cassidy in."

"Given the circumstances," replied Savoy, "I'm not certain Child Services is the answer."

Cassidy backed away from the door and sat on the stool behind the sales counter. She felt drained. That, like the shop, someone had come in and pulled her life off the shelves and trampled all over it. She didn't know if she could survive it. If not for good people like Emily and the random kindness of strangers like Detective Savoy, she knew she couldn't.

"Are you all right, dear?" asked Emily. She and Detective Savoy had entered the shop and were looking at her with guarded concern.

Cassidy nodded and let out a deep sigh.

"Don't worry," said Emily. "We'll set this place to rights in no time. You'll see." She said nothing of the visit from Child Welfare.

· 8 ·

Straka

The television blared some documentary about growing crime in the city and how the streets were no longer safe to walk at night. On an empty, lamp-lit street a sober-faced man with a microphone calmly explained how gang members skulked around every corner, waiting to stab or shoot anyone who violated their *turf*.

Straka turned the television off and sat staring at the wall.

He had been flipping through the channels since six a.m. hoping to find a report of the break-in in the Valley business district, but while there had been non-stop reports of crime and violence of every stripe, there was no mention of *Faith's Candles and Things*.

The void of information was irksome. Was it safe? Dangerous? A year ago he wouldn't even be asking these questions. A year ago Straka had been immortal.

He frowned at his reflection in the black mirror of the television. Even this murky image could not hide the obscenity he was becoming, the swollen face, the distorted features. There was no question, his body was decaying.

There was a time when he had thought there could be no end. That the smoke from Milos Radimir's candles would sustain him forever. The centuries had left him ageless and impervious to physical injury. He was a god, or as near a god as this world could create. There was nothing he could not do, and very little he did not try.

Power had been Straka's first ambition; even before he found true magic he had joined the Church, not through any belief in a cruel or benevolent god, but because he desired the power that, in those days, only Churchmen held.

Ironically, it was the imagined power of the Church that led him to the true power of magic. As an eager and ambitious novice Straka had been the ideal choice to the calling of witch-hunter. For a time he had amused himself with the burning of harmless crones and meting revenge on comely wives who refused his advances. And the Church rewarded him for it! They even made him Bishop and then sent him to steward over the most pagan-infested province of the Empire. It was there, outside Prague, where he was again astonished. He found real witches!

Of course, Milos Radimir denied any association with what the Church deemed witchcraft. And Straka believed him. Radimir no more believed in devils than Straka himself did. But the man did wield magic. He had been working miracles in the town for years.

Back then, Straka had only a vague idea of how the magic worked. Performing cures and curses with candles was common to the area, though most practitioners were pure charlatans. Those few with any confirmable talent he questioned vigorously before burning them at the stake, until, finally, he felt ready to move on Radimir. Radimir was the only one Straka had feared.

Making the candles had been a risk. None of those he questioned could predict the results. Most were horrified by the prospect. Straka thought it likely that nothing would happen.

Worst case he'd have a few dead townsmen and some worthless candles to amuse himself with. What did happen went beyond his imagining. From Milos' death he had gained immortality. And once he shed the fear of death... he became unstoppable.

His rise through the Church had been unprecedented. From Bishop to Cardinal to Apostle to Pope. He had actually been several Popes at various times, and had shaped the course of history. If anyone could be credited with ending the dark ages and bringing about the Renaissance, it would be him. But Straka had accepted no recognition, had in fact hidden his role. It was power he craved, not fame, and he was smart enough to know how fame could hinder power.

And when the power of the Church waned it was a smooth transition from pope to monarch. And in the secular courts he learned a renewed appreciation for the term *decadence*. Women, fine foods, exotic entertainments. He had witnessed the Dance of the Seven Veils innumerable times and had bathed in the blood of virgins until its iron-sweetness no longer moved him.

His increasing dissatisfaction with power came as a surprise. Those who crave power have no sense of how empty it is. Or perhaps it simply takes several hundred years of pulling the strings of nations to realize that the nations simply weren't worth the effort.

And so the monarchy, too, lost its amusements, and Straka learned new trades: soldier, highwayman, assassin, torturer. For a time he had roamed the streets of London reaping the still-beating hearts from young women for no better reason than that he was bored. He found it ironic that the only souls-ease an immortal could find was to rip the very life from others. It was power still, but on a more personal level.

Yet after a time even that had failed to stir him.

Briefly he turned his mind to riches and soon owned most of Europe. But wealth, too, lost its luster. He explored the world, from deepest Amazonia to darkest Africa, and visited both poles, unimpressed by what he found. In the end he sat alone on a deserted isle for a hundred years, contemplating his own death.

Oh, he had no desire to die. That would be absurd. But it was the one thing withheld from him. Perhaps that was why his last true passion had been to explore the various means and ways that a man or woman could die.

On his island he reached a kind of balance. His life and mode of existence had removed him from humanity. He no longer considered them his peers; living among them had become intolerable. He preferred solitude. Just himself and the wind and the sea.

Straka held no regrets for what he had become. Yes, the candles made from Milos' corpse had changed him and, though immortality came with a price, the price of his own immortality was one he could live with.

Once a year he would leave his island and move among the race that had spawned him. For though he was immortal, his vitality would fail without occasional renewal. For his amusement he would visit a different port each year, tasting what entertainment was new or the current style. His visits all ended the same, in murder. A citizen gone missing or found headless or disemboweled. Only Straka knew the motive for the deaths. A motive that no police investigator would ever postulate. Using the necromancer candles, Straka stole their very life essence and took it into himself.

His last few visits to civilization, however, had been less amusing. Vienna, Trinidad, San Paulo. In all these places the people had increasingly shunned him. Then three years ago in Shanghai they hailed him with insults. Monster. Demon. *Gui.*

Only then did he look at himself in a mirror, really look, and notice the change. His skin had begun to melt, like wax left in the sun. The wasting had occurred so slowly he had not even noticed it. The questions of why and how had occupied his mind for many months.

He searched the world for answers. Clues. He sought out secret cabals and societies of sorcerers. He sought out magicians and healers. He returned to Prague and turned the city upside down. But there was no magic. His was the only magic left in the world, and it was failing him.

His skin continued to melt, and the nails of his hands and feet grew crooked. It was difficult to find shoes he could wear comfortably. He began wearing long coats, and hats, and scarves, and gloves, and lurked in the shadows.

Then one morning he awoke and knew what was wrong. Milos Radimir had tricked him. Somehow, from the depths of a boiling pot of flesh and bone, the wily sorcerer had conspired to withhold some portion of his magic, enough to make Straka believe he had won, and still destroy him in the end.

Straka had laughed and bought cheap wine and toasted Milos' name. Milos had bested him fair and square, and after nine hundred years Straka felt himself ready to cede the game.

Until it occurred to him how Milos had won. There must be another candle somewhere. It was the old boneman outside Prague who had cheated him.

Too late for repercussions now. Straka had already murdered the old fool, and anyone else who had been there that night, though he seemed to recall that the boneman's apprentice had fled and not been found. With a thirteenth candle, Straka now realized. Fool. He should have had his dogs look harder. But how could he have known? He had received Milos' magic, after all.

And now he was here in Los Angeles, hot on the trail of the missing thirteenth candle. The irony of it was, it was Milos' magic that allowed him to track it. Radimir had not won yet.

Yes, Straka was weak and growing weaker, but the magic was still strong. And it could do more than just extend his life. Tonight he would try again. The candle was close. Soon it would be his. And Straka would be whole again.

With the remote control he turned the television back on. There were still many things about Los Angeles he wished to learn.

· δ ·

William

William Faith stood on the steps of Valley Hospital staring up at the tall glass doors. A year had passed since he last stood on this spot. Now, as then, he did not have the courage to go inside.

It was more than a phobia. As a teenager he had spent months in this very hospital, sitting at his mother's bedside, waiting for her to die of the same insidious disease that had returned to take Cassie. Those months had been the worst in his life. The constant pain and steady deterioration that had turned his mother into an empty, half-dead husk was something he just couldn't bring himself to witness again.

And so instead of entering the hospital he had left town. Ashamed. Hating himself. His one saving grace was that Cassie still had her mother to see her through. But now Carolyn was gone and she no longer had even that.

Leaving Cassie had been hard. Leaving Carolyn had been harder. Though he never expected her forgiveness, he had expected to see her again. Only that, too, was now taken from him. He hadn't even been there for the funeral.

It was Emily who had found him, running through the phone list from the house after Carolyn's death, calling friends of friends of friends for days until finally she tracked him down.

Her phone call had been as distressing as it had been unexpected.

"Cassidy needs you."

"Cassie?" He thought she would be gone by now. It had been over a year. His mother had died six months following her diagnosis. Cassie had already suffered twice that long!

"Carolyn is dead," Emily told him next.

"Carolyn? When? How?"

"Six nights ago. There was a break-in. She must have surprised the thief. Cassidy needs you now."

After hanging up the phone William drove straight to the airport. He didn't even pack a suitcase. Twelve hundred miles and ten hours later found him wrinkled, smelly, and with a day's growth of beard, standing once again outside the doors of Valley Hospital. He had come full circle.

During the flight he tried not to think about Cassie. Concentrated instead on Carolyn and the life they had shared. The life he had abandoned. He felt like a heel.

He had been wrong. Wrong to leave. Wrong to stay away. And now it was too late to make things right with Carolyn. Was it too late for Cassie? How could she still be alive?

The glass doors continued to loom before him. William took a deep breath and forced himself to focus on the concrete steps, to close his mind to everything but the pavement directly in front of him. Slowly, he moved one step forward, eyes on the concrete.

Before he even realized it, the concrete turned to linoleum and he was through the doors.

When William was admitted into Dr. Kinman's office he immediately recognized the middle-aged man as an older version of same the young intern who had looked in on his mother almost daily twenty years earlier. William knew the recognition would not be returned, as he looked nothing like the gangly teenager who had cried at his mother's bedside. Yet the doctor's eyes widened in disbelief.

"Mr. Faith," Kinman said in a cool, even voice. "I'm glad to finally meet you."

"You— you know me?" asked William.

Kinman waved him into a chair. "Yes. And no. Carolyn, your wife, told me much about you, and showed me pictures." His forehead wrinkled. "Your leaving was difficult for her, though she did feel a little better when I told her about your mother."

"You told her! You had no right."

"No. I didn't. I'm sorry. But she was so distraught and angry. She couldn't understand why you left. How you could leave."

William pressed his face into his hands. "It's all my fault. Cassie's illness. She inherited it from me, from my mother."

"Carolyn understood that, after I told her. How you blamed yourself."

William looked up. "Does Cassie know?"

The doctor frowned. "We told her. But your leaving upset her... on top of everything else. She doesn't talk about you. After you left, Carolyn and Cassidy made a life for themselves without you."

"Can I... can I see her?" William asked. Already he could envision his sweet little girl lying twig-like in a hospital bed, chained to a life-support machine, emaciated, barely alive, eyes filled with pain. A year? How could they drag her agony out like that?

"Cassidy?" said the doctor. "Why would I stop you? You're her father. She's been through a lot. I don't know if your turning up will be a good thing or bad. My advice is to go gently with her."

William stood up and looked toward the door. He knew the way to the room where his mother had died, he had been there so often. Cassie would be near there. Maybe even the same room. "Where is she?"

The doctor looked at his watch. "It's three o'clock. She's probably at the shop."

"The shop?" echoed William. How could...?

"Candles & Things," answered the doctor. "The shop you ran with your wife before... before Cassidy took ill."

"You mean she's not in the hospital?"

"Cassidy *should* be here," said the doctor. "She needs personal care. But I can't confine her against her will. If you can convince her to come in, I'd appreciate it. I really do think she'd be better off here."

William staggered out of Dr. Kinman's office and down the sanitized corridor toward the elevator. She's not even in the hospital. She's sick and she's dying and her mother's dead and she's working at the shop. And her father is the biggest reprobate that ever lived.

"Are you all right?"

William focused his eyes and found a concerned face above a nurse's uniform looking at him.

"Yes," he said. "No. I'm suffering from terminal stupidity. But I'll get by, somehow. I hope."

The nurse blinked, unable to respond as William lurched the rest of the way to the elevator. What can I possibly say to Cassie to make things right?

· δ ·

Family Reunion

The shop was exactly as William remembered it: a quaint, one-storey building on a quiet business street, with wide glass windows displaying books and candles and soaps and inexpensive jewelry boxes. A cornucopia of coziness. The shop had been Carolyn's dream and together they had made it a reality. They had been happy there. In many ways the shop had become more of a home than most houses do.

Then William looked closer at the wooden sign and the trim around the door and windows, and he frowned. The once-white paint had faded to the color of old bones, and in places it had cracked and flaked. He had never seen the shop in such poor condition. How could...?

Then he cursed himself. Paint was his responsibility. Carolyn loved to make candles and soaps, but she wouldn't go near a can of paint or wood stain. It was one of the little quirks that had endeared her to him.

His throat tightened as he remembered that he wouldn't find Carolyn behind the sales counter reading the latest issue of *Country Candle* magazine. She wouldn't smile as he entered and blow him a kiss, or remind him of a chair or lamp that needed mending around the shop.

What awaited him was not the world he had known and was comfortable with. It was unknown territory. And he a stranger. Likely an unwelcome stranger.

Grimly, he opened the shop door and stepped inside. It was not as difficult as entering Valley Hospital. Almost, but not quite.

William frowned again as his eyes took in the familiar shelves and aisle displays. He knew them, but at the same time they were foreign to him. The books and soaps were in disarray as though hastily pushed against each other, knick-knacks all in the wrong places or missing entirely. He saw candles with long scratches along the sides. There were bare places along the shelves and a few shelves were missing entirely, leaving ugly outlines along the walls and on the floor of where they used to be. Surely in the days since Carolyn's murder the shop would not have fallen into such a state. Cassie would have... But no, Cassie would be in no condition to straighten the shelves. Why was she even here instead of in the hospital?

He continued his journey through the unruly aisles until he came to the sales counter, behind which stood Emily, Carolyn's best friend in all the world. Emily's eyes boggled when she saw him looking, he supposed, like some beggar come in off the street. Which was true in a sense. He had come to beg forgiveness.

"Will!" Emily rushed around the counter and gave him a big hug. "Thank God you're here. They want to take Cassidy away!"

"Cassie? Who wants to take her?"

"Child Services," said Emily. "They want to lock her away in a home for discarded children."

This news momentarily stunned William. He forgot about the cancer. And the disrepair of the shop. Forgot about everything. They wanted to put Cassie away. How dare they? Anger flared within him. "Over my dead body," he said. Then he sagged. Discarded children. Isn't that what he had done to Cassie?

"You have no idea how glad I am to hear that," Emily said. "Cassidy is in the back room clearing things. She'll be so overjoyed to—"

"—see me?" William finished. "I don't know why she should. I won't blame her if she tells me to get out and never come back. Lord knows I deserve it."

"Times have changed," said Emily. "Despite what happened in the past we have a new kettle of trouble today. Cassidy needs you now like she never has. The real question is: are you up to it?"

William took in a big swallow of air and let it out slowly. "I've come this far. All I can do is try."

He steeled himself as he walked resolutely to the back room door. Emily was right. The past was the past. He needed to deal with today, however hard it was. However much it hurt.

When William entered the back room, however, he was ill-prepared for what he found. The place was a calamity of debris: broken chairs and shelves and lamps, a flurry of paper, and boxes filled to overflowing with damaged candles and soaps and books. A broken music box was open on the candle-making table, a sad song clinking out as a contorted dancer hobbled about her pedestal. Cassie stood among the jumble, emptying damaged goods from one box and sorting them into others.

She looked far older than he remembered, but certainly no taller. She had obviously lost weight. Her hair was short and ragged-looking, and she had always grown it long. Pale strands stood out like cobwebs. She turned to look at him and froze, her expression blank.

"Cassie," he said. He couldn't think of anything else.

His daughter didn't respond. She just continued to stare at him. Was she paler now than when he had entered?

Finally she spoke. "Customers aren't allowed back here when classes aren't in session."

William suppressed a chuckle. Had Cassie told a joke? "I taught you that," he said. "When you were about six years old and took upon yourself the job of traffic cop."

But now he wasn't sure it had been a joke. Cassie continued to stare. And her skin had turned whiter. He could see now that she was trembling.

"Customer's aren't allowed," she said again.

William didn't know what to do. "Cassie, it's me, your father." Then he rushed to catch her as she collapsed onto the boxes of debris.

· δ ·

Doctor Straka

Straka tied the mask across his mouth and nose and then adjusted the green gown so that it looked like he knew how to wear one. The surgical gloves were the real problem. They were size extra-extra large, but still squeezed tightly over the deformity of his thick fingers.

Somehow the candle had moved to the hospital. Last night it was in the woman's shop while several days ago it was in her home. Straka had the horrible sense that it somehow knew he was tracking it, and even now was trying to stay one step ahead of him. Well, that would only work for so long. He was closing in.

Straka looked into the mirror and studied his eyes. They had been dark once. Black as coal. Now they were a startling blue. His entire body was pale. The flesh around his eyes was puffy and hairless, but with the surgical garb he could pass himself off as an elderly doctor, provided no one demanded he identify himself.

Leaving the first floor washroom, Straka walked briskly to the stairs and up to the cancer ward on the fifth floor. The nurses and patients cast him odd looks as he scanned the roster at the nurses station then marched to room 516 where Cassidy was listed. Surgery was on the second floor and unfamiliar hospital staff were always viewed with suspicion.

Straka halted outside the door to Cassidy's room. There was a doctor and another man inside with her. Barging in on them wasn't likely to get him anywhere.

"It's the trauma of seeing you again," the doctor was saying. "It shook her up some. I'm sure she'll be fine."

"I feel so bad," the man said. He looked like a street person with his wrinkled clothes and unshaven face. "If I had been thinking at all I wouldn't have walked in like that. I would have sent Emily in to warn her."

"Excuse me?"

Straka turned to find a stout, white-haired woman eyeing him up and down. "Is this Cassidy-Ann Faith's room?"

Straka didn't know what to say to the woman, and he could hear the two men inside coming out to investigate. There was a clipboard on the wall and he took it down and pretended to study it.

"Dr. Kinman," said the woman as the two men approached. "Is that Cassidy-Ann Faith lying in that bed? I was beginning to think she didn't exist."

"Estelle Walker," said the doctor. "I'd like you to meet William Faith, Cassidy's father."

The woman eyed the other man up and down, much as she had Straka. "Really?" she said. "I can't say that I'm impressed."

"These past few days have been trying," said the man. "I usually look more presentable."

"You don't have to convince me," said the woman. "The Board will examine your case at the Hearing."

"Hearing?" said the man. "What Hearing?"

"I assume you'll want a Hearing," said the woman. "You did come back for your daughter, did you not?"

"Of course I've come back for my daughter. Why do I need a Hearing? I'm her father."

"But are you a fit father? You abandoned your family last year. It's in our records."

"Well, I'm back now." Straka could see the man was growing angry. His face had flushed and his words were growing louder.

"I think we need to take this discussion to my office," suggested the doctor. He took the two combatants by the elbow and forcefully led them away.

Perfect, Straka decided. I can search this room in a matter of seconds.

"Doctor!" came another voice. "We need you in 502. Code yellow."

A male nurse stood a short distance down the hall. He was looking critically at Straka. Straka could see the question forming on his lips.

"On my way," Straka said, with enough authority to dissuade the young intern. He strode toward the man and, seeing an empty patient room, quickly pressed his hand over the surprised intern's mouth and pulled him inside.

Straka had killed a thousand men in a thousand different ways. On this occasion he utilized a sharp twist of the neck that severed the spinal cord bringing instant death. Pushing aside the sheet from the bed, Straka laid the intern out and then pulled the sheet back in place: a sleeping patient. It would do.

In retrospect, Straka's disguise was a poorer choice than he first thought. He was lucky to have gotten this far. He would kill the girl and frisk the room, taking anything that wasn't nailed down.

Only, when he returned to Cassidy's room, the girl was gone.

· δ ·

Mother's Candle

Never in his life had William met a woman like Estelle "Holier Than Thou" Walker.

"If you want to be Cassidy-Ann's father you will need to earn the right," the irritable woman said after they entered Dr. Kinman's office.

"Earn the right! I'm her father! Flesh and blood. No government can take that away from me."

"Mr. Faith," the woman said coldly. "The government takes that away from men like you every day. We have zero tolerance for deadbeats."

"I'm not—" but William stopped. There was no point arguing with the woman. She had decided that he was a villain and in many ways he couldn't blame her; she was right. But he was still Cassie's father no matter what anyone said.

The woman smiled, sensing she had won something, and turned to Dr. Kinman. "Has Cassidy-Ann signed herself over to the care of this or any other hospital?"

Dr. Kinman slowly shook his head.

"Then I will be return shortly with custody papers and a transportation nurse. Good day." With that she turned and left.

The doctor looked at William as if to say: It's out of my hands. Then he spoke. "I hope you will consider convincing Cassidy to stay here at the hospital. I cannot speak for Child Welfare, but I can assure you that *Fountain Valley* will provide your daughter the best care possible."

William struggled with the memory of watching his mother die in this very hospital and then envisioned Ms Walker escorting Cassie away, never to be seen again. He couldn't decide which was worse. At last he said, "I don't even know if Cassie will speak to me, never mind let me convince her of anything."

Dr. Kinman nodded. "I see your point. It might be best if the first person Cassidy sees when she wakes up isn't her long lost father. Why don't you go home and clean yourself up? By the time you get back Cassidy will be awake and I'll have spoken with her."

"But that Walker woman said she'd be right back." William couldn't stop clenching his fists. He had never struck a woman in his life, but that woman had sorely tempted him.

The doctor let out a small chuckle. "The wheels of government turn slowly my friend. First she has to find a temporary care home that will take Cassidy, and then she has to find an available nurse to escort Cassidy to that home. Estelle Walker will be lucky if she can do that by this time tomorrow, never mind *shortly*."

William decided to take Dr. Kinman at his word. It was clear that he cared for Cassie and had no love for women like Estelle Walker. And William did need to get cleaned up. He would go to the house and take a shower. Hopefully, Carolyn hadn't thrown out his clothes and shaving kit. Otherwise, he'd have to go shopping. But none of that would take long. He'd be away from Cassie for at most two hours. Cassie would need that time.

On the way home he pulled his rental car against the curb outside the candle shop. He wanted to let Emily know Cassie was all right.

"I'm so glad," Emily said when he told her the news. "I should have spoken to her before you walked in. What was I thinking?"

"It's alright," said William. "It's all water under the bridge now." What a stupid thing to say. Was his abandoning Cassie and Carolyn this past year *all water under the bridge*?

"I'm sorry about the mess," said Emily, looking around her. "What with the break-in—"

"What break-in?" William demanded.

Emily looked at him quizzically. "I thought you knew. The shop was vandalized last night. That's why Cassidy was sorting things in the back."

William raced into the back room and pushed his way through the boxes. He went to a lower cupboard and shuffled through its contents. "Emily!" he shouted, trying to stay calm and failing miserably. "My mother's candle? Do you know where it is?"

Emily stood in the back room doorway, her eyes wide with concern. For his sanity, no doubt. The candle would mean nothing to her.

"Carolyn always kept it in that cupboard," she said. "Is it not there?"

"No." William stared hopelessly at the boxes of ruined wax. He had failed even in that.

· δ ·

William Versus The State

Cassidy's head throbbed with the bouncing of the bus as it trundled from stop to stop toward home. She felt that at any moment she would vomit onto the red plastic seat.

She still wasn't certain why she had sneaked out of the hospital after feigning to still be asleep while Dr. Kinman and her father discussed her. It wasn't because Ms. "In the Best Interest of the Child" had shown up. Dr. Kinman had taken that well in hand. Nor was it because her father had suddenly walked back into her life. Her father! Though his sudden disheveled appearance at the shop had thrown her for a loop, she had dealt with bigger problems since her illness. If she could survive her mother's funeral, she could survive anything.

No. It was the strange doctor out in the hall that had made her flee. Though he was a doctor, and he healed people, and he belonged there, just as she belonged there as a sick person in need of healing, the man somehow reminded her of the horrible figure last night outside the shop, and the day before at her mother's grave. She just knew she had to leave.

I'm being silly, she told herself. One of my cancer-induced sillinesses. Later I'll look back and shake my head: That couldn't have been me doing that! I would never....

The bus bumped to a stop and a tall man in a dark raincoat climbed quietly up the two steps into the bus. He dropped some change into the coin box and then scanned the seats with fierce blue eyes. His face was runneled, his hair a mop of straw. He strode slowly down the aisle, past empty seats, toward her.

Cassidy blinked. The rumpled man. He's found me. She looked left, then right, but there was nowhere to go. The bus was already moving.

His eyes seemed to stare through her as he approached. And then he was there, standing by her seat. Slowly he smiled, revealing a mouth missing several teeth, and nodded. "Afternoon" he chirped, and his eyes sparkled.

Cassidy watched as the man changed, aging decades in seconds, the smooth, lumpy flesh his face wrinkling and drooping until folds of thin skin hung loosely from his jaw and throat. His straw hair thinned and receded until it was grey and balding. Even his eyes changed, green now instead of blue, and no longer bright.

"Move along," called the bus driver.

The old man, who looked nothing like the one Cassidy had watched board the bus, grumbled and continued along the aisle. Cassidy watched him slump into a seat and then turned back to face the front.

Maybe *silly* was too mild a word for the delusions her mind sometimes created. This man looked nothing like the one she had seen outside the shop and among the tombs. Or in the hospital dressed as a doctor. Perhaps none of them had been real. Cassidy took a deep breath and stared out the window.

She had ridden this bus between home and hospital a hundred times in the year since her diagnosis. This was not the first delusion she had had while riding the bus. But it was the first that had scared her. That had to mean something. But what?

The bus turned down Aspen Avenue and drove past the candle shop. She imagined her mother working inside, cheerfully discussing soaps and scents with her customers. Then she remembered there was only Emily left, and she felt like vomiting again. Cassidy tightened her throat and closed her eyes, and by shear force of will settled her stomach. She focused on the movement of the bus and sound of the road beneath the wheels, and hummed softly to herself until the bus shrieked to a halt.

Cassidy had not pulled the bell cord, but the driver knew her and her habits. If she didn't get out at the shop, she got out at home. He gave her a brief smile as she stepped down onto the sidewalk in front of her house; the actual stop was three doors down. He had long ago stopped charging a fare.

There was a car in the driveway, a Toyota Camry with rental plates.

As the bus drove off, Cassidy walked down the sidewalk to the house next door, up the walkway and then to the side of her own house and around to the back yard, keeping in the shadows of the Mulberry bushes and peering in at the windows.

She didn't really expect to see burglars, despite the two break-ins. What burglar in his right mind would rent a car and park it in the driveway of the house he was robbing? No, it would be her father. After discovering her flight from the hospital he would have called Emily and then come here to wait for her.

Cassidy didn't know what to make of her father. He'd abandoned her when she became ill and as a result she had all but blocked him from her mind. It was difficult coming to terms with her cancer. The added burden of being rejected by her father, whom she had loved and who she thought had loved her, had been too much to bear. So she had locked him away, forgotten his face, and his love. And by doing so she had learned to deal with her illness. It was Cassidy against the world, one day at a time, with only her mother to love her.

The loss her mother had been easier to deal with than she had thought. Carolyn Faith was gone, dead, and Cassidy had expected to be inconsolable. But instead, she felt a new kinship with her mother. Cassidy herself was half-dead and gone, and felt she now had more in common with her mother than with any living soul.

The return of her father was much more difficult to digest.

Through her bedroom window, Cassidy spied William Faith pawing through her dresser drawers. His face was a dark mask, an expression of savagery her foggy memories could not reconcile with the man who had been her father. He shoved a drawer shut and turned to the closet, dumping out a box of shoes and pushing the inoffensive footwear about with the toe of his foot.

Cassidy was stunned at first, and then angry. How dare he? How dare he violate her belongings? A man who had become a stranger?

Cassidy abandoned all semblance of stealth and marched through the backyard door and down the hall to her room.

"Get out!" she said.

William Faith turned from rummaging the closet and stared at her.

"Get out!" Cassidy repeated. "How dare you go through my things like this?"

Cassidy could feel her skin flush with anger as adrenaline surged through her blood. She could feel herself begin to wobble as her hammering heart and deep breathing robbed her of the little strength she had. But she stood firm. She would not be violated this way.

"Cassie..." her father squeaked. He dropped the clothing on hangers to the closet floor and held his arms out toward her. Finally his hands dropped to his sides and he lowered his gaze. "I'm sorry," he said. "I'm sorry for everything."

"You picked a damn fine way of showing it," said Cassidy, who rarely swore and never in front of her father, back when they had been a family. "You're as bad as the burglars."

William Faith shook his head and then sagged onto the bed. "You have to let me explain. The candle. The old candle from the shop. I have to find it."

This was the last excuse Cassidy expected to hear. The candle? The one her parents had argued about?

"You need a candle so bad that you have to tear apart my things?" she demanded. She felt herself falling and wished she could sit on the bed. But wouldn't. Not with her father there.

"It's important," said William. "It was my mother's candle. And her father's before that."

Cassidy couldn't believe what she was hearing. William Faith had not returned because his wife had died. He had not returned for his dying orphaned daughter. He had come back for a smelly old candle.

She fought for words, but none would come. Her father was a monster. But to simply tell him so seemed so... inadequate. Laughable, even.

William Faith, too, seemed lost for words. He shook his head and stared at the confusion of shoes on the floor. "It's...," he floundered, "been in our family for generations. More than that. It's a sacred trust. We have to keep it safe."

"Keep it safe?" Cassidy echoed. "From who?"

Before William Faith could answer, the doorbell rang.

Cassidy stood back in the hallway while her father, still unshaven and unshowered, answered the door.

On the doorstep stood Estelle Walker and a dull-eyed, broad-shouldered man who looked like he might have retired from professional boxing to become a Child Welfare enforcer.

"Is Cassidy-Ann Faith here?" demanded Ms. Walker. "Or do I have to send the police out looking for her? For the record, I hold you responsible for that vanishing act at the hospital."

"Cassie is here and she's fine," William told her, "though it really is none of your business."

"I think the state of California will disagree with you on that count, Mr. Faith."

"Well, the State is welcome to come here and discuss it with me," William retorted.

Estelle Walker wasn't amused. "The State does not look kindly upon deadbeat dads. If you even dream of regaining custody of your daughter I suggest you begin cooperating. If you play by the rules and prove to be more reliable than you appear, you may just get her back in twelve months. Maybe ten. For now you are required to hand her over to us. It's for the best."

William Faith stepped outside with his fists clenched. Cassidy had never seen an angrier look. The two day's growth of beard on his chin stood out like tiny spikes, and Cassidy swore she could hear his teeth grinding.

The hulking enforcer was first to back down the step, with Ms. Walker reluctantly following suit.

"No one," said William Faith, his voice carrying like a hammer though it was little more than a whisper, "is coming near my daughter. For god's sake! She has terminal cancer and her mother was just brutally killed! What can you people do for her? Go get your police. Better bring the National Guard while you're at it. No one is taking away my Cassie. Not while I have anything to say about it!"

Wordlessly, the Child Welfare enforcer took Estelle Walker's elbow and pulled her away toward the street.

"I'll be back," the woman said.

The enforcer whispered something to her and pulled her away faster.

"I'll be waiting," answered William. He stepped back inside the house, and then closed and locked the door.

Cassidy's father no longer stared down at his shoes. His shoulders were not hunched and the wrinkled clothes and unkempt hair no longer made him look like a hobo. What he looked like was the father Cassidy remembered, back before the cancer, before her world came crashing down.

But she wasn't ready to trust him, to accept him back. Instead, Cassidy reached into her blue Medi-Pack and pulled out a plastic bag filled with brown paper and an ugly candle, the ugliest candle she had ever seen.

Her father stared at it, his expression frozen with shocked disbelief. Then, slowly, he smiled, white teeth stark against his unwashed face. "That's my Cassie."

· δ ·

Candle Magic

Straka locked the motel room door and pulled down the blinds, leaving the room cloaked in darkness. The red glow of the clock-radio on the nightstand reported five minutes to midnight. The time of day wasn't important for the working of magic, but down through the centuries Straka had grown comfortable with the deep hours of the night.

During his time alone on his island he had pondered the attraction of quiet and darkness. Earlier in his life he had craved just the opposite: bright lights and colors, men cheering his name. Women whispering his name. He had eschewed the darkness and being alone. He had reveled in that life. But eventually, after several hundred years, it had all simply become noise.

Midnight on a deserted beach. With clouds overhead so there is neither moon nor stars. No noise but the gentle lapping of waves against the shore, rhythmic like a mother's heartbeat from inside the womb.

That was Straka's ideal. To be once again inside the womb, waiting to be born. Darkness. Warmth. The steady beat of a heart not his own.

Once, during a time when he had still enjoyed religious trappings and the adoration of men, he had spent time in Egypt looking for this sort of magic, but had found only disappointment. The followers of the Horus cult had no magic. Their diversions had been just that: diversions. Straka had gone through the rites, learning their so-called magic, and quickly became their high priest. He had taken concubines and lain with them while bathing in the warmth of their life's blood; but when the heartbeats ceased, the blood turned cold and cloying.

So great was his disappointment that, before leaving Egypt, he killed every last one of his followers, bringing the Horus cult to an end. It was a chapter in his life he would sooner forget. The island suited him better. He had been happy there, until he learned he was dying.

Striking a match, Straka paced around the room, lighting the twelve candles he had arranged in a rough circle. The candles smoked, filling the room with an acrid stench, but the tallow refused to burn. After the many hundreds of times he had lit the candles, the tallow never diminished and the wicks only become blackened. Now here was magic, the only magic Straka had ever found that lasted. Had Milos, the simple healer, even known what he possessed? Wasting himself in that tiny Central European town treating fevers and salving wounds. Oh, to have that magic within himself, as Milos had, instead being required to light the candles and consume a life.

On the bed rested a bird cage, and from within the cage two eyes blinked against the smoky candlelight.

Straka waited while smoke permeated the air, the flickering of the flames growing indistinct as the smoke thickened. But he grew impatient. The visit to the hospital had been a disaster, just like the house and the candle shop. He'd been in Los Angeles now for ten days, and as far as he was concerned, ten days too long. He missed the quiet of his island.

He opened the cage and hauled out an orange and white tabby, some family pet that had made the mistake of wandering too far from the safety of its home. The cat hissed and scratched with its claws, but Straka felt no pain. Thanks to the magic the scratches healed almost as quickly as they were formed.

Annoyed, Straka broke the animal's legs and set it on the center of the floor. He watched in amusement as it twitched and jerked, trying to get its useless feet under it and make a get-away. It didn't know yet that it was dead.

He pulled an ancient Keris dagger from his belt, a little something he had picked up in Malaysia during the Second World War. For the Moslems it carried great ritual significance. For Straka, it was just a sharp blade that he liked. That he used it for his own rituals was pure coincidence.

The cat cast him a peeved look and then howled as he reached down and slit the animal's belly from neck to pelvis— not a deep wound, just enough to let the life's blood slowly leak away and mingle with the smoke in the room.

As the scent of living blood mixed with the magic of the candles, the candle flames flared and smoke whirled about the room. Straka breathed deep, taking the smoke into his lungs, absorbing the life essence of the cat into himself. At once he felt stronger, the weight of centuries falling away from his bones, his sinews, his soul.

The cat mewed where it lay dying on the floor, unaware of the gift it bestowed upon Straka by means of the candles.

Straka knew his time was short; the small animal would quickly bleed out and die, and the magic would cease. He turned to the desktop where he had unfolded a map of the city. The map, though new ten days ago, now contained the cuts and stains of earlier searches. Straka closed his eyes and concentrated on his goal, holding his blooded knife over the map. The smoke filled his lungs, permeating his being with the life essence of the cat, briefly renewing his own ages-old essence, strengthening it beyond that of ordinary men. This was the magic that kept him alive, allowing his body to heal and survive wounds that to others would be fatal. This was the necromancer's gift that Straka had taken so many lifetimes ago in the boneworks of that nameless town near Prague. And, while the cat still lived, there were other magics he could call upon.

The knife descended with such force that it pierced the map and sank a good half inch into the wood of the desk. Behind him, on the floor, lying in a pool of cooling blood, the cat breathed its last and the magic was gone. But it was enough.

Straka opened his eyes and was at once angry and delighted. The lost candle had moved again, but only a short distance. It seemed obvious now that its owner was not trying to hide it. Protect it. That Straka had failed to recover the candle three times in ten days was simple bad luck. He'd seen enough whimsy of fate in his long life to not be overly concerned. Luck turned. It always did. Perhaps this time. Perhaps the next. And then the magic would be his.

· δ ·

Flaky Synapses

Cassidy came awake from a sound sleep, alerted by the scent of smoke. The clock on the night stand proclaimed midnight. Outside her room all was quiet.

Sitting up, she sniffed the air, testing it. It did not smell like a house fire. Neither did the smoke come from outside, a burning rubbish heap or field. She imagined, briefly, her father somewhere in the house smoking a cigarette or cigar, though she had never known him to smoke in the time before he had abandoned her.

And yet, earlier that day he had sent the Child Welfare woman packing. Did that not mean that he was still her father? That somehow, despite everything, he still loved her? No matter how she tried, Cassidy couldn't reconcile his leaving a year ago and his fierce unwillingness to give her up now. And then there was his obsession with the candle.

Cassidy had listened quietly as her father explained that the candle was very old, passed down through his family from generation to generation along with an obligation to keep it safe, though the reason had been lost long ago.

"I have to keep it safe," he said.

"Why?" Cassidy asked.

Her father just looked at her, his mouth moving though no words came out.

"It's just an ugly old candle," she added, turning the candle this way and that on the coffee table. "Even mother kept it hidden in a cupboard, and she loves candles."

William Faith shook his head. "Your mother never understood."

"I can believe that, not if you never explained it to her any better than you're explaining it to me."

"It's a sacred duty," he asserted. "To abandon it is to undo all of the efforts made by those who came before, to negate all of their sacrifices."

Cassidy thought about that. There seemed to be something in what her father was saying, but she couldn't put it into words any better than he could.

"It's your responsibility, too," he added.

"Not for long," she said. And then she told him something that apparently Dr. Kinman had not— just how little time she had left.

Cassidy had never seen her father cry. At least she had no memory of it. The moment was awkward, and she still didn't know if she could trust him. She had left him there in the living room, sitting on the sofa with his face in his hands, his ancestral candle on the coffee table, and had returned to her room to clean up the mess he had made. She had no idea what to make of this man she knew so well, yet didn't know at all.

The scent of smoke returned, distracting Cassidy from her thoughts. She climbed out of bed, pulled a nightgown over her pajamas, and stepped into the hall to investigate.

She found William Faith asleep on the sofa in the living room, an open book lying next to him. She was somewhat mollified that he chose not to sleep in mother's bed, in the bed her parents had shared before he abandoned his family. He had showered and shaved and put on fresh clothing, and looked almost like the man she remembered from before her illness.

The curtains were open and a full, harvest moon illuminated the front yard and the contents of the room. Pale light conjured sharp outlines and harsh shadows.

On the living room table stood the source of the smoke that had awakened her: father's candle. It was unlit, the wick still pale yellow from having never been lit since the day it was made. Who would light such a thing? If it burned at all, the dirty tallow would stink and shed very little light.

And yet the unlit candle emitted smoke, a thin, grey cloud that rose up and swirled about the table, though certainly not enough smoke to have wafted down the hall to her room and wake her.

The smoke was most likely a dream induced by her diseased brain, like the old man she had seen on the bus who, for a moment, had looked like a completely different man, quite possibly a man who didn't even exist. She'd had such dreams before — a vague, surreal mix of the real and the unreal — both waking and asleep. And they occurred more frequently as the cancer progressed. Dying synapses.

That was what Dr. Kinman had called it. The cancer would kill certain synapses and Cassidy's brain would make alternate connections so that it could go on thinking. Sometimes those connections would make her see things that weren't there, or remember things that never happened, or forget what had happened five minutes ago. It was why she sometimes found herself sitting in a bus not knowing where she had just come from or where she was going. Cassidy had learned to accept it. And to hide it. She usually succeeded.

The candle continued to smoke, and Cassidy pinched herself, trying to decide if she was really standing in her living room watching her father asleep on the sofa, or if she was still in bed having a vivid dream. For all she knew she was sitting on the bus coming home from the hospital, staring out the window, not seeing the quiet streets, but instead imagining her living room at midnight. Any moment now the driver would shake her shoulder, urging her back to the here and now.

It was even possible that her father had never really returned. That the confused new connections in her brain had drawn past memories of him into the current tragedy of her life, and that in the morning she would awaken to discover he had never been here, that Dr. Kinman, Emily, and even the Child Welfare woman would deny having seen him.

Real or not, the smoke continued to twist and roil, and it seemed to Cassidy that a shape was taking form in the moonlight: a man, haggard like her father had been when he surprised her at the shop, though extremely lean, and with long, unkempt hair. The smoke figure waved its ethereal arms, as if beckoning her to light the candle.

Now Cassidy knew she was dreaming. She should laugh, but felt too afraid. The idea of lighting the candle scared her.

"Cassie?"

Cassidy turned from the candle and saw her father sitting on the sofa, rubbing his eyes.

William Faith yawned and then switched on the light in the brass stand by the sofa. "Why are you up? Are you okay?"

Cassidy looked back at the candle, but the smoke was gone. There was no sign of there ever having been smoke. The air smelled dry and clean, with perhaps a hint of coming rain.

"Flaky synapses," she said, and then returned to her room and her bed, leaving her father to stare after her in confusion.

· δ ·

Natural Healing

William watched Cassie wander back to her room and wondered for the hundredth time if he was doing the right thing. Should she be here? Or should he have taken her back to the hospital? Where she was supposed to have been earlier that day instead of coming home and finding him searching her room. After all the stupid things he had done, why did he have to disappoint her like that? And she rewarded his bad judgment by presenting him with his mother's candle, safe and sound.

But William's relief had withered as Cassie told him what Dr. Kinman had avoided telling him at the hospital, that her time was nearly up.

They had spoken little after that. William silent as he tried to decide if he should do as Dr. Kinman asked and urge Cassidy to check herself into the hospital, permanently, and as he waited for Cassie to ask the question he knew she had to ask before he could hope to be her father again: Why had he left?

Cassie's silence could be for a hundred different reasons. Was it because she hated him? Or she didn't *want* to know why he had left? Or didn't care? Or was she too ill to talk? He hoped that was not the reason. His mother had spoken little during her final weeks. But neither had she energy to move, while Cassie was running around town all on her own.

After some much needed grocery shopping he had made French Toast for dinner, something Cassie had always loved as a child. She had smiled, but hardly ate two forkfuls, and had spoken little. His mother couldn't eat in her final days, and had taken nourishment through a tube.

The circumstances were different, but the similarities were there. Cassie was dying, just like her grandmother when William was Cassie's age. He would watch his daughter die, just as he had watched his mother die.

These thoughts had haunted him for the past hours and William was no closer to knowing what to do,

He looked down at the book he had been reading before falling asleep: *Natural Healing on the Western Plains*. William had always been a reader, but this past year he had done little else.

Modern medicine had failed both his mother and his daughter. Cancer treatments, at least for the type of cancer that ravaged his family, were painful and mostly useless. It had surprised him to learn that Cassie's treatments were an improvement over his mother's, but in the end they still failed. Cassie would still die.

When he had run away a year ago, he had also been running to. There was a whole world of alternative medicine out there. Some even claimed to defeat cancer. But every approach he studied had a low success rate. Usually low enough to be sheer luck.

He had started out with great optimism. He would find a treatment and come home and cure his daughter. Carolyn would understand and welcome him back. Cassie would live.

But nothing had turned out the way he thought it would. He had failed to find a cure. Carolyn was dead. Cassie was still alive, but for how long? It was too late to help, yet it wasn't over. Dr. Kinman. He would speak with Kinman. Find out what he could do in the time Cassie had left. Everything William had done up to now had been wrong. Surely he could do *something* right. Before the end.

A noise outside the window drew his attention. William cocked his head and heard it again. Rising from the sofa he walked to the sliding glass door and listened. Several raindrops fell onto the cement patio blocks with a tap-tap-tap. The wind shifted and drops began striking the window glass. The sound had only been the rain.

And then something smashed through the glass and William felt himself tackled to the floor.

· δ ·

Housebreak

The clock on the night stand indicated twelve fourteen when Cassidy came awake again. She had slept five minutes, if that. Ominous sounds crept in from the living room, squeaks from the floor and furniture moving. Cassidy sat bolt upright at what sounded like a lamp smashing, and she quickly climbed out from the blankets and put on her nightgown for a second time.

The living room was in darkness. The curtains were still drawn and wind through broken glass brushed her face and the patter of rain on concrete and grass echoed in her ears. Moonlight illuminated two figures grappling near the sofa: her father and a taller man in a long cloak. At first Cassidy thought the stranger might be the enforcer from Child Welfare, come to take her away, but then she got the sense that this man was far more dangerous.

Her father grunted as they fought, arm on arm like wrestlers. He lifted one foot and kicked at the cloaked man's knee, then quickly returned his foot to the floor for balance. The other man made no sound, and the kick seemed to have no effect. He merely bore down with his superior weight, patently waiting for an opportunity to strike.

"Cassie! Run!" William Faith had spotted her standing in the hallway outside the living room. He grunted as the stranger took advantage of his distraction and punched him in the stomach.

Cassidy turned to flee through the kitchen and out the back door into the yard, but her feet wouldn't carry her. She felt like she was falling. Her father grunted again as the intruder brought up his knee, and then she could see something metallic shining in the moonlight. It looked like a knife.

"Run!" her father shouted again.

Now Cassidy did run. Into the living room. On the coffee table was the book on candle-making she had brought home from the shop. She had intended to read it, but hadn't had an opportunity yet. Now an opportunity of a different sort presented itself. It was a large, hardcover book, with many glossy photographs of candles. It weighed maybe five pounds. Cassidy took the book off the table, lifted it high with both hands, and slammed it against the back of the intruder's head.

The intruder did not even falter. He turned from her father to stare at her in amazement, and she recognized immediately the waxen face and straw hair. It was the disheveled man who had watched her mother's funeral and hammered at the shop door. He smiled at her with thick, uneven lips. Cassidy had never felt so cold in her life.

The man's smile slipped as his eyes rolled up into his skull and he sank to the living room floor. Cassidy's father stood behind him with the broken lamp in his hand, the bulb and canopy had been smashed, but the brass stand was as strong as ever.

"Are you okay?" William asked. He was breathing hard and was hunched over like he was injured.

Cassidy nodded, though the stress and interrupted sleep had left her feeling weak as a kitten. She gazed down at the disheveled man lying on the floor. Beside him lay a silver knife shining pale in the moonlight. The man looked like a stale corpse, his flesh dead and bloated. Who is he? Why is he here?

"I'll call the police," her father said, lurching toward the kitchen. "See if you can turn on some lights."

Cassidy nodded, but instead of going to the light switch she lifted the ancient candle off the coffee table and took it to her room, rewrapped it in packing paper, and placed it inside her Medi-Pack. For some reason the image in the smoke seemed more real than the disheveled man lying unconscious on the living room floor. Who were these two men? And why had the smoke man wanted her to light the candle?

She returned to the hallway to turn on the light and saw a police car sitting outside in the street. The doorbell rang just as she hit the light switch. "That was fast."

Her father emerged from the kitchen, wincing as he moved. "I haven't called them yet."

That was when they both saw that the intruder and his knife were gone. "The candle—" began William Faith, seeing that it was no longer on the coffee table. The doorbell rang again, more insistent this time.

Cassidy was about to say that the candle was safe when her father opened the door and two policemen stepped inside followed by Estelle Walker, a triumphant grin on her face. The enforcer was not with her.

Cassidy's father glared at her. "Ms. Walker? It's the middle of the night."

"I told you I'd be back with the police," she purred. "I have a document here requiring you to hand over your daughter."

One of the policemen frowned and, after taking in William Faith's condition, peered past him into the living room, noting the jumbled furniture, broken lamp and sliding glass door and the discarded book on candle-making. "Is there a problem, here?" he asked.

Cassidy stood back in the hallway shadows, listening as her father described the attack and the stolen candle. Neither the police nor Ms. Walker seemed to notice her.

"Are you certain he had a knife?" asked the officer.

William nodded and described the curved blade, then displayed a long slash on his arm where the shirt was torn leaving a long red gash from wrist to elbow. In the moonlit darkness Cassidy had not even noticed he'd been cut.

"You should get that looked at," the officer suggested. "It could get infected."

"This is all secondary!" exclaimed Estelle Walker. "We came here to collect the girl, and the sooner the better given the circumstances. Where is your daughter, Mr. Faith?"

William gawked as Ms. Walker stamped her foot and waved the document in her fist like a weapon.

The second officer, who until this point had said nothing, cleared his throat. "Perhaps it's for the best, sir. I understand the child's mother was attacked and killed in this very house less than two weeks ago. Your daughter will be much safer in Ms. Walker's care."

Cassidy's father continued to gawk. He stared at all of them and his shoulders seemed to slump. Cassidy did not wait to see what would happen next.

In stocking feet she slipped back down the hall to her bedroom, grabbed some clothes, tossed her Medi-Pack through the bedroom window and climbed out after it. Soon she was through the neighbor's yard, across the alley, and away down the street. The night was calm with a post-rain ozone smell in the air and the harvest moon dipping behind broken clouds.

· δ ·

Safe Haven

Cassidy couldn't recall ever visiting the hospital voluntarily. She had either gone with her mother or alone on the bus for a scheduled examination or procedure, or, more recently, had woken up in a hospital bed after having a spell. Over time the hospital had become sort of a third home after the shop and her house. She supposed that is why she had come.

Waiting near her house for the police and Child Welfare to leave, hadn't been an option. Something in the slump of her father's shoulders made her wonder if he wouldn't just call them back.

She would have gone to the shop. Even at night with the *Closed* sign up and the door locked and no customers, she had always felt comfortable with the soaps and candles for company. But the shop had been broken into the night before and the place was still a mess, despite Emily's attempts to return it to normality.

No. Both house and the shop had been violated, making Cassidy feel violated. Only the hospital felt safe.

Since the buses had stopped running she had found a taxi after walking two blocks. The driver, noting her haggard appearance and her destination had refused to take her money. "Take care," he said as he let her out.

The nurses and orderlies all smiled at her as she walked along the hallways and past the nurse's station. The light in Dr. Richard Kinman's office was off, the first indication Cassidy had ever seen that the doctor had a life outside the hospital.

In the cancer ward most of the beds were in use with many of the occupants asleep though some read books or magazines while a few simply stared dull-eyed at the ceiling.

Cassidy slumped into a chair in the waiting area that afforded a good view of an unoccupied bed. In a few minutes, after the orderlies had forgotten about her and the coast was clear, she would climb into that bed and get some much needed sleep. At least, that was the plan.

She didn't know if she had fallen asleep in the chair or had simply lost four hours while the synapses in her brain sought new connections. All she did know was that she was still sitting in the chair in the hospital lounge when Dr. Kinman shook her shoulder and softly spoke her name.

"Cassidy?"

The clock on the wall at the nurse's station said it was just after five. She assumed a.m.

"Cassidy? Are you all right?" Dr. Kinman sat in the chair next to her and waited patiently for Cassidy to collect herself.

"Child Welfare came to my house in the middle of the night," she said at last. She didn't want to tell Dr. Kinman about the disheveled man, or about the candle. He would think it was one of her brain dreams. Dementia, he called it. "That Walker woman brought the police to take me away. Like I was a criminal."

"And you ran away." Dr. Kinman nodded. "I'm glad you came here. You can always come here, Cassidy. Always remember that."

"My father can't stop them," Cassidy said, feeling her eyes grow wet with tears. "He wants to. But he can't."

Dr. Kinman nodded again. "I'm sure he does. But he abandoned you before, and that gives people like Estelle Walker the power to take you away. But they can't take you from the hospital. Not if you wish to stay here."

More tears flowed. Cassidy didn't want to stay in the hospital. And she didn't want to go to a strange home. She was dying and she wanted to spend her last days at her own home and the candle shop, remembering her mother. And maybe even get to know her father again while there was still a chance. She didn't need Ms. Walker or the police trying to take her away, or that horrible disheveled man breaking into her house. Why couldn't they just leave her alone?

"You need something to eat," said Dr. Kinman. "Let's get you some food and some medication and then you can sleep in a private room. Once you've rested you can decide what to do next." He smiled at her. "How does that sound?"

Cassidy smiled back through her tears. "Yes. I could use some rest. Thank you Dr. Kinman."

"You're welcome Cassidy. Remember. You can come to me for anything."

· δ ·

Straka Buys A Gun

After last night's brief rain the day had turned hot. Sweat oozed from Straka's runneled forehead, running down his face like rivulets of melted wax. Despite the heat he still wore his bulky, ankle-length raincoat; the shapeless garment helped to hide the growing deformities of his body.

He grunted as he shuffled along the sidewalk of LA's seedier industrial core. The city was no place for a man to live. Smog-stained buildings brooded along the streets, blocking the horizon and the sky and the wind. The air was stagnant and tasted of garbage and gasoline. Every second door was a pawn shop or a third-rate strip club. The hot July sun, when it crept between buildings, burned down on the asphalt streets and concrete walls, choking the life out of the place.

A documentary he had watched on television in his motel room called this the modern age. Straka had seen ages come and go; each worse than the last. The narrator had called it progress.

Straka was tired. He wanted to get this Milos business over with so he could return to his island and sit beneath a shady tree, basking in the cool ocean breeze. His home of the past hundred years was a paradise, a tiny deserted island in the Aleutians. No people, no plumbing, no modern. Now that, Straka decided, was true progress.

A super-bus tore along the street, kicking up dust and gum wrappers in its wake. Straka closed his eyes and turned his head, covering his mouth and nose with the sleeve of his coat. When he opened his eyes again, he squinted at the street signs and then down at the torn paper he clutched in his thick fingers. The address was blurred from sweat, but still legible. This was the place.

A gap between two buildings opened into an oil-stained alley. The smell of garbage rose around him, but at least it was out of the sun. He slouched across the expanse of broken concrete and gravel until the alley turned behind one of the buildings into a sun-scorched yard of chain-link fence and wilted grass littered with newspaper, broken bottles, and smashed crates. In the midst of the ruin waited Straka's objective.

The peddler and his cart suited their environment. Both were worn, tattered, and scratched, neither of them worth the time it took to look at them. The cart was a 70's Oldsmobile Cutlass, patched together from parts of maybe six different vehicles. The peddler wore an open leather vest and no shirt, with tattoos crawling down from his neck over a scrawny chest and emaciated stomach into faded jeans. Undoubtedly, the tattoos continued down into a pair of ancient, alligator skin cowboy boots. His grey-blond hair was long and greasy. All and all an absolute waste of a human being. Straka would be loathe to use his blood with the candles for fear of contamination.

The peddler sat next to his cart in a beat-up lawn chair drinking warm beer and eyeing Straka warily from behind dark sunglasses.

Straka uttered the phrase that, along with the scrap of paper, had cost him fifty dollars from a young hoodlum in a video arcade: "Joe sent me."

The peddler returned a gap-toothed smile. "Any friend of Joe is a friend of mine. What can I do you for?"

Straka gritted his teeth, but kept his annoyance from his face. "You know what I want. Let's get it done."

The peddler tipped his head and made a show of getting out of his chair. The man's slow, cocky movements were an attempt at intimidation. Straka let it go. He was willing to let the peddler believe anything he wanted in order to get this done quickly.

The peddler pulled a screwdriver out from beneath his cart and stuck the business end into a hole in the trunk where a lock should have been. An artful twist popped the trunk lid open. Inside lay several Army Surplus wool blankets cradling a ragtag collection of assault rifles, handguns, knives and blackjacks. There were even a couple of hand grenades, though Straka wouldn't trust one in his hand for any price. At one time his magic would have healed even a hand lost to a faulty grenade, but he no longer believed this was true. His body was failing, and the magic — incomplete as it was — could no longer sustain him.

"Take yer pick," the peddler drawled, waving a tattooed hand at his wares. "Every one's a beauty. And untraceable."

Straka doubted both statements, and was beginning to have second thoughts about using a gun at all. He had never liked guns. They were too impersonal. Half the time people never even knew who was killing them. He considered himself a knife man. Nothing beat the look in a man's eyes as he stood toe to toe with the one who was turning a blade in his belly.

It angered Straka that he was even considering a gun. Last night, though, he had learned a harsh lesson of just how weak he had become. He had gone one on one with William Faith, and lost. And William Faith was no fighter. For one of the few times in his life, Straka was ashamed. And angry. Inwardly, he cursed Milos Radimir for bringing him to this. The weakness, the shame, the blasted heat.

"That one," he said, pointing.

"Excellent choice," chimed the peddler. His hand reached down and came back holding a short-nose Luger P-08. "These were used by the SS in WWII. Most efficient weapon in the war. And just as efficient today."

"I know," said Straka. He had carried one during the war, but had rarely used it. At the time he was a ranking SS officer, respected for his ability to extract information from even the most reluctant of prisoners. But he never used his gun. There were better ways of putting holes into people when you wanted them to talk.

Straka took the two pounds of tooled steel into his hands and popped out the 8-round magazine: empty. He peered down the barrel, which was straight enough, and decided that the gun would probably fire.

"Only $600," said the peddler. "Though a fine weapon like this is a bargain at any price."

Straka reached into his pocket and thrust a ring toward the peddler. It was solid gold and held a ruby the size of a walnut.

The peddler's eyes bulged in his head. "I don't know," he said, though he took the ring readily enough and scratched the gold to see if it was real. "This could be junk."

"As could this gun," answered Straka. "But it isn't. Men with guns like this one liberated that ring from a Jewish merchant as they loaded him onto a train to Auschwitz. It's worth more than this gun, or all your guns, and probably this whole city block."

"So you say," said the peddler, clearly unimpressed. This didn't stop him from slipping the ring onto his left middle finger.

Straka had never planned on staying in the city this long and was running out of cash. Baubles and rings no longer meant anything to him, so he didn't give the loss of the ring a second thought. What annoyed him was the peddler's attitude. Treating him, Straka, as an inferior.

Earlier in the day he had gone to a gun store and then a pawn shop, only to discover that while he would have no problem buying a gun, he would have to wait four weeks for the paperwork to clear. Apparently it didn't matter what lies were on the papers, so long as the shopkeepers made a show of propriety.

Straka wasn't about to wait four weeks.

It was the pawn shop owner who had put him onto the boy in the arcade. After Straka agreed to purchase a box of 9mm Parabellum ammunition. Apparently he could buy all the ammunition he wanted without paperwork.

"Make it the ring plus a hundred," said the peddler. "And we'll call it even."

During the peddler's examination of the ring Straka's had managed, even with his thick fingers, to discretely load a single bullet into the Luger's firing chamber. "How about the ring and a bullet?" he suggested.

"Huh?" said the peddler.

Straka shot the gun from hip level hitting the peddler in the belly at close range. The noise of the shot echoed between the tall buildings, and the smell of gunpowder sweetened the stench of the alley. "One bullet should be sufficient," he explained.

The peddler groaned and pressed one hand to his stomach, the other he slid into his vest pocket, where he no doubt kept a loaded pistol.

Straka shook his head and, reversing the P-08 in his hand, smashed the weapon's handle against the peddler's skull, bringing him to his knees. From the sheath at his belt he pulled free his knife and finished the job. "You just can't trust a gun," he said.

He wiped the blade on the dead man's vest and returned it to its sheath. Then he slid the Luger into his coat pocket, yanked the ring from the peddler's finger, and shuffled back into the alley. The sun beat down on the empty yard like a furnace.

· δ ·

Healing Smoke

It was nearing noon when Dr. Kinman awakened Cassidy with a sandwich and a warning that Child Welfare was on their way over. Cassidy had to sign a waver placing her in the hospital's care, or leave before they got there. Dr. Kinman did not push for Cassidy to sign the waver, though she could see in his eyes that he wished she would.

"Not yet," Cassidy told him. Then she collected her Medi-Pack, took the elevator downstairs, and hid behind an equipment cart as Estelle Walker, the Enforcer, and three policemen besieged the front desk before being taken upstairs by Dr. Kinman.

The bus dropped her outside *Faith's Candle's & Things* beneath a sky that was clear and warm. Cassidy could almost forget the horrors of the past few days.

The shop was looking much better that it had yesterday. Emily had been busy and her father had arrived to help after Dr. Kinman called him from the hospital that morning and reassured him that Cassidy was fine.

THE NECROMANCER CANDLE

Emily arranged candles that needed no arranging in the front window display while William stood on a ladder returning overstock on the top shelves. Cassidy, feeling relatively energetic after sleeping half the day, passed up the boxes. It was almost like old times, except that mother was gone and Emily's eyes scoured the street, looking out for Child Welfare, the police, and who knows what else. Terrorists?

"I didn't mean to leave you," William said when he had finished with the boxes. He climbed down the ladder and sat on the third step. Cassidy was sitting on one of the boxes, catching her breath.

He told her about grandma Faith, about her six months of anguish and the final release of death. "I couldn't bear watching you suffer the way I watched your grandmother."

"So you went looking for a cure?" Cassidy asked. This was the hardest part to believe. There was no cure. Dr. Kinman had said so. There were only drugs to slow the disease and dull the pain.

William nodded. "I was desperate. Modern medicine couldn't help you, so I went looking for ancient medicine. I visited Native Americans and spoke with their medicine men." He shook his head. "But they didn't trust me. Not at first, anyway. When they did finally begin to teach me, it was too late. Months had passed and I thought you were dead. Your mother... I was too ashamed to face her."

"Ow!" Emily stood back from the window and shook her hand. "A paper cut," she said. "It's nothing."

"Let me see," said William.

Cassidy stood and followed him to the front of the shop where he took a plastic bag from his pocket, dumped a pinch of its contents into an empty candle-holder, and lit it with a match. It burned like tinder but smelled like incense.

"Calendula leaves," he said. "Hold your finger over the smoke."

Seeing no danger in this, Emily held her cut finger over the burning leaves. It was a thin cut, but deep, with very little blood. As Cassidy watched, the line of the cut shrank and disappeared.

"You learned that from Indians?" Cassidy asked. She'd never seen anything like it.

William smiled and shrugged. "The Native peoples live close to the land. They know better then we how nature works. The medicine men taught me a few tricks."

"But no cure for cancer," said Emily with sadness.

William shook his head.

"Something smells good," said a voice from the doorway. Detective Savoy stood there grinning at them. "I wouldn't mind buying some of that incense myself."

Cassidy feared she was slipping again. She hadn't heard the door chimes when the detective entered. But neither, apparently, had Emily and William. Was she having another dementia? Maybe her father hadn't really healed Emily's finger after all. Had never gone off to live with the Indians.

Detective Savoy nodded at her and then grimaced at the others. "I have some bad news. Child Welfare has issued a general warrant for Cassidy to be brought into custody. They're making threats of obstruction against you, Mr. Faith. If they do, that'll go against you in a custody hearing."

"What right do they have to take a child from her family?" Emily demanded. "This is an outrage!"

Savoy sighed. "In this case I agree with you. Unfortunately, I'm not the judge. I'm not going to tell you what to do. I just wanted to let you know what's happening."

"So you're not taking Cassidy in?" asked Emily.

Detective Savoy smiled. "Me? I was never here." Then he stepped out through the door and was gone.

"I'll get a hotel room and Cassie can I can stay there," suggested William. Then he shook his head. "No. That's no good. Hiding in a hotel is no better than being taken away."

Cassidy touched his hand, thankful that he had said it first.

"You'll stay with me, won't you Cassidy," said Emily. "They haven't come looking for you at my place. Not yet, at any rate."

They both looked at her. Their expressions said there were no good options, and that, in the end, only Cassidy could decide what to do.

Cassidy returned to her seat on the box. She felt like giving up. She was too tired to fight. She had been standing all of two minutes and her legs were already turning to jelly. There were no options. Fate had taken her health, her mother, her home, and now even her final days were not her own. There was nothing, really, that she could do.

"All right," she said. "Tonight I'll stay with Emily." She owed her that much for all her friendship and support. "Then tomorrow

THE NECROMANCER CANDLE

I'll admit myself to the hospital. They can't touch me there. And it's probably for the best." Those last words, when she said them, she believed to be true, which was the worst part of it.

· δ ·

The Evening News

Another night. Another rented motel room. Another cage with an animal. Whoever occupied the next room had the TV on, loud, and it was getting on Straka's nerves. It was almost one o'clock in the morning and Straka was impatient to make his next move.

Earlier in the evening he had watched TV himself. The news had carried a special report on a string of bizarre crimes in the city. The police were mystified. It had begun with the home invasion and murder of Carolyn Faith two weeks ago. Then, more recently, the dead woman's candle shop had been vandalized, followed by a disguised attacker in the dead woman's home. The attacker had been described as a large man wearing a rubber mask and gloves, the kind worn on Halloween. Police suspected that the same man had checked into various motels and performed animal sacrifices, the link being that candles were apparently used in the sacrifice rituals. Police concluded that the man (or men) was a deranged satanic cultist and that people should safeguard their pets.

Straka had laughed. Safeguard your pets! Were the police stupid? Or just incompetent? They had described the death of the gun peddler as *gang related*. No wonder criminals lived so free and easy. Straka might learn to like this city, if he didn't miss the peace of his island.

In the next room, the TV blared.

"Enough," he said. The candles were ready. The map was on the dresser. He opened the cage and let the cat go free. It sped through the open apartment door and out into the night with blinding speed. Safeguard your pets.

Straka took his gun and hammered on the next apartment's door. He wondered if its occupant had watched the evening news.

· δ ·

The Warning

Cassidy wrinkled her nose. Smoke. She was tempted to ignore it. It wasn't real. Just her damaged synapses inventing memories. She turned her face into the sofa bed and tried to go back to sleep, but the smell just got stronger.

"All right," she said and sat up.

It took a moment to remember where she was, in Emily's living room. After her mother had died, Emily had tried everything short of crying to get Cassidy to sleep in her bedroom while Emily took the sofa bed, but Cassidy wouldn't hear it. Bed. Sofa bed. It made no difference to her, but she wouldn't have Emily give up her own bedroom. In the end, as she always did, Emily let Cassidy have her way.

There was no moonlight filtering through the window, but there was a night light plugged into a wall socket out in the hallway. Cassidy looked around, searching for the source of the smoke, and eventually found it: her blue Medi-Pack. The candle. She had forgotten about it.

Slowly, for her arms felt almost lifeless, she fumbled inside the pack, eventually unwrapping the old candle and setting it on the coffee table. Smoke drifted around the ancient tallow like mist, until, eventually, a man-like figure in smoke hovered above the candle.

Again it gestured, as it had the night before, for Cassidy to light the candle. Cassidy was reluctant. According to her father, the candle had been in their family for generations, the task falling on each generation to protect it and keep it safe. From what, William Faith had no idea.

Emily's living room had a brick fireplace with a broad oak mantle, upon which stood photos and glass ornaments and, of course, candles. A box of matches sat at one end of the mantle. Cassidy had retrieved the box and was back sitting on the sofa before she even realized what she had done. She held a burning match in her fingers.

The smoke figure gestured for Cassidy to light the wick and, before the match burned down to her fingers, she did just that.

The ancient wick sputtered and flared, died out, then rekindled itself, and suddenly the smoke in the air was real. It was just as acrid and pungent as Cassidy had always expected it would be.

"Thank you."

THE NECROMANCER CANDLE

Cassidy started and looked around. It was a man's voice that spoke. It sounded vaguely like her father, but felt rough from lack of use. The smoke man above the candle grinned at her, looking more and more solid the longer the candle burned.

"You are in danger," the shadow said.

Cassidy couldn't help herself. "Well, duh! I don't know how things could get much worse."

"The one who seeks you," continued the shadow, "is a very dangerous man. He killed your mother and searched your home and property. It was he who fought your father and who will shortly come to the place you are now. You must flee along with all who are with you."

"Dementia," said Cassidy. "None of this is real."

"The danger is very real," the voice responded, more quietly now. The smoke seemed to be dissipating.

"Why is this man after me?" Cassidy demanded. "What did I do?"

The man in the smoke turned away, and the smoke swirled and almost broke up. But then the man reformed and looked at her. "It is me he wants. Or rather this candle, which holds my soul. I am the cause of your troubles. I am sorry."

Cassidy didn't know what to say. She wanted to destroy the candle. To break it into pieces with her fists and flush it down the toilet. To throw it in the fireplace and light a bonfire. But she knew that wouldn't help. Destroying the candle wouldn't stop the disheveled man from looking for it.

"My time is short." The voice was but a whisper, and Cassidy could see that the smoke was nearly gone, even thought the wick still burned.

"The other candles are being extinguished and the magic that sustains me returns to slumber. You must bring the candles together. All thirteen. And light them in the presence of a healer. Only then can the evil one be stopped."

"What?" said Cassidy. "How?"

"He comes now. Flee!" And with that the smoke was gone.

"Who are you talking to, dear?"

Emily stood in the hallway, wrapped in a checkered robe and squinting into the candle-lit living room. "Where did you get that horrible candle?" she exclaimed. "The stink!"

Cassidy reached with her fingers and pinched out the wick. Only then did she notice that the candle itself had not burned.

"We have to leave," Cassidy said abruptly. "Now." Feeling energy she did not have, she rewrapped the candle and pushed it into her Medi-Pack.

"Leave?" said Emily. "It's the middle of the night. Go back to sleep, dear. Everything will be all right in the morning."

"No," said Cassidy. "It won't. The man who came to my house last night and fought with my father. He's coming here. Now. We have to go!"

"Cassidy, child. You're not making any sense. Where would we go? Can't it wait till morning?"

"The shop," said Cassidy. "We'll go there." She looked at Emily, her eyes pleading. "Call my father. Ask him to meet us there."

"In the middle of the night?" Emily shook her head, but in the end gave in.

Cassidy knew she didn't believe her. Her fears were just dementia. But Emily was a good friend and was willing to humor a sick child. And perhaps she was doing just that. The man in the smoke couldn't be real. Cassidy was sinking into madness.

· δ ·

The Plan

William was waiting for them when they arrived at the shop. He looked tired and irritable, but welcomed them inside and gave Cassidy a hug. "The police are watching the house. I had to sneak out the back door and walk here."

"You'd think we were criminals," said Emily. "Skulking around in the night."

Cassidy claimed the stool behind the sales counter and took the candle from her Medi-Pack. She set it in front of her and then nearly collapsed with fatigue. This was her second night with interrupted sleep and it was taking a heavy toll.

William Faith stared at the candle on the sales counter. Cassidy knew he thought that last night's attacker had disappeared with the candle. Perhaps if that were true, that would be the end of it, and they wouldn't all be hiding in the shop in the middle of the night.

Quickly, Cassidy repeated what the smoke man had told her.

While she spoke, her father examined the candle. "You say you lit it?"

Cassidy nodded. "In Emily's living room. The man in the smoke wanted me to."

William poked his finger around the wick. "It doesn't look like it's been lit."

"It smoked before it was lit," Cassidy added. "But the smoke couldn't talk until I lit the candle."

Emily stood apart from them looking nervous. Cassidy knew she thought she was speaking nonsense, that it was her brain cancer speaking, but her father seemed open to the idea. Maybe his experiences with the Indians made him less of a skeptic.

"No one in our family has ever lit the candle," William muttered. "We've always been afraid to."

Outside, a car sped past the shop, its headlights momentarily illuminating the front windows. It was two in the morning and even a single car was enough to startle them.

"Should we light it again?" William asked.

Cassidy thought about this then shook her head. "The smoke man went away even before I snuffed out the wick. I think all the candles have to be lit for it to work."

"And there are thirteen, you say?" asked William.

Cassidy smiled weakly. "The candle said there are thirteen. And that the evil man has the others."

"Who is he?" William asked, more to himself than as a request for an answer.

Cassidy wondered who he meant: the man in the candle? Or the man who had killed her mother?

Emily cleared her throat. "This evil man. Won't he find us here as well? What are we going to do?"

"I have a plan," Cassidy said.

Emily and her father looked at her.

"It's not a very good plan," she admitted, and suddenly she felt exhausted. So much could go wrong.

"I'm sure it will be fine," said William.

"First," said Cassidy, "we need a business card."

· δ ·

Foiled Again

Straka kicked at the coffee table, sending it scraping across the hardwood floor. The candle had been here. And recently. He could smell its presence in the air. He searched the rooms, one by one, but found nothing. No one. He desperately needed to question someone, to find out where the candle was now, and how it kept eluding his grasp.

In the bathroom he stopped to look in the mirror. Surely his face appeared more melted than it had even earlier that day. Soon his strangeness would be too obvious. It would be impossible for him to go anywhere without being instantly noticed and remembered.

"The man who rented the room, officer? Why, yes sir. It was the elephant man. Big fellow. Face like a pudding. All runny like. How was I to know he'd gut his neighbor? Sure I'll talk to a sketch artist. Hard to forget a face like that."

He had run out of time. He'd have to start taking risks.

Straka closed the drapes in the living room and cleared space for the candles. He then went out to his car and drove slowly through the neighborhood, but there wasn't a cat or a dog loose within a dozen blocks.

Guard your pets. People in this town must actually pay attention to the news. There was, however, a late night pub that had just made last call.

Straka waited in an alley one block away and watched the last few customers stagger outside. Most left in pairs or trios, but soon a loner wandered down the sidewalk in his direction.

The man was an obvious alcoholic. Probably owned a stool in the pub and sat there from 4 pm till closing on a daily basis, drinking his welfare check while his wife and children went barefoot and starving. He'd be doing them a favor by curing the sot of his alcoholism.

Straka stood hard against the brick wall in the alley, listening to the uneven footfalls of the approaching drunkard. When he reached the mouth of the alley, Straka pistol-whipped him hard and pulled his collapsing form out of sight. He tumbled the man into the open trunk of his rental car and hammered the lid down. Then he jumped into the driver's seat and started up the engine. Two minutes later he was back at the empty house hauling the man inside.

Nothing had changed in his absence. No police. No one had returned home. The neighborhood still slept.

Straka went back out to the car and brought in the steel case the held his candles.

He set them about the living room in a rough circle. In the center of the floor the man came awake to find himself bound and gagged. Straka was certain he sobered quickly. The man began squirming like a worm, attempting to loosen his bonds. Straka could hear him screaming against the cloth gag. It was distracting.

He showed him his gun, hoping it would silence the man, but he only squirmed all the more.

Straka shook his head. "Guns are so useless." Then he smashed the man on the head with the handle sending him back to oblivion, and resumed lighting the candles.

· δ ·

The Trap

"Maybe we should go to the police," Emily suggested. She stood near the window looking out into the dark street.

Cassidy and William looked at her. Cassidy could see how frightened she was. Emily doesn't believe me, she thought. She's humored me this far, but talk of mother's killer knowing where to find us has shaken her. She's afraid I'm delusional and that father believes my delusion. Which could, of course, be exactly what is happening. Cassidy had to admit that she couldn't be sure that her perceptions echoed reality.

"You heard what that detective said," William told Emily. "If we go to the police they will take Cassie away. I don't think you want that any more than I do."

"No. Of course not," said Emily. "The hospital, then. We can go there."

William Faith held his breath for a moment. "You haven't heard, have you? There was an intern murdered in the hospital. In a room near Cassie's. About the same time that she ran away the other day."

"What?" demanded Cassidy. "No one told me!"

William looked at her. "I didn't want to worry you, sweetheart. It could have nothing to do with you."

"My god!" said Emily. "What if Cassidy hadn't run away?"

"I've asked myself that very question," said William.

"Then we must go to the police," insisted Emily.

"And who would believe us?" William asked her.

"Look!" said Cassidy. The candle on the table had begun to smoke.

Emily and William crowded around the candle, staring and sniffing.

"I never would have believed it," said Emily, "if I wasn't seeing it with my own eyes. I'm sorry for doubting you, dear."

Cassidy had already begun searching for matches, and quickly found some in a counter drawer.

"Are you sure you want to do this?" William asked her.

"Do you have a better idea?" she said.

William shook his head and Cassidy struck a match.

The smoke from the candle swirled with what Cassidy felt was increased urgency. Sharp tongues of darkness twisted in a rapid dance until the vague outline of a man turned this way then that in the air above the candle.

"Flee!" rasped the voice of a throat not yet fully formed. "Evil comes!"

The words drained all the strength that Cassidy had remaining. Flee? She needed to sleep. To lie down and close her eyes. The last few days had been emotionally as well as physically draining, and it was all Cassidy could do to concentrate on what was happening around her.

"No," she complained to the candle. "We fled an hour ago. We can't keep running. There's no place to go."

"Brave one," said the candle. "The man who comes is a madman and a murderer. Leave me here and go. Perhaps he will be satisfied and leave you be."

Cassidy listened to the words, and knew the candle was wrong. The disheveled man would never leave her be. And gaining the candle would make him stronger somehow, more dangerous. The candle was trying to get her to run so that she could live another day. And then run again. Even if that meant giving himself up. Cassidy couldn't live like that. Not for another day. Not for another minute. Then she remembered the words the candle had spoken in Emily's living room.

"Soon you will be free," she told the candle, and then snuffed out the wick.

· δ ·

The Confrontation

Straka sat in the driver's seat of the rented Chevy and watched the lights and movement inside the shop. His hands trembled where they rested on the steering wheel. He had them! They hadn't moved on. He should have done this the first night when he rolled into town, repeated scrying until the candle was his. Damn the police! He felt foolish now. His first scry had brought him to this very shop. And instead of persisting until the candle was his, he had followed the owner, the woman, to her home and demanded she give it up.

Ah, but he thought he had time then. The candle would be his soon enough and he could afford a little sport. He had wanted to question the woman, to watch her slowly die beneath his hands. That she knew nothing about the candle was unimportant. He had enjoyed their time together.

But then he had made his mistake. He should have performed a scrying with the woman's blood, gone after the candle immediately. He should never have allowed this farce to go on this long.

Well, it would end now. He would have the candle, deal with those inside, and then he would leave. Go back to his island and bask in the cool, nighttime darkness, and explore the magic anew now he had all of it.

Straka swallowed saliva and checked the gun in his coat pocket. He would allow no more mistakes. As much as he detested the cold impersonality of guns, he would stoop to shooting everyone dead if it meant the candle would be his.

He climbed out of the rental, opened the trunk, and lifted the crowbar from where it rested next to the spare tire. Then he walked around the building to the back.

The door had been repaired after his earlier visit, but there was still police tape clinging to the wall. Straka wedged the crowbar into the doorjamb and easily ripped the door free of its frame. He had absorbed the life essence of two grown men in the last few hours, and it left him stronger than he had felt in years.

Straka entered the darkened back room with his gun in his right hand and the crowbar in his left. He moved forward slowly, working his way through the stacked boxes of damaged goods, fruits of his earlier visit, toward the main room of the store. He pushed the door open quickly and entered the room.

The lights were on and the girl and her father were sitting at the shop counter. They looked at him when he entered, surprise and fear painted on their faces.

"Where is the other one?" he demanded. "The Sanderson woman?"

"How dare you come in here like this!" William Faith roared. "This is private property."

Straka pointed his gun at him and grinned. "I do as I please. Where is the candle?"

William Faith's eyes boggled at the gun and his face went pale. He hadn't expected a gun. Straka had surprised him. Surprise was nice.

"I—I'm not sure what you mean," William told him. "There are lots of candles here. Take what you want."

Straka redirected the gun so that it pointed at the girl. What a sickly creature she was. Killing her would be doing her a favor.

"All right. All right," said William. He reached slowly and carefully beneath the counter and held up the candle.

Straka knew it instantly for what it was. The size and coloring were right. Its great age was obvious. But in addition he could feel its resonance: Milos. Yes, the magic was there. And something more. The candle might be more useful than he even guessed.

"Take your bloody candle," William Faith growled. "You vandalized our home and shop for a candle. You killed my wife, and God knows who else."

Straka couldn't help but laugh. "I would gladly kill a thousand wives for such a candle. Life is cheap. That candle is one of a kind."

"I've heard enough," said a voice from the front doorway.

Straka turned his head to the sound and saw a man with a gun. For a moment he was too surprised to react. Then he turned his gun on him and fired.

Slow. Perhaps it had been a mistake to avoid guns these past decades. Once he had been a crack shot, but now his reflexes were off, as was his aim. Both guns had fired at the same time.

Straka felt a sudden pressure in his chest. And then a burning flame. The burning spread and he felt his legs collapse beneath him. He was no longer looking at the man in the doorway, but was staring at the hardwood floor.

He felt warm all over, and could hear a heartbeat ringing in his ears. He knew it was his own heart, but it sounded distant somehow, remote. His hot skin grew cool as darkness closed in around him. Nice, he thought. If this is death, I like it.

· δ ·

The Healer

"Are you all right?"

Cassidy sat on her stool at the sales counter, resting her head in her hands. She felt like vomiting. The gun in the disheveled man's hands had not scared her, neither had the loud POPs as the guns fired. Cassidy didn't even feel like she was present in the room. I'm dying, she thought. The next time I go to sleep, I won't be waking up. And Cassidy so much wanted to go to sleep.

"I'm fine," she whispered.

But the question had not been for her. She was just so used to being asked that she had automatically answered. William Faith was holding Detective Savoy up, urging him to sit on the raised floor near the front window.

"It's okay," said Savoy. He gripped his left arm with his right hand. "Nothing that some bandages and a bottle of Scotch won't fix."

Emily entered through the front door carrying a large metal chest. "I heard shots," she said. Then she saw Savoy and put down the box to look after his arm.

Cassidy watched all this as through a fog. Savoy waving Emily away, insisting he was fine. William picking up the metal box and testing its lock. A sound like moaning echoed throughout the room. At first Cassidy thought the sounds came from her, but then she followed the gaze of the others to where the disheveled man lay on the floor.

"He can't be alive," she heard Savoy say. "I shot him in the heart, or damn near."

There was movement in the room, and when next her eyes focused, William Faith stood holding the disheveled man's gun and Detective Savoy was standing again. Both had weapons trained on the man on the floor.

"Open the box," Cassidy whispered.

"What?" William looked at her and Cassidy watched her father's expression sag. "We have to call an ambulance," he said. "Now."

There were two shot and bleeding men in the room, but Cassidy knew her father meant the ambulance for her.

"No time," she said. "No use." Cassidy so much wanted to sleep, but knew she had something important to do. If she failed, the smoke man would never be free.

"The candles in the chest," she managed to say. "We have to light them. All of them."

"Please, dear." Emily was there, holding her hands. "Your father is right. We need to take you to the hospital. We can deal with the candles tomorrow."

"Can't," Cassidy whispered. She could say no more.

There was a loud PING and that brought Cassidy back from the dark well she had been sinking into. She blinked and saw that her father had tried using the evil man's crowbar to snap the latch on the strong box. Apart from putting a small dent in its shining surface, he had accomplished exactly nothing.

"Better let a professional do that," someone said. Detective Savoy.

There was another shot, and this time the box lid popped open. There were candles inside. Cassidy's vision was too foggy to count them but she knew there were twelve. Her father's candle made thirteen.

"Light them," she said.

Savoy was saying something that Cassidy couldn't make out, Emily arguing with him. There was a beeping noise like buttons being pushed on a cell phone. Soon the small shop would be flooded with police and medics, with no one to tell them what was needed. Cassidy had failed. Out with a whimper, she thought, and at last rested her head on the counter.

Death smells like smoke.

It was an odd thought. All around Cassidy was darkness. There was no sound. She couldn't feel her arms or her legs or hear her heartbeat. She felt light. Free. No sensations. But she could smell smoke.

"Brave one?"

Cassidy still could see nothing, hear nothing, but there was a clear voice ringing inside her head, a sound that had nothing to do with her ears. "Who's there?" she asked, and was surprised when she heard her own voice.

"The candles are lit," the smoke man answered. "I can feel them. The smoke mingles and I am whole."

There was silence for a time. How long, Cassidy couldn't say. Then the voice spoke again.

"Have you brought a healer?"

"I...." Cassidy didn't know how to respond. The shop could be full of healers by now, paramedics. They could be working on her right now, fruitlessly applying electricity to her failing heart. "I don't know," she finished. "I can't see."

More silence. And then her vision began to clear. Weight returned and with it a terrible exhaustion. Sound returned to Cassidy's ears, harsh and loud.

"Hold on, dear." It was Emily's voice, hard as a hammer.

With enormous effort, Cassidy lifted her head. A few feet away from her stood Detective Savoy. His face was grim as he held his gun in both hands pointed toward a place on the floor. Cassidy followed the line of fire to where the disheveled man lay glaring up at him.

A voice spoke in Cassidy's head and she echoed the words: "Bullets will not harm him and the candles give him strength."

"Cassie?"

William Faith entered her field of vision holding an expended match in one hand and a gun in the other. His face was haggard and there were tears in his eyes.

"Cassie? I've lit the candles like you asked. Now what do I do?"

Even in the full light of the room, Cassidy could see the smoke figure swirling above the candles. "He brought me back," she said aloud. Cassidy knew she had lost consciousness, had started down that long dark road, and that the man in the smoke had brought her back. But for how long?

"A healer," Cassidy said. "He needs a healer."

Detective Savoy flicked his gaze at her. "The paramedics are on their way. But if this bastard dies, I won't lose any sleep."

"Not for him," Cassidy managed to say. "The man in the smoke."

There was a rough laugh and then the disheveled man spoke. "Milos Radimir is well beyond the ministrations of a healer. He died nine hundred years ago. I should know. I'm the one who killed him."

Somehow, despite the blood pumping from his chest, the disheveled man climbed to his feet. He glared at Savoy. "I wish to thank you for shooting me. It was a pleasurable experience. Had I known, I would have tried it sooner. But even the pleasure of dying, like all pleasures, is fleeting. And now I shall have to seek other entertainments." He took a step forward.

Detective Savoy fired. And when the man kept coming, he fired again, and again, until his gun was out of bullets.

Straka laughed. To say that the bullets had no effect would be a lie. Blood wept from every hole, and Straka lurched as he moved forward, like a caricature from a Mummy movie. Savoy backed away from him, looking for another weapon.

"Straka." The voice came from the smoke.

The disheveled man stopped and peered about the room. "Milos?"

"You are an evil man, Straka. Have you not done enough?"

Straka laughed. "Enough? How much is enough? There is no joy in ending, in death. Recently I thought there might be but, alas, I was wrong. So now I shall seek out other, unexplored amusements. And you shall help me. I'll let you know when I've had enough."

There was silence for a moment, and then a word: "No."

"No?" Straka echoed. "What do you mean, no? None can stop me. He gestured to the holes in his chest. I have become too strong. I have the smoke of the candles in my lungs— *all* of the candles, now, after so many years. None can stop me."

"I can stop you."

Cassidy spotted a flicker of doubt and fear in Straka's eyes as he absorbed these words. Then he shook his head. "No, not even you."

"I can," said Milos. And for a moment Cassidy thought she saw a flesh and blood man in the air above the candles, an honest, gentle man with soft, sad eyes. "And I will."

"How?" demanded Straka. "Is this a new magic? Something I have not yet seen?"

The man in the smoke smiled. "Not magic. Just life. And death. Now that my soul is united I can free it from the candles. I can, at last, truly die."

"No!" shrieked Straka, and he ran forward as if to somehow pull Milos out of the air, contain the man of smoke in his hands.

But the smoke was, in the end, only smoke and the man dissipated. Cassidy thought she heard a whispered: "Goodbye, Brave One," and then the room grew suddenly brighter.

"The candles," said Emily. "They're burning!"

Cassidy looked and it was true. The green wicks were burning black and stale. Rancid tallow melted and ran down the sides of the candles.

Straka shrieked and began flailing with his fists. There was a loud POP and the disheveled man slumped to the floor, his eyes staring up to the ceiling. Cassidy looked and saw her father holding the evil man's gun in his hand. His face was white. "It just went off," he said. "I didn't mean to pull the trigger."

"Just as well," said Savoy, taking the gun from William. "This will be difficult enough to explain with Straka dead. Alive and full of holes would be near impossible."

Cassidy found she was holding her breath, and released it. She had won. The man in the smoke was free and the monster who killed her mother was dead. She could die now with no regrets. She closed her eyes and rested her head on the counter. Peace.

Again death smelled of smoke. Darkness, quiet, and smoke.

It had a different flavor this time. Sweet, like the leaves her father had used to heal Emily's paper cut. Cassidy breathed deep and the scent entered her lungs, and she felt tingly all over. The darkness began to brighten.

"Brave One?"

Had he returned? The man in the smoke? But he was gone now, sacrificed his soul so that Straka would finally die.

"Cassie?"

Not the smoke man. Her father. And it was his leaves she smelled. Calendula. Cassidy opened her eyes.

"The paramedics are here, sweetheart," said her father. He and Emily crowded close to her. She could hear Detective Savoy talking to someone at the door. On the counter in front of her stood a pile of smoking ashes and an empty plastic bag. He had burned all of his leaves in the hope their healing properties would help her to hang on.

Somehow, Cassidy knew she wouldn't need the paramedics. The cancer was gone. She didn't know how or why. She was exhausted, but she also felt stronger than she ever remembered feeling.

"I'm hungry," she said. "Is there any food around here?"

· δ ·

A New Beginning

Cassidy stood beside Emily on the sidewalk, holding the ladder steady as William Faith hung the new sign on the hooks: *Faith's Candles and Natural Healing*.

"How does it look?" he asked as he climbed down the ladder.

"I think Milos would be proud," Cassidy said.

William stood on the pavement and smiled up at the new sign. Sunlight glinted off the ring on the middle finger of his right hand.

After the police had removed the crime scene tape and the three of them had begun cleaning up, William had found the ring in the remains of the melted candle. Cassidy had insisted he wear it.

"You're the healer," she told him. "It's your ring now."

Cassidy had resisted when the paramedics came and carted her off to the hospital, and was still arguing when Dr. Kinman came to meet her at the emergency entrance and ordered the medics to unstrap her from the gurney.

"Where is your father?" Dr. Kinman asked as they walked together into the hospital.

"The police needed him as a witness. He said he'd meet us here after making his statement. They got the man who killed mother."

Dr. Kinman looked startled and relieved, and then gave her a long, serious look. "I think I know just what you need." Instead of taking her to the cancer ward he took her to the hospital cafeteria.

Cassidy would have eaten everything in sight if Dr. Kinman hadn't expressed caution. "Cassidy, I'd like to try a few tests." He smiled at the look she gave him. "Just to confirm what I think I already know."

"That I'm cured?" Cassidy asked him.

He nodded. "I work with the ill and dying on a daily basis. I've watched you for the past year. I've never seen you this… vital. Cassidy, despite everything we think we know, every now and then something happens that we can only describe as a miracle. There is no medical way that you should be healthy, but everything that I'm seeing tells me that you are."

"Yes," Cassidy agreed. "A miracle is exactly what it is."

It was then that she knew. The man in the smoke had wanted a healer. But not for himself. For her. When he gave up his soul he would pass on his magic, and he wanted to pass it on to a healer. Her father.

William Faith folded up the ladder and carried it through the doorway into the shop. Cassidy and Emily followed him inside. The shelves were full of candles and soaps and music boxes, all the things Cassidy had come to love as she helped her parents run the shop growing up. And alongside them were new items: leaves and oils and bright round stones, bead chains with feathers.

Dr. Kinman stood near a shelf of books on aromatherapy and stress stones and had selected half a dozen. He smiled as Cassidy went behind the counter to process the sale.

"Hello Cassidy. I understand your father passed the preliminary competency hearing with flying colors."

Cassidy laughed. "It will take the State longer to accept him back as my father than it took me, but it's all working out."

"That woman," suggested Dr. Kinman, "Estelle Walker. I hear she nearly had a stroke when the board decided that you could remain in your father's care during the proceedings."

"If she does have a stroke," said Cassidy, "I know a good doctor I can recommend."

Dr. Kinman shook his head. "No thanks, please. I think I've seen as much of that woman as I care to. Maybe we should send her some of these stress stones." He winked. "I hear they can work miracles."

Then he turned serious. "Your own tests show that the cancer is gone. Instantaneous remission. But you've still got some cell damage from when you were ill. That won't go away overnight. Have you had any seizures? Or strange dreams?"

Cassidy smiled and flashed a grin at her father where he sorted books on one of the shelves. "I've never felt better. And all my dreams now are good ones."

· δ ·

FULL
HOUSE

On The Plains Of Camlaen, 645 AD

Near the lake's edge, a short distance from the fighting, three women knelt by a supine form. Two of the women cut bandages from a blanket while the third mixed herbs from string-drawn pouches at her belt. Druidic magic!

"Stop!" Galahad cried, running toward them and falling to his knees before Arthur. The king's face was pale. Pale as death. Galahad looked up at the witches. Witches! "Arthur is a Christian king. You cannot work your magic on him!"

The witch with the herbs — the eldest Galahad thought, though with youthful eyes — cast him a penetrating glare. "We do what we must, young knight. If Arthur dies, so too dies Britain. So it is written in the stars."

Galahad looked to his King. So pale. "Yes, he cannot die. But neither can you use your magic. It will change him."

"Galahad?" The word was deep and slow, the king's breath ragged. "Ah, Galahad, it is well what they do. Merlin warned me before I banished him. He foretold all. Mordred's deceit. My wounding. Even of you."

"The magician told of me?"

"Peace, my King," cautioned the elder witch. "You must save your strength." The other two witches began stripping away Arthur's surcoat, readying him for the herbs and bandages.

"But this is druid magic!" Galahad cried. "Mordred's magic."

"Aye," said the elder witch. "There is only one magic. Just as there is only one Christ. Blood and death will continue so long as this truth remains unembarrassed."

"I—I don't understand," said Galahad.

"Are you daft boy!" cried one of the younger witches. "This is what Arthur is meant to do: join the old ways with the new. So long as past and future fight against each other there can only be death."

"Join?" Galahad echoed. He didn't understand. Arthur's chest was bare now and he could see the wound. So near his heart. How could his King still be alive?

The elder witch took no time to smear away the blood, but applied the herbs directly into the wound, urging her companions to bind the King's chest. Arthur made no sound during this, though Galahad could see his king clench his teeth.

The task done, Arthur beckoned him closer. Galahad leaned down, as from the corner of his eye he watched the three witches move off to prepare a small boat on the lake. Would they take Arthur away?

"Galahad," Arthur whispered. "For you I have a task. The Grail. Galahad of Camelot, I charge you to protect the Grail until I return."

A shadow fell across the King's face and Galahad looked up to see the three witches waiting to lift Arthur into the boat.

"And return he shall," said the elder witch. "Once he is healed the King shall return and take up the Grail, then the world itself shall be healed."

Galahad pondered these words as he helped the witches lift his King into the boat, and then watched as they took up the oars and rowed away from shore.

"The Grail shall be safe," Galahad called out.

And it seemed to the knight errant that he could hear Arthur's whispered voice return across the slap and the dip of the oars, and above the clash of blades on the plain. "Galahad. Be true."

· δ ·

DAY 1

A Tale of Two Houses

Jonas turned his 2005 Buick LeSabre off Crowchild Trail onto Richmond Road. It was 11 a.m. on a Friday. Too early to be going home.

He lived in an older part of Calgary, a well-treed suburb adjacent to the bustling downtown core. It was the best of both worlds: wide, quiet streets with shrub-strewn lawns, but only ten minutes from the hub of skyscrapers and big business.

Jonas slowed as he drove past the Badlin place, a wood and brick manor house that marked the beginning of his street. While all the houses on Richmond Court sported bright colors — whites, yellows, blues — the Badlin place was a deep earth-red, with the mortar so grayed it was almost as dark as the stone. Despite that people lived there, many claimed the house was haunted. Jonas figured the occupants were just peculiar. No crime in that.

As he cruised past the house, the living room curtains parted slightly and a ghostly figure peered out at him. Jonas shivered and hit the gas.

Jonas didn't know why the house made him curious. For the past fifteen years he'd slowed whenever he passed the place. Usually there was nothing to see. Sometimes, like today, a curtain would move. On rare occasions he'd glimpse one of the Badlin clan slipping between the house and the ancient Edsel parked in the gravel driveway. Black-haired and always dressed in black, the Badlins were a frequent topic of discussion in the neighborhood.

Six houses down from the Badlin's he pulled into the paved driveway of his half-duplex, a faded yellow monstrosity of angled gables and jutting bay windows. The home's most unique feature was a shack-shaped attic room squatting like some large, sick bird on top of the house, its single window a glass eye that glared at the entire neighborhood. A previous owner had added the attic to the existing three floors. He didn't doubt that some people gawked at *his* house as much as at the Badlin's.

He'd been saying for years that he was going to repaint the exterior, make the place look respectable, but he'd never found the time.

A decade and a half ago he and Gwen, his wife, had moved to Calgary from Toronto after Jonas accepted a job with Trans-Alta Pipeline as a *flow analyst*, a fancy name for a computer jockey who monitored thousands of mechanical sensors mounted on the insides of oil pipelines that measured how fast the oil was moving. It was a brain-dead job but it paid well. Over time Jonas had become good at it.

Even back then the house had been old, with faded yellow paint and a cracked front porch. The Badlin place had been there too, dark, secretive. Looking back, Jonas tried to think of anything in the neighborhood that had changed over the years, but he drew a blank. Everything had just gotten older.

"Jonas?"

Gwen must have heard the car drive up. She stood in the front doorway looking surprised and a bit worried. Her dusty blond hair was tied up with a white band. That, along with faded jeans and an old t-shirt, suggested that she had been doing some cleaning.

Jonas sighed and opened the car door. Gwen's appearance had solved a problem; he hadn't known how he was going to bring himself to go inside.

Stepping deftly down the porch step, avoiding the crack in the cement, Gwen approached the driver's side of the LeSabre. She spoke in a quiet, cautious voice: "Did you hear? One of the Badlin boys was murdered."

Jonas stared at her. In fifteen years nothing had happened in this neighborhood. Now here were two front page stories in one day. "What happened?"

"It was Ricky Henders. In number 22. Looks like he sat on his porch all morning with a handgun. When one of the Badlins stepped out of the house, Ricky shot him."

Jonas could only gape at his wife. Where would a kid like Ricky Henders get a handgun? Where would he learn to shoot it? And why would Ricky shoot anyone, never mind a Badlin?

"What's with the box?" Gwen asked, looking past him into the passenger seat.

And now the other news. There was no easy way to say it, so he just said it: "I've been laid off."

· δ ·

A View From The Attic

"Bastards." Larry took another gulp of his Coors, looked at Jonas, then said it again. "Bastards."

Jonas had just told his friend and neighbor that Trans-Alta had handed him his walking papers. They were sitting in his attic room, a deck of untouched playing cards on the round table between them.

"How many years did you give them?" Larry asked.

Jonas gazed out the window. "Fifteen, give or take."

"Sounds like they did the taking. What excuse did they give?"

Jonas snorted. "They said I was redundant. Everything's automatic now. They don't need someone telling them when there's a problem. The computer tells them. But they're right. Last few years all I did was confirm what the computer was saying. I *am* redundant."

Larry drained his beer and tossed the can into the blue recycle bin next to the mini-fridge. The aluminum clinked against other empties. "So watcha gonna do?"

Jonas shrugged. "Paint the house."

"Not much of a career move," said Larry.

"No, but the house needs painting."

"What does Gwen think?"

"She agrees about the paint." Jonas picked up a pair of binoculars that hung from a nail by the window and looked out and down the street.

"Badlin's?" asked Larry.

"Got some activity," said Jonas. "Looks like Mr. Badlin going out to the car."

"He wearing that pale blue suit today?" Larry chortled, his thick gut shaking.

"Black suit. Black hat," said Jonas.

"I'd say he was dressed for mourning," suggested Larry, "except that's what he always wears. All of them Badlins. You think it's a religious thing? Like Amish or something?"

"They don't go to church," said Jonas. "There goes the Edsel. He's off somewhere. Maybe the morgue."

"Weird about Ricky," said Larry. "That boy was always a bit off. Didn't know he was paranoid."

Jonas hung up the binoculars and began shuffling the cards. "What do you mean?"

"Scuttlebutt says Ricky thought the Badlins were out to get him. They were going to sacrifice him to the devil or something."

"Says who?" asked Jonas. This was news to him.

"No one specific," said Larry. "It's just rumor. People talk when stuff like this happens. So what are you really going to do?"

"Really?" Jonas paused, not sure of what to say. He'd been asking himself that question all afternoon. "I have no idea. Beyond being a flow analyst I don't know how to do much of anything." Returning the cards to the table, Jonas picked up the binoculars and looked out the window. "Edsel's back."

"Jesus," said Larry. "That's hardly enough time to drive around the block. Where do you think he went?"

Jonas had no idea. "He's going back into the house. I don't see any groceries or anything."

Larry picked up the cards and began dealing. "That family gives me the creeps. If I was half as witless as Ricky, I might take a shot at them myself."

"No, you wouldn't," said Jonas, putting the spyglass away again and picking up his hand. "You and I are normal people. Normal people don't shoot their neighbors."

Larry threw two cards on the table and drew two off the deck. "It might surprise you what normal people do."

· 8 ·

All In The Family

Dinner was awkward.

Jonas hadn't said anything to the rest of the family about his job situation, but knew Gwen must have spread the word and told everyone to behave. Their idea of good behavior tended toward dead silence. The clang of forks on porcelain was deafening.

Their daughter, Susan, had been ten when they moved to Calgary. Four years ago she had married a bum. Literally. Dennis had no job when they were married, and was still unemployed three years later when they divorced. Susan had moved back in after the divorce. The details of how she and Dennis had survived their time together was not a topic for discussion.

Jonas had to admit he now felt a bit like Dennis: unemployed. But at least he had some savings put away and had received a golden handshake along with his dismissal. That and the offer of a cab ride home, which he graciously refused. It would be a while before things got tight.

Gwen's sister, Ann, had moved in when Susan got married. She had come out for the wedding and had never returned to Toronto.

The end result was that Jonas lived in cramped quarters with three women. His friends joked about being envious, but Jonas knew it was no laughing matter. Susan's marriage had scarred her and Jonas didn't know how long it would take the wounds to heal.

As for Ann, Gwen's sister was insane. Always had been. Not in a dangerous sense, but she had strange notions and was frequently doing something incomprehensible. Jonas had been subtly urging Gwen to evict her sister, especially with Susan back in the house, but to no avail. Gwen had the kindest heart of anyone Jonas knew and wouldn't hear of sending her sister away.

"These carrots are delicious," said Ann, breaking the silence.

Jonas would have been grateful had there actually been carrots on the table. What *was* on the table was Salisbury steak, mashed potatoes, peas, and gravy.

"Thank you, dear," said Gwen, smiling encouragingly.

"Did any of you know Ricky Henders?" It was Susan, the first words she had spoken all evening.

Ann nodded vigorously. "Delightful boy. Lives down the street, don't you know."

Susan nodded. She always took Ann at face value, treating her as though she weren't a raving loon.

Ann continued. "Mrs. Luis next door to the Henders says Mrs. Henders told her that Ricky doesn't know why he shot the Badlin boy. He doesn't know where the gun came from and can't remember pulling the trigger. He only remembers sitting there with the gun in his hand and William Badlin lying in a heap across the street."

Everyone at the table stared at Gwen's sister.

"It must have been a traumatic experience for the boy," said Susan. "Did Ricky and this William fight at school?"

"The Badlin boys don't go to school," said Jonas.

"That's right," said Ann. "They're in home school. As is the daughter."

"There's a daughter?" Jonas knew about the boys because he had seen them. He also knew they didn't go to school because they rarely left the house. He had never seen a daughter.

"Priscilla Badlin," said Ann. "The remaining two boys are George and Jonathan."

"How do you know all this?" Jonas asked. "You don't speak with them do you?"

Ann laughed. "On no. You'd have to be mad to speak to the Badlins. I asked Mrs. Luis. She speaks to them. She's quite mad, you know."

Jonas speared a Salisbury streak and began hacking it to pieces. He wasn't sure the table discussion was appropriate. Talk of murder and motives was best left for coffee on the porch.

Ann must have read his mind. "Oh, but this is dreary talk. We need a change of subject." She looked at Jonas. "What about you, dear? Any job prospects on the horizon?"

· δ ·

Dogs Playing Poker

"She actually said that?" Larry shook his head. "You've been off the job, what? Half a day? And your daft sister-in-law thinks you should be beating the streets?"

"Quit stalling and make your bet," said Andy from the seat nearest the window. He was clutching his cards as though he feared they would run away. It was eight o'clock and the start of the nightly poker game. Andy was Jonas' dad's age. Retired for real and living the good life on Patterson Way two blocks over. He was ex-military, Intelligence Division or something, and had arrived for tonight's game with army surplus night-vision goggles strapped across the top of his bald pate.

Larry took one look at Andy's card-clutching demeanor and folded.

"I'm out too," said Jonas.

Phil, the game's forth who lived two doors down, also threw down his cards.

"Damn," said Andy, collecting up the ante. "A whole buck. If you guys don't start bleeding cash soon I'm going to have to find another game."

"I'm getting another beer," said Larry, standing up and walking over to the mini-fridge. "Anyone with me?"

Andy shook his head and pulled the goggles down over his eyes. He pressed his face against the attic window and looked out through the evening darkness at the Badlin place. "Twenty-O-Five and all's quiet. Man, these goggles work great! Like it was daylight. Are you sure there was a murder there today? There's not even police tape."

"It was all cut and dried," said Phil. "The killer gave himself up right after the shooting. Didn't even leave the scene. Police came and went in less than an hour. I doubt it got more than a minute's mention on the news."

Andy pulled up his goggles and began shuffling the cards. "I've been watching that house for sixty years. Three generations of Badlins and nothing like this ever happened. Wish I'd been there to see it."

"It's kind of sad, really," said Jonas. "The Badlin boy was just that, a boy. And Ricky Henders is just a kid, too. A shame."

Larry sat back down and passed beers all around even though no one had asked for them. "Well, I'm not broken up to see one less Badlin. There's something wrong with those people."

"You don't know the half of it," said Phil. "This isn't the first murder at that house." Then he sat back, waiting for the others to ask for it.

"All right," said Andy. "I'll bite. Give us a history lesson."

Phil was a high school history teacher and delighted in all things past. "The Badlin house was built at the turn of the century by one Charles Tucker Badlin who owned most of the land around here. It's said he was a Freemason or some such and swindled his neighbors out of life and luxury. He was found one night with a knife in his back and his safe empty. Never did figure out who killed him. His son kept the house and the family has never left."

"What?" said Jonas. "No one stays in a house where family was killed. They always move on."

Phil shrugged. "What can I tell you? The Badlins stayed. Everyone has shunned them ever since."

Larry popped his Coors. "Like I always said: Total nut bars." He plucked his cards as Andy dealt them, rearranging his hand with each new card.

Phil waited till all the cards were dealt before looking at his hand and managed to keep his face expressionless as he pondered its value before returning the cards face down to the table. "I fold."

Andy frowned at him. "You're not even going to draw?"

"No point," said Phil. "You've just dealt the worst hand of all time."

Jonas looked at his own cards and covered his surprise by choking a laugh at Phil. "You could at least *try* to play the game."

While Larry and Andy goaded Phil into drawing two cards, Jonas practiced his poker face: three knights, a queen, and a four. He had a good chance of winning this hand.

With a great show of reluctance, Phil discarded, drew two cards off the deck, considered his new hand, and then tossed it down on the table. "Told you," he said. "Complete waste of time. Not to mention I'm now down another dime."

Jonas tossed a nickel on the table and discarded the four. "I'm going to regret this," he said, trying to look angry with his hand, "but I'll draw one."

Larry grinned at him. "Trying for a straight? You'll never make it."

"Probably not," Jonas admitted. He feigned disappointment as he drew a replacement off the deck and saw it was a second queen. Full House. He couldn't even remember the last time he drew a full house.

Frowning, he studied the stack of change at his elbow. He had a good chance of winning the hand, but if he bid too high his friends would fold, thinking he got Larry's suggested straight. He nudged a single quarter to the center of the table.

"I'm in too," said Andy, after drawing two cards.

Larry held pat. "I'll see your quarter and raise you fifty cents." He wore a Cheshire cat expression as he pushed silver to the middle of the table.

Jonas' false disappointment turned real. He finally gets a decent hand and Larry gets a better one. Or is he bluffing? Jonas had no option but to play along. "I'll see you." Coins clinked as he added to the ante.

"I'm out," said Andy. He put down his cards and pressed his night-vision goggles against the window.

"Looks like it's just you and me little buddy." Larry pushed four more quarters into the pot. "Are you good for another dollar?"

"Seeing as I'm now unemployed," Jonas said, "I'll have to see your dollar and call the hand. It's all I can afford to lose."

The two men stared each other down, hoping to measure each other out and predict the winner before revealing their cards.

· δ ·

Dancing In The Dark

"We've got movement," Andy announced.

"Really?" said Phil. "Which is it? Police? Badlins? A torch-bearing mob?"

Jonas pressed his cards against his chest and joined Andy at the window. Phil and Larry quickly followed.

"I can't see anything," said Phil. "Edsel's in the driveway. Porch light is out."

"Not the front yard," said Andy. "The back yard."

"You can't see into the Badlin's back yard at night," said Jonas. "Too many trees and not enough light."

Andy passed him the night-vision goggles. "You can with these. Should have gotten them years ago."

Jonas stuffed his cards into his shirt pocket and slipped the goggles over his head. He was forced to blink when the street appeared almost as bright as during the day. Lights in living room windows shone out like suns, so he tried not to look at them. Instead he focused on the Badlin place. It looked quiet. The curtains were drawn, but with the goggles he could see wisps of lamplight sneaking through here and there. He turned his attention to the back yard.

The Badlins was a corner lot with an oversized back yard. While most of the neighborhood sported yards with gardens, grass, and BBQs, the Badlin back yard was a forest grown wild. Jonas had never seen anyone back there. There were no gardens to tend. No BBQ. Near the forest's center stood a fountain or marble bird-feeder.

Watching the yard at night for the first time, he looked carefully, and in a moment saw movement. Someone was behind the fountain. Then they moved away and seemed to be ducking stealthily among the trees. Why would anyone be hiding in the Badlin's backyard?

Jonas squinted through the goggles, trying to make out details, but there were too many trees in the way.

"What do you see?" said Phil.

"Just wait." He followed the figure from tree to tree. What was it doing? And then the figure moved to a place in front of the fountain and Jonas saw that it wasn't sneaking, but dancing. He also saw it was a woman. Jonas took off the goggles and passed them to Phil.

Then he sat down at the card table, alone, and considered its roundness. When he and Gwen moved in the table was already here, left behind by the previous owner. The neighborhood card game took a while to get started, but when it did Jonas had considered taking the old table to the dump and getting a proper square poker table. He had never gotten around to it, of course, and soon everyone was used to playing cards at a round table.

Larry sat down across from Jonas and spread his cards. "Five Hearts. Beats your straight." He reached out for the pile of change.

Jonas didn't stop him. His full house beat Larry's flush, but he couldn't think about poker just now.

Andy pressed a hand on Jonas' shoulder. "I think you'll want to have a talk with Gwen."

Jonas nodded.

Andy sighed. "I wonder if she knows what her sister does in the evenings."

FULL HOUSE

Sister? Jonas summoned back the image he had seen through the night-vision goggles. A woman dancing in the Badlins' backyard forest. Ann? Hadn't the woman been younger? Wasn't it Susan he had seen?

· δ ·

DAY 2

Another Shade Of Pale

Breakfast came and went without Jonas bringing up last night's discovery with Gwen. If he knew for sure who it was, Susan or Ann dancing in the Badlin's backyard, he would have spoken with Gwen right away. He was certain it was Susan he had seen: long flowing hair, youthful movements— Susan dancing on her wedding night. But the others had all seen Ann. And now in his minds' eye, Jonas could see Ann, hair let down, waltzing among the Badlin trees loony as a drunken crow.

It had to be Ann, hadn't it? It was something Gwen's sister would do.

In the end he decided to think on it a while. Things would become clear with time. Wouldn't they?

And so now Jonas stood in his front yard gazing up at jutting angles of faded yellow. In fifteen years he had not once taken a good long look at the house. If he had, surely he would have done something before now. It wasn't just the paint, so faded after two decades that it was almost white. The whole structure was, well, ugly. Most duplexes were symmetric cookie-cutter shapes, compact, stylish, quaint. This building was an ungainly albatross.

Larry's side of the house was bone white, square, and featureless. No trim around the windows. No welcome mat on the bleached concrete porch. Not a shrub or flower in the yard. Bleak.

Jonas' side was much the opposite. The once bright yellow walls sat at odd angles, with looming bay windows, ten inch trim, and of course the *crow's-nest* addition up top. It was a Lego experiment gone horribly wrong.

Combining the two half-houses just made things worse. Who in the world designed this monstrosity? Jonas doubted a mere coat of paint could improve things and idly wondered what effort would be involved in a façade remake.

"Beautiful, isn't it."

Jonas neither saw nor heard Ann come up to stand beside him. He nearly had a heart attack.

"I love this old place," Ann continued. "Much nicer than my apartment back in Toronto."

"You still have your apartment?" Jonas asked.

Ann looked at him. "Of course I still have my apartment. I'm only here for a visit."

Jonas tried not to look too dumbfounded. "Your visit is going into its fifth year," he suggested to Gwen's sister.

"Oh! Have I been away so long? I really must start thinking about heading back. Of course, I can't leave with this murder business unresolved. Leaving town so quickly, the police may think *I* killed the Badlin boy."

Jonas couldn't believe his ears. He was *this* close to getting Ann to move out. After so long. "Well, they have arrested Ricky Henders."

Ann laughed, that high, shrill titter he found so irritating. "Oh, Ricky didn't do it. The police will figure that out soon enough. Then they'll come looking for the real killer. But by then more mischief may have happened. No, the police are too slow. You'll have to find the villain first."

"Me?"

"You are a pipeline detective," Ann said. "You're supposed to be able to spot evidence and reach conclusions."

"I'm a flow analyst," said Jonas. "An ex-flow analyst." But it surprised him how well insane Ann understood his work. She never seemed to understand anything.

Ann waved her hands. "Names mean nothing. You have the skills to solve the murder, so you should use them."

"I should what?"

But Ann was no longer looking at him. Instead she was back to considering the house. "Blue," she said, then walked away.

Just as suddenly as Ann departed, Larry from next door appeared at his elbow. It was just after breakfast, yet Larry stood there with an open Coors in his hand. He was a day trader or a stock broker working out of his home. Something like that. He lived the life of Riley, drinking beer for breakfast while honest men went off to work each morning.

"What color should I go with?" Jonas asked. "And don't say white. Gwen will never go for it."

Larry set his beer can on the grass and stuck his hands in the air, fingers and thumbs together making a square— a camera frame. "I don't know, little buddy. I'm kind of partial to white." He turned his hand camera, panning across the neighboring houses, a flower garden of color, until he stopped facing the Badlin place at the end of the street. "Blood red seems to be in vogue."

Jonas studied the brooding, dark red exterior of the Badlin place. It didn't look so frightening from a distance. In fact, the house looked damn respectable compared to his awkward half-duplex. Maybe Gwen would go for red.

Just then a car turned onto the street and puttered past the Badlin place. A rusted, vintage Honda Civic. Jonas frowned, thinking it looked familiar. The Honda drove slowly past his driveway and Jonas got a good look at the driver— Susan's ex-husband, Dennis. Dennis looked back at him, his unshaven face pinched and his blue eyes glaring.

Larry spoke: "How about sky blue?"

· δ ·

Dennis The Menace

Later that morning Jonas found himself in the basement looking through old clothes for the ideal painter's outfit. The boxes were marked Salvation Army, carefully packed and labeled by the ever efficient Gwen, but not yet delivered. That wasn't like her.

Gwen spent half her life helping with charitable causes. Salvation Army. Food Bank. Drop-In Center. She was always helping someone in need. It was one of the things he loved best about her.

Possibly Ann had kept Gwen from delivering the boxes. It would be just like Ann to squirrel away old clothes in the basement. There must be four years worth of useless Jonas-clothes. Dress shirts, jeans, old shoes. Things Jonas had worn out and replaced, only not quite replaced because they were still here, stacked neatly against a wall. A blast from the past.

Jonas pulled out a Hawaiian shirt that was so neon-ugly he had only worn it once. Deeper in the box was a white, long sleeve turtleneck that would be perfect under the Hawaiian shirt. It had a hole in one elbow, but that only gave it charm. He added a pair of jeans with the knees worn out and some old runners. He'd be the talk of the neighborhood.

Then all at once it struck him why the old clothes were stockpiled in the basement. Four years worth. Ann had nothing to do with it. They were meant for Dennis. Gwen had collected them and tried to pass them on to Dennis over the years while Dennis, unwilling to owe anything to anyone but also unwilling to work to support his wife, had refused. He took every penny he could get from the government, but not an ounce of charity from anyone with a face who could look down their nose at him.

Jonas looked for any clothes that might not be his and found none. There was nothing of Gwen or Ann's. Those had gone to Susan who, unlike Dennis, had accepted them. Jonas remembered seeing Susan in Gwen's hand-me-downs on those rare occasions when Dennis had let her out.

Already angry from realizing why the clothes were here, memories of Susan locked up in that bum's low-rent apartment made his blood boil. Calm, he told himself. Calm. No use dwelling on it. That's what Gwen always told him. The past is the past. Nothing to be done.

With enormous resolve he turned his thoughts to re-packing the clothes. Gwen had labeled them for the Salvation Army. Recently, he was sure, or they would already be gone. He couldn't leave a mess down here, undoing Gwen's hard work. He had his painter's clothes. Goal accomplished. Life was good.

In the middle of cleaning up, the phone rang.

"Gwen, can you answer that? Susan? Ann?"

The phone continued to ring so he ran up the stairs from the basement into the kitchen.

"Hello."

The line was open, but all Jonas could hear was his own heavy breathing from running up the stairs.

"Hello?" he said again.

Still nothing. Then it occurred to him that the breathing on the phone wasn't his. He slammed the phone back into its cradle and swore, wishing he had spent the few extra cents for call display. Who the hell was making obscene phone calls?

Marching into the living room, Jonas saw that the car was gone from the driveway. The women must be out. Then he turned and saw Susan standing in the hallway.

"Was that Dennis?" he demanded, his anger from the basement returned tenfold.

Susan froze, a deer in the headlights, and then dropped her head. "I stopped answering the phone when the calls started a few days ago."

Jonas immediately regretted the tone he had used. It wasn't Susan he was angry at. It was that bastard, Dennis. In Susan's fragile state, speaking to her that way was the last thing he should do. He softened his voice. "Sorry. Sorry. Why didn't you tell anyone?"

"I did. Mom."

Jonas rubbed his eyes. "Well, your mother didn't tell me."

"Dennis only calls in the daytime. You were at work."

"I still need to know."

"I guess."

Jonas sighed and sat on the couch, motioning for his daughter to join him. "I thought we were done with that bum. Do you know why he started calling? It's been a year since the divorce."

Susan shook her head. "I don't know. The first time he called he said I still belong to him. I hung up and haven't answered since."

Jonas sighed and gave her a hug. "Well, you got that right."

As they sat there, he wondered if he should bring up last night's forest dancing. It was the perfect opportunity. Susan could say whether or not it was her in the Badlin yard and, if so, why she was there. But as he considered his daughter, leaning silently against his shoulder, he realized that it couldn't have been Susan last night. He hadn't seen Susan dance since her wedding night, not once, and couldn't for the life of him imagine her dancing now. So instead he just held her, father and daughter enjoying the comfort of each other's presence.

They were still sitting there when Gwen and Ann came home. Gwen's expression revealed she understood what had happened.

"It would have been nice to know about the phone calls back when they started," Jonas suggested.

"I didn't want to worry you," Gwen said. "I thought if we ignored him, he'd stop."

"Dennis drove by the house today."

"What!" Gwen's eyes grew wide. "We need to call the police."

Ann scowled. "The police won't do anything. Jonas should handle it."

"Handle it?" Jonas echoed.

But Ann had already moved on and was taking something from a shopping bag. "Look what Gwen bought you. A suit to wear on your job interviews." Ann's face beamed as she held up a pair of shiny white painter's overalls.

· δ ·

Paint Heaven

One of the nice things about Larry was that he owned a truck. A sparkling white quarter-ton Toyota. Just right for hauling stuff around. Like paint supplies.

Jonas and Larry pushed a cart down one of the aisles of the local Paint Heaven superstore, tossing in tape and brushes and canvas gloves. They had already taken a twenty-four foot extension ladder out to the truck and had set the store staff to mixing up twenty gallons of sky blue water-based latex paint.

"Sounds to me," said Larry, "like this Dennis fellow is in need of a good beating."

Jonas had just told Larry about the phone calls. "I seem to remember you saying something like that during the wedding."

"I never liked the guy," agreed Larry. "So I guess this beating business is overdue."

"You know I don't agree with violence. Violence never solved anything."

"Actually," said Larry. "If you look at history, violence solved pretty much everything. Don't take my word for it. Ask Andy or Phil. Pacifists refuse to learn from history."

Jonas tried on a painting cap and added it to the basket. "We've had this debate before, Larry. Nothing was resolved then. Nothing will be resolved now. You see how I learn from history?"

"Touché," admitted Larry. "So you think a stern warning will make Dennis back off?"

"I'm hoping."

Larry shook his head. "If wishes were fishes."

"How about the threat of police?"

"No effect on the Dennises of the world. Like a dog in training they need a strong hand. You put any thought yet into gainful employment?"

Jonas slowed the cart and drew a heavy sigh. "I went through the morning paper. Careers section. Want ads. I'm not qualified for anything beyond flow analysis and no one's hiring. Computers do everything these days. And I'm too old to go back to school. About the only thing I saw that I'd have a shot at is a door greeter at Wal-Mart."

Larry laughed. "I love those guys. But you're too young. They'd never hire you."

"Great," said Jonas. "So I guess I'll be on the dole like Dennis."

"Nah. There's always work for those who want it. Why don't you do what I do?"

Jonas looked at his friend. "And what is it, exactly, that you do?"

Larry grinned. "I thought you knew. Stock speculation. Buy low, sell high. Pocket the difference."

"You make any money?"

Larry shrugged. "Most days. I get by."

"I've got a family to feed," said Jonas. "I don't think the life of a professional gambler will fly."

"Gambler!" Larry looked shocked. "Playing the market isn't… Well, actually, now that you mention it, I suppose it is. Buddy, you just made my day. I'm a gambling man, gambling ma-an." Larry sang the tune of a song Jonas couldn't quite recognize.

"Thanks, Larry. You've been a big help."

"We'll think of something, little buddy. No worries."

· δ ·

A Question Of Motive

Andy threw down his cards and dug in his pocket for more change. "If my luck keeps on like this I'm going to have to go back to work."

Phil laughed. "An old war dog like you? The military would never take you back."

Larry folded as well. "I think Andy is thinking of Wal-Mart. They have a door greeter posting with his name on it. Don't they, Jonas?" Larry winked.

Jonas threw in four quarters and looked at Phil. "I'll see you. And I hope you're bluffing. A few more winning hands and I'll be able to afford a down payment on the painting supplies I picked up today."

"Isn't it a little late in the year for painting?" suggested Phil. "September can be hit or miss weather-wise."

Jonas shrugged. "Perhaps I should go back to work and ask them to post-pone laying me off until next summer."

"I'm just saying," offered Phil. Then silence settled across the table as Phil slowly lowered his cards to reveal two pair, ten high.

"I could have beaten that," complained Larry.

"As can I." Jonas laid down a queen high straight and drew the small pile of coins toward him.

Andy gathered up the cards and began shuffling. "My contacts down at the cop shop say the police aren't convinced of Ricky's guilt."

Larry shook his head. "They got Ricky standing over the body with the smoking gun in his hand. What more can they want?"

"Little things," suggested Andy. "Ricky has no memory of how he got the gun or of pulling the trigger. There were some odd drugs in his system. And I understand the gunshot residue test isn't conclusive. They'll probably have to let him go."

"Let him go!" Larry stood and went to the fridge for a beer. "I don't want a killer back in the neighborhood."

"Well," said Andy. "If Ricky didn't do it, we may still have a killer in the neighborhood."

Jonas listened to all this, remembering what Ann had said, that Ricky hadn't killed William Badlin. And her challenge to him to find the real killer. What possible motive could Ricky have? What possible motive could anyone have? As far as Jonas could tell this was just a random killing. Some punk kid shooting a stranger as part of some crazy gang initiation. Things like that were happening more often these days.

"Earth to Jonas," said Phil.

"What?" Jonas looked down and saw five cards face down on the table in front of him. The others had cards in their hands.

"We lost you there, little buddy," said Larry. "Ante up."

Jonas pushed a dime to the center of the table and picked up his cards. Ten high. He discarded two and picked up nothing. He briefly considered bluffing then decided to fold. He was a lousy bluffer. What if it wasn't a random drive-by? What if there really was a killer in the neighborhood? What if his neighbors weren't who he had always thought they were?

Andy slipped his night vision goggles over his eyes and peered out the window. "We've got movement!"

Phil left his chair and squinted out the window into evening's darkness. "Where? The Badlins?"

Andy chuckled. "Nope. Front yard. Looks like Jonas' sister-in-law has moved her nocturnal activities from the Badlin place closer to home."

Jonas joined them at the window and looked down into his front yard. Three stories below, Ann lay on her back on the grass waving a candle at the sky.

"Did she happen to say what she was doing at the Badlin's when Gwen spoke to her?" Andy asked.

Jonas shook his head. "Nothing intelligible." But that was a lie. He hadn't spoken to Gwen about the dancer in Badlin's back yard.

· δ ·

DAY 3

A Firm Hand

Sanding and taping the windows was slower going than Jonas had expected. Scraping out the frame edge with a wire brush, then tearing and applying painters' tape to the glass was easy enough, but he found he had to move and adjust the ladder twenty times just to finish one window. And the house had more windows than he ever thought possible.

On the other hand, the weather was perfect. Sunny, but not hot. Not even a cloud in the sky. And very little wind.

Jonas found he was enjoying the physical activity. His work at Trans-Alta had kept him tied to a desk, and over his time there he had put on thirty pounds. Two pounds a year. He wondered if he could find a new profession where he would lose two pounds a year.

He was taping one of the living room bay windows when he heard the phone ring and watched through the glass as Gwen answered it. The vehemence with which she slammed the phone down surprised him. He didn't think he had ever seen Gwen so angry.

Climbing down the ladder he put the roll of tape on one of the steps and went inside the house. "Dennis?" he asked.

Gwen made a good show of curbing her anger. "What is wrong with that man?"

"I'll go ask," Jonas told her.

"Should you?" Gwen's expression changed to one of concern. Dennis was two decades younger than Jonas and twenty pounds heavier, none of it fat. The man had never worked a day in his life, but he spent enough time at the gym. Jonas had joked once, asking if Dennis' tattoos were of the prison variety. Susan had taken him to task for that one. That, of course, was before the divorce.

"Perhaps we should call the police," Gwen suggested.

Jonas laid his proverbial cards on the table. "I already called the police and they can't do anything. Phoning and driving past the house aren't illegal. Unless Dennis enters our property there isn't much they can do."

"But…" Gwen didn't finish the sentence. Jonas could think of several *buts* as well.

"I'll go talk to him. He's left us alone for a year. No reason that can't continue."

· δ ·

Dennis still lived in the small apartment he and Susan had shared during their brief marriage. Jonas suspected it was subsidized by the city or province or some organization that found virtue in enabling the lifestyle of the fit and lazy. Jonas understood Dennis' philosophy exactly. A roof over his head and beer money was all he needed. Why work when society would provide for his needs?

The apartment was in a run-down neighborhood twenty minutes drive from Jonas' neck of the woods. He had hated it when Susan lived here, and suspected that his harping on Dennis to get a job and make a better home for Susan had contributed to their break-up. If so, he didn't regret it. Susan was better off without Dennis.

The rusted Honda Civic sat in its oil-stained stall, so Dennis was probably home. There was no security system — the place was too squalid for that — so Jonas was able to walk up to the second of three floors and pound on Dennis' door.

The building hadn't lost the familiar stink Jonas remembered from when Susan lived here. He had never figured out what it was. Mold? Unwashed laundry? Foreign cooking? A combination of all three? Susan said she had gotten used to it, but Jonas couldn't see how. It was a smell he could never grow used to.

The door opened and there stood Dennis in all his glory. He wore a stained T-shirt that displayed a skull with a knife through it. His arms boasted a range of tattoos that, though colorful, were quite meaningless to Jonas. There was nothing as recognizable as a flower or a heart among the lot. His hair was a bird's nest.

During Susan's dating and engagement Dennis had always worn clean, inexpensive, long sleeve shirts that hid his tattoos. He had smiled and spoken with care. He had pulled the wool over everyone's eyes, especially Susan's.

He made no effort to put on a show now. "I was wondering when you'd show up."

"Look, Dennis." Jonas spoke as firmly as he could. "Susan left you almost a year ago and she isn't receptive to your attentions now. Leave her alone or I'll call the police."

Dennis shook his head. "Susan still loves me. It's you and her bitch mother that have poisoned her against me. If you'd let Susan answer the phone, I could convince her to come back."

Jonas just stared. Was the man delusional? "Susan..." he began, trying to figure some way to get it home to Dennis that Susan was afraid to answer the phone. But then he was pushed aside as someone swept past him and planted a fist in Dennis' face.

That first punch was just an appetizer. Jonas stood there, not knowing what to do as the attacker, dressed in sweats and a ski mask, rained a hail of blows so fast that Dennis was too surprised to fight back. By the time Dennis did think to react, the attacker had the upper hand and forced Dennis to the ground. Fists were replaced by booted feet as the attacker brutally kicked at Dennis' side and legs and arms. Dennis gave up the fight and brought his arms up to protect his face. The attacker gave him a final hard kick, shouted: "Leave Susan alone!" and then ran along the corridor to the stairs and down.

"What?" Jonas blurted. He glanced down at Dennis, roiling in a puddle of pain, and then took off after the attacker. Jonas exited the apartment building just as the sweats-cloaked man jump into a white Toyota pickup and roared off down the street.

Jonas ran to his LeSabre intending to follow the Toyota, but by the time he was on the road the other vehicle was gone. No matter. Jonas knew where it was going. It was Larry's truck. Just as it was Larry's voice behind the ski mask. Dennis had gotten his long overdue beating after all.

· δ ·

An Interview With The Police

Jonas arrived home to find a white Toyota pickup sitting in Larry's driveway and three police cars parked along the street. Two officers were standing in his yard speaking with Gwen and inspecting the painters' tape on the windows.

"This is my husband, Jonas," Gwen told the officers. "He was at work when it happened."

The male officer tipped his head toward Jonas. "We're interviewing the neighborhood regarding the shooting two days ago. If you were away at work I suppose you didn't see or hear anything."

"That's right," said Jonas. "By the time I got home the police had come and gone."

"I see. Do you know the Badlin family?"

Jonas felt a bit embarrassed by the question. "I've never spoken to them."

"Your wife says you've lived here for fifteen years. The Badlins live six houses away. None of you have spoken to them in fifteen years?"

"The Badlins keep pretty much to themselves," Jonas explained. He glanced at the female officer who hadn't said a word. He got the impression that she was acting as a human lie detector while her partner asked the questions.

The male officer spoke again. "Your neighbors say pretty much the same thing. Do you know your other neighbors?"

"Most of them," Jonas admitted. He found himself consciously trying to sound honest. He didn't want the police to mistake nervousness for deceit. "Some of us play poker in the evenings."

The human lie detector raised an eyebrow. Jonas mentally kicked himself. Interview skills 101: never offer information that hasn't been asked for.

"Do your neighbors talk about the murder?" asked the male officer.

Now Jonas was starting to get annoyed. Why ask questions you already know the answer to? "Of course my neighbors talk about the murder. How can they not talk about the murder? It happened on our street."

Then came the real question. "What do they say?"

Jonas thought about that for a moment, and was surprised to discover that despite two days of talk, not a lot had actually been said. "Well," he began. "Everyone pretty much agrees that Ricky Henders looks guilty as Hell, but can't imagine him doing it. Frankly we can't imagine anyone in the neighborhood shooting a Badlin or anyone else. It must be someone from outside the neighborhood."

No one had suggested that last bit. It was Jonas' own thinking, provided Ricky was innocent. "Could this be some random drive-by thing? Gang related?"

"Anything is possible," the officer responded. Jonas noted what he didn't say. That the neighborhood has no history of gang activity. Or that William Badlin obviously didn't belong to a gang.

"The Badlins have had trouble before," the officer suggested. "Do you know anything about that?"

"I heard there was another murder at the house over a hundred years ago," Jonas told him. "But that was before we moved here from Toronto."

Another raised eyebrow. Jonas hadn't intended to sound cheeky, but knew he had as soon as the words left his lips. "So there's been other, more recent trouble?" he asked, trying to cover up.

The police ignored him and, apparently done with their questions, looked prepared to move on. "What about Ricky Henders?" Jonas asked. "Are you letting him go?"

"Thank you, Mr. Smith," was the officers' only answer. The male policeman handed him a business card with the name Detective Bradley on it. "Please call us if you remember anything else."

The pair of them then walked across the grass to Larry's side of the duplex and rang the buzzer. Larry came out wearing jeans and a T-shirt. He wore painters gloves on his hands. "I'll be there to help in a minute, little buddy," he called to Jonas, and then turned grave as he answered the policemen's questions.

Jonas hadn't asked Larry for help painting. And he certainly hadn't asked Larry to give Dennis a beating. Seeing Larry now, acting all innocent, wearing gloves over his bruised knuckles, Jonas felt tempted to call the police back and tell them what had happened. He was still mulling over this impulse when Gwen spoke to him.

"What was that, dear?" he asked.

"I said, how did it go with Dennis?"

· δ ·

Criminals Rights

"I don't know," said Andy. "Seems to me that criminals these days have more rights than their victims." He was at the window and had put on his night vision goggles, even though it was not quite dark enough to need them yet.

Jonas shuffled the cards while they waited for Larry, who was late. Andy, unable to wait, had already told Jonas and Phil the news. The police had released Ricky. Too little evidence.

"I like kids," Phil said. "God knows I like kids. I teach rooms full of them every day. But letting a teen murderer go free because he was too stoned to remember pulling the trigger just doesn't sound reasonable. I'm sorry."

Andy, not turning from the window, said: "No sign of drugs in his system. Well, not drug drugs. Just some kind of sleeping pill."

"Kids try anything to get high these days," said Phil. "I know. You wouldn't believe some of the crap I've confiscated in class. Some of these kids are too stupid to live."

"Ricky's always been a good kid," Jonas suggested. "So Susan says."

"Did I miss anything?" Larry bounded through the doorway, grabbed a beer from the fridge, and took his place at the table.

Jonas' eyes went immediately to his knuckles, which were bruised and bandaged.

"Ricky's on the loose," Phil blurted.

"Actually," said Andy. "He's sitting in his living room with his mom, probably telling her about all the neat things in the detention center. In two days he's probably learned how to pick pockets like a pro and get high on bubble gum."

Larry's jaw tightened. "How do you find out all these things, Andy? Did you bug the police station?"

Andy kept his eyes on the Henders place. "Between military service and retirement I worked for a while at the youth detention center. Learned a few things. Made a few contacts."

"Must have been a walk in the park after the military," Larry suggested.

This time Andy did turn away from the window. He raised his goggles. "That's what I thought when I made the move. I couldn't have been more wrong. Youth detention is dangerous. I retired much earlier than originally planned."

Silence ensued as Andy returned to his surveillance.

"Ah, so, how come you're late?" Phil asked Larry.

Larry held up his hands. "One-handed bandaging took longer than I expected."

"Ouch," said Phil. "How'd you do that?"

Jonas answered. "Beating my ex-son-in-law to a pulp."

Larry grinned.

"Did he deserve it?" Phil asked.

"Long overdue," said Larry.

Phil nodded sagely. "Better late than never."

"You're all good with this?" Jonas asked, looking around the room. "I'm not saying Dennis didn't have it coming. But how appropriate is beating him within an inch of his life?"

"It's the only thing some kids understand," Phil suggested.

"Dennis is twenty-seven."

"It's the only thing some adults understand," Phil amended. "I see it all the time in the schools. The only way to put a bully in his place is to have a bigger bully punch his lights out."

"I think it's more complicated than that," said Jonas. "Andy? What say you?"

Andy stood for a moment, pondering. With the night-vision goggles pulled down over his eyes he looked like some kind of giant insect. At last he spoke. "Sometimes the only solution is a bullet to the brain."

A moment of silence.

"So," said Phil. "I haven't seen Dennis around here in quite a while. What did he do to come to your attention?"

Jonas told them about the phone calls and the drive-by.

"A beating is too good for him," Phil said. "I hear tar and feathers is coming back in style."

"Really?" said Larry. "I know a good pillow store. Genuine goose."

"Fire," said Andy.

"I don't think we can set Dennis on fire," said Phil. "You have to draw the line somewhere."

"No," said Andy. He took off his goggles and pulled out his cell phone. "Fire at the Badlin house." He punched in 9-1-1.

· δ ·

DAY 4

A Breakfast Of Arson And Murder

Breakfast was quieter than usual. Ann made no comments about food that wasn't there, and you could still smell wet ash in the air.

Last night after calling 9-1-1, Jonas and his poker buddies had run down the street and watched as the fire engine rolled in and hosed down the Badlin house. At first it looked as though the whole place would go up. The heat and the smoke and the flames were considerable. But once the firemen put it out it Jonas saw that the fire hadn't started inside the house, but had been set against an outside wall. It was deliberate arson. The end result was a large patch of burned grass and a section of burned and blackened siding.

It was an act no less senseless than the Badlin boy's murder. Jonas couldn't fathom why anyone would do either, but had to believe it was the same person. So much for his random drive-by theory.

"Ricky Henders is back home," said Susan, looking for something cheerful to say.

Gwen smiled. "I knew he couldn't have done it."

"Someone did it," said Ann, sounding not the least bit strange. "Someone shot and killed William Badlin and someone tried to burn down the Badlin house. Probably the same someone."

Was the woman reading his mind? Gwen's sister was becoming a bigger mystery than the Badlins.

Gwen sat over her breakfast wearing an uncomfortable expression. "You don't suppose Ricky...."

"No," said Jonas. "Not Ricky Henders. Yes, he was just released, but he was sitting all evening in his living room. He didn't sneak out to start a fire."

Everyone looked at him.

"How...?" began Gwen.

Ann grinned like a demon. "Of course not Ricky. And you knew, Jonas. Good. Very good. Keep that up and you'll find our villain."

Jonas couldn't help feeling buoyed by the praise, even considering its source.

Ann tapped a finger against her lips. "I think it's time. Yes. Jonas, you should visit the Badlins to check on things."

"I should what?"

"They've been through a lot," said Ann. "They need some neighborly support."

"I'll go," said Susan.

Jonas couldn't believe his ears. Susan? Meek, gentle Susan volunteering to visit the Badlins? Nobody visited the Badlins. But if that *had* been Susan dancing in the Badlin's back yard...? Perhaps she visited them all the time.

Ann smiled. "That's sweet, child. It really is. But your father should go. He needs to understand."

· δ ·

The Merits Of Break And Enter

"You know," said Larry, pulling a pair of gloves over his bandaged knuckles and then steadying the ladder. "This Badlin thing is beginning to scare me. First the murder. Then the arson. And now it looks like maybe Ricky Henders didn't do it. If not Ricky, who? And what will happen next? Someone else in the neighborhood might get hurt, not just the Badlins."

Jonas looked at his neighbor. "I didn't think anything scared you."

Larry grinned. "Not me personally. I'm just a middle aged, single guy. If something happened to me no one would care. But what will your family do if something happens to you? What will you do if something happens to Gwen? Or Susan?"

Jonas cringed inside. Larry had hit on something Jonas had been avoiding for days. Not just since the murder, but since being laid off from work. What will Gwen do if he doesn't find new work? What about Susan? Will they be reduced to living like Dennis? The life Susan had endured for three years before escaping? Will they have to sell the house and live in some low-rent apartment, standing in line every month for a dole check?

"But what can we do?" Jonas asked. "Until the police arrest whoever's responsible, we'll just have to be on guard."

Larry spat into the grass. "Bah. The police can't do anything. You saw them asking their useless questions yesterday. They know nothing. And they won't know anything until it falls in their lap. They'll do no better solving this murder than they did the one in 1900."

Jonas hated to admit it, but he agreed. The police appeared stymied. They had been around twice yesterday asking about the murder. Then last night asking about the arson. No one knew or saw anything. It had always been such a quiet neighborhood.

"I have an idea," Larry whispered, his voice low and conspiratorial.

For a moment Jonas had visions of Larry dragging one of the remaining Badlin boys out of the house and beating answers out of him. "What idea is that?" he whispered back.

"The two of us," said Larry, "should go have a look around the house."

"The Badlin place? We can't do that!"

"Shsssh," whispered Larry. "Maybe I should get Andy. I'm sure he knows how to keep quiet while discussing break and enter."

"But that's just it," Jonas whispered back, "Break and enter is illegal."

"Not as illegal as murder and arson," said Larry. "A little B & E will fall under the radar."

Jonas thought about that. Truth is, he was worried about Gwen and Susan. Even Ann. The murderer-arsonist needed to be caught and the police were running in circles. How could a little fact-finding hurt? Then he remembered Ann's words at breakfast, that he should check on the Badlins. Maybe this is what she meant.

"I'm in," Jonas whispered, even though saying so left a bad taste in his mouth. He didn't like Larry's methods, but he had to admit they were effective. There had been no more phone calls from Dennis.

Larry excused himself to go bet on the markets or the horses or whatever it was he really did for a living and Jonas took off his cap & gloves to join Gwen for lunch. Before he could go inside, a police car drove up and two officers got out. Different ones than Detective Bradley and his nameless female partner.

"Not more questions about the fire," he told them. "I told the police everything I know last night."

The two officers looked at each other. "We don't know anything about a fire. Apparently you were a witness yesterday to an intruder assaulting your son-in-law. We'd like to hear what you have to say."

· δ ·

Trouble Follows Wherever You Go

Jonas sat at the poker table, the deck of worn cards protected beneath his fingers. His friends looked at him, anticipating a shuffle and deal. Jonas was of no mind to appease them.

He had spent the afternoon brooding about what had been happening in the neighborhood. Physical labor, such as painting, did that. It gave you time to think.

"Look guys," he said, "I hate to put a damper on things, but I'm really concerned about what's been going on around here lately. We've got murder, arson, and Dennis stalking my daughter. And the police are powerless to do anything. The neighborhood is in trouble."

Larry smirked. "I doubt we have to worry about Dennis anymore. That's one trouble solved."

"I'm not sure we need to extend the Badlins' troubles to the whole neighborhood," suggested Phil. "The Badlins have always had trouble. I've continued my investigations and have discovered that before coming to Calgary in the late 1800s they owned farmlands in Newfoundland. They came west as part of the first wave of Dominion Act homesteaders when they were burned out and forced to leave their property behind."

"But if they were forced to leave everything behind," asked Jonas, "How is it they still had wealth when they came to Alberta?"

"They conned their neighbors," asserted Larry. "They no sooner arrived in Calgary and they were swindling and cheating everyone in sight. That's probably why they were burned out in Newfoundland."

Andy shook his head. "I don't see how hundred year old events have any bearing on what's happening today." He donned his goggles and looked out the window.

"Past events," said Phil, "always shape what happens today. Especially regarding the Badlins. They have a history."

"Well, they aren't making history tonight," replied Andy, removing his goggles and taking his seat. "Nothing going on out there. Are we playing cards or what?"

"What's that smell?" Larry asked as Jonas reluctantly dealt out the cards.

Jonas sniffed and at first wasn't sure what Larry was talking about. Was the Badlin house on fire again? Then he realized that Larry was referring to a less nefarious odor. "Ann has new candles," he said.

Phil snorted. "I don't much care for this month's scent."

Andy picked up his cards. "I've heard that aromatherapy can accomplish miracles."

"She just likes candles," Jonas said, examining his cards: four hearts and a spade. "If she could work miracles I'd be winning more hands."

"Well, I wish she'd go back to liking her old candles," Phil said, discarding two. "The old ones didn't bother my sinuses."
Jonas tossed his spade and picked up a diamond. A lost gamble. Phil and Andy both held pat and Larry bet a dollar.
Throwing down his cards Jonas sat back and a sniffed at the candle scent rising from Ann's room. Phil was right; it wasn't a particularly pleasant smell. Ann had always been crazy about candles, burning them at odd hours and often sitting in her room just to smell them, which he didn't mind. She said the rose milk scent allowed her to be one with the universe or some such Zen nonsense. Tonight she wasn't burning rose milk. What did that mean?
"I'll see your dollar and raise you another," said Andy. He wore a look that dared Larry to fold.
Larry just smiled and threw two dollars on the table.

· δ ·

Jonas called the game early. He wasn't really in the mood. After Andy's full house took ten dollars from Larry's ace high two pair, none of the hands had been interesting and his thoughts had wandered to what might follow murder and arson. Ann's new candles were also giving him a headache.
Larry lingered in the yard as Andy and Phil left.
"You're right," said Larry. "Now is the perfect time."
"Time for what?"
Larry lowered his voice to a whisper. "Time to take a closer look at the Badlin place."
"I'm not sure," said Jonas. What had sounded like a good idea that morning had appealed less and less as the day wore on.
Larry let out a sigh. "Look, the police are useless. If we're going to protect the neighborhood, we're going to have to do it ourselves."
Jonas couldn't argue with that. "But it could be dangerous."
Larry shook his head. "A little harmless looking around. We're looking for motive, not the villain. And if by some microscopic coincidence he does show, he won't be after us. He won't even know we're there. Maybe we'll catch him in the act."
Jonas still had reservations, but Larry had an answer for everything.
"Go put on some dark clothes," Larry suggested. "I'll do the same and be right back."

Soon the two of them were skulking among the lilac bushes of the house across the street. This late in September the leaves were mostly gone, but the bush was still thick with branches. It was a dark night, not especially late, but late enough that everyone was indoors for the evening watching television. Even so, had Andy still been up in the attic room, Jonas knew that he'd be watching them with his night vision goggles.

Larry made a quick hand sign that meant nothing to Jonas and darted toward the next clump of bushes. Jonas followed and before he knew it they were crouched among the thick Nanking cherry bushes in the Badlin's front yard. Light from the street lamps bathed half the yard in shadows. Larry pointed to the side of the house marked by police tape. The bushes that had once run up against the house had burned away, so there was no cover there.

Jonas shook his head. He wasn't going to go out in the open. He didn't see what examining the burned wall would accomplish anyway. They'd be better off checking out the back yard. See what they could learn about the Badlins. Did they have a small garden hidden among the trees? A swing? A row of family tombstones?

Larry leaned in close and whispered in his ear. "I'm going to check out the house. You watch from here. If anyone comes, hoot like an owl."

Before Jonas could tell him that he had no idea how to sound like a convincing owl, Larry slipped up to the burned section of the wall and began tapping with his knuckles, tearing down police tape when it got in his way. He pushed at a spot low on the wall and, with only a little noise, widened out a hole through which he pushed himself and disappeared. This really was break and enter!

Jonas had no way to measure time. He wore an old fashioned analog watch that didn't glow in the dark. Barbaric, but he never understood the attraction of luminous hands or cheap plastic digital watches. Perhaps he didn't skulk around in the dark as much as most people. He had no idea how much time had passed when a light went on in the house.

"Hoo."

That wasn't very loud. Jonas tried again.

"Hoo!"

He waited and listened. Another light came on.

"Hoo!"

Some noise from near the burned out wall. Larry.

Jonas turned and dashed toward the bushes of the next yard, and then the yard after that. He didn't stop in the lilac bushes across from his house, but kept going for three more houses, until he ran out of bushes.

Larry caught up to him and they waited several minutes watching for activity in the street. When there was none, they crossed to the other side and walked down the sidewalk to Jonas' house and then went inside and up to the attic room.

Larry grabbed them each a beer from the fridge and began muttering curses.

"What's wrong?" Jonas asked.

"I had hardly any time at all to look around. I was quiet as a mouse and still managed to rouse the household."

"What did you find?" It had better be something, Jonas decided, to make this whole adventure worthwhile.

Larry looked at him for a moment. "I was down in the basement," he said. "There was a big pentagram on the floor, with candles on the five points and others along the walls. None of them were lit, of course."

Jonas realized his jaw had dropped open. Even with news stories of devil worship and strange cults, more so in British Columbia than Alberta, he was having trouble buying this. "If the candles weren't lit, how did you see anything?"

Larry took a penlight from his pocket and flashed it in Jonas' eyes. "Every cat burglar needs his tools."

That would have solved his watch problem, Jonas realized, without even resorting to digital watches. "So what do we do next?" he asked.

Larry clicked off the light and put it away. "I don't know. I think we have to get the Badlins out of the house."

· δ ·

DAY 5

A Direct Approach Is Needed

After a sleepless night haunted by half-dreams of black cloaked figures, fiery pentagrams, and curved knives dripping with blood, Jonas found himself more confused than ever. Had he really spent the last fifteen years living just a few houses away from a family of devil worshipers? Had he raised a young daughter from childhood, through her teens, and into a failed marriage while just down the street in a basement, innocent people were being sacrificed to Satan? Where would these victims come from? He'd never seen anyone enter the Badlin house who wasn't a Badlin.

Jonas considered these things as he painted through the morning. By noon he had decided that he couldn't believe a word of it. Sure, Larry had seen *something* in the Badlin's basement, but a pentagram with candles? Candles he could understand. He had emergency candles in his own basement. Ann had candles. And so maybe there was some tape on the floor that looked like a pentagram. Even if it was a pentagram, that didn't mean anything. Maybe it was just art. It could mean any of a hundred things. Assuming devil worship was a stretch. Human sacrifice an even further stretch. Too big a stretch for Jonas to make. He needed more information.

A direct approach was needed. He would have to actually visit the Badlins and talk to them. Just as Ann had suggested. Insane Ann, who sometimes seemed saner than anyone. Somehow he found the prospect of visiting the Badlins more frightening than skulking in their yard at night and finding signs of devil worship in their basement.

After a quick lunch and a change out of his painting gear, Jonas marched over to the Badlin place before he could change his mind. He noted that the police tape was still disturbed, but that plywood now covered the hole where Larry had entered last night. Jonas would have noticed if the police had been back, so the Badlins obviously hadn't called them about last night's break in. Perhaps they had given up on the police as well.

He stood on the front step for an unnaturally long time before pressing the doorbell, and then waited an additional unnaturally long time before the door opened.

Up close Badlin appeared older than he looked at a distance, sixty-something, his dark hair graying, his skin oddly weathered for an indoor recluse. He didn't have a beard, but sported several days' growth of salt and pepper facial hair. Jonas supposed he hadn't shaved since the murder of his eldest son. Given the age of his boys, he had to have been past forty when he began siring them.

"Mr. Badlin," Jonas said haltingly. "I'm Jonas Smith from down the street. May I come in?"

Badlin said nothing for a moment. His expression remained stern and otherwise emotionless. "I know who you are." Then he turned and walked away.

Jonas entered the house, closing the door behind him. He belatedly wondered if he should have told Gwen where he was going. Visions of being led down to the basement and being staked inside a pentagram filled his head.

Badlin didn't take him to the basement, but past a stairway leading to the upper floor and into a sitting room at the front of the house. The room was filled with antique furniture and paintings and small statuary and felt very comfortable. There was a large stone fireplace in one corner and several shelves filled with dusty books. The paintings and cloth hangings depicted ancient forests and leather-clad men with swords.

Badlin motioned him to sit on the couch while he sat himself in a soft armchair. He said nothing.

Jonas cleared his throat. "I just want to express my condolences for your recent troubles. It must be hard on you and Mrs. Badlin and the rest of your family to lose William the way you did."

Badlin considered him a moment, his expression still unchanged from the greeting at the door. "Yes," he said at last. "It is hard." He paused. "Fortunately, William's mother passed away several years ago. She didn't live to see her eldest son taken from us. It's better that way, I think."

"I didn't realize," Jonas said. "That your wife had passed away, I mean."

Another long pause from Badlin. "How would you know? We keep pretty much to ourselves. No need to share our troubles with strangers."

"Do you have any idea?" Jonas asked. "Who would want to hurt your family, I mean? It's such a terrible thing."

Badlin kept his expression unchanged, but Jonas detected a fire in his eyes. "It is terrible, yes. And no, we have no idea who would do this. As I said, we keep pretty much to ourselves."

"How are your other children holding up?" Jonas asked, needing to keep the conversation going.

Again a pause. "George and Jonathan are doing as well as can be expected."

"And your daughter?"

The fire in Badlin's eyes flared. "I have no daughter. It is just the three of us now." Badlin rose from his chair. "Thank you for your visit, Mr. Smith. Few of our neighbors have made the effort. I appreciate that you have." He directed Jonas to the door.

· δ ·

About The Daughter

Ann was waiting when he returned from the Badlins. "Well?"

"Well what?"

Ann turned her mouth into a scowl. "Have you solved the murder?"

What did Ann think? That Badlin himself murdered his own son? How was a five minute talk with the man supposed to solve a murder? "I just offered my condolences," Jonas told her. "That's all."

Ann shook her head. "What kind of detective are you?"

"I'm not any kind of detective. Today I'm a house painter."

"And not a very good one," Ann suggested. "There's more paint on the lawn than on the house."

For a woman who couldn't tell the difference between carrots and peas, Gwen's sister was suddenly very astute. "He did say one thing that was odd," Jonas suggested. "He claimed not to have a daughter."

Ann looked thoughtful. "He might at that." Then her face turned stern once again. "Try harder." And then she was gone.

Jonas found himself more confused than ever as he changed back into his painting overalls. Two days ago they were snowflake white. Today they were sky blue and weighed ten extra pounds. It was entirely possible that Jonas was wearing a full can of paint.

Why was Ann so urgent about solving the murder? Was she also scared that the Badlin troubles might boil over into the neighborhood? Did she feel herself at risk? Or Gwen? Or Susan? She was right though. Jonas did have to try harder. Even if the Badlins were the target, anyone in the neighborhood could get hurt. If only he knew where to begin.

Back outside, Jonas popped open a fresh can of paint and was stirring it with a stick when a rusted Honda Civic pulled up and Dennis jumped out. Well, jump is perhaps too energetic a word. Dennis limped out. But he looked as belligerent as ever, even with his arm in a sling and tape and bandages littering his wardrobe. A little more bandage than necessary considering the damage consisted of nothing more than bruises. It stank of a pity play, confirmed by the fact that Dennis' hair was washed and combed.

"Bring her out!" Dennis demanded. "I insist you let Susan talk to me."

Jonas left off stirring and stood up straight. "Susan doesn't want to see you, Dennis. She doesn't want to hear from you. Please. Just go away and don't come back."

"You've brainwashed her." Dennis took several steps across the grass. "Or you're keeping her locked up. You don't let her answer the phone!"

"She won't answer the phone because she's afraid you're on the other end. You're terrorizing her. If it doesn't stop, there'll be hell to pay."

Dennis took several more steps and scowled even harder than his usual scowl. "It was you, wasn't it? Hired some goon to put a beating on me. Well, I don't need no goon. I can put out a beating with the best of them. Maybe I should give you a demonstration."

Jonas glanced casually about. Painting supplies made poor weapons. "Are you threatening me? Because if you are, that's a crime. The police—"

"—the police can't tie their own shoes." Dennis stood right in front of him now. There was a wildness in his eyes that Jonas hadn't seen since Susan, flanked by her parents, told him they were getting divorced.

Then from the house: "Go away."

Both of them turned to see three women standing on the porch: Gwen, Ann, and Susan. It was Susan who spoke. "I don't want to see you, Dennis. It's over. Go away."

"They're making you say that," Dennis asserted. "If they weren't twisting your arm, you'd come back to me."

"You're only saying that because that's what *you* do. You twisted my arm so that I wouldn't leave you. But I did leave you. It's over. I'm not coming back."

Dennis took several steps toward the porch. "You will come back."

This was getting out of hand. Jonas looked around again for a weapon. The best he could find was an unopened can of paint. If he could smash Dennis in the back of the head with it, this might end well.

He picked up the can as Dennis took several more steps toward the porch. Then there was a flash of lights and a short blare of a siren as a police car pulled up against the curb. Detective Bradley and his partner stepped out.

A lengthy discussion between Dennis and Bradley ensued, with Bradley's female partner silently keeping score. Apparently Bradley won, as the discussion ended with Dennis led away in handcuffs and a recommendation by Bradley that Susan apply for a restraining order.

As the police drove off Larry ambled over, scowling at Dennis' rusted Honda. "Did they have to leave his car behind?"

"How did they get here so quick?" Gwen asked. "I only just called them before we came outside."

"I called them when Dennis first drove up," Larry explained. "He's trouble on wheels." He turned to Jonas. "What say you and I take his car back to his place? We don't need to give him an excuse to come back here."

This was the first idea of Larry's that Jonas actually liked. "We don't have keys."

Larry grinned. "Not a problem, good buddy. Anybody can hotwire a Honda."

· δ ·

A Prince Of Wales

"He'll be back," said Andy. The ex-military, youth detention retiree stood at the window surveying the street through his night vision goggles. "A restraining order means nothing until the restrained tests the waters. I suggest you tap your phone and record his calls. Even if he doesn't say anything the tap will record the times and the police will be able to trace it back to Dennis. I can set it up if you like."

"Well, I'm not sure—" Jonas began.

"He'll gladly take you up on your offer," said Larry. "Come on, Jonas. Get with the program. Wimp out now and Dennis will win."

"This isn't a contest."

"It is to Dennis," said Larry. "You need to show him his place in the pecking order. It's basic human nature."

"Then sure," Jonas acquiesced. "A tap on my phone is just what I need."

"Maybe a few days in jail will help Dennis see the light," said Larry.

"I have some news as well," said Phil. "I've been able to trace the Badlins back to Wales, where they were a prominent family named Badlaen. At one point, back in the twelve hundreds, they even contended for the English throne. If things had gone differently, young William Badlin would have been the King of England."

"Pah!" said Larry. "Re-write history and anyone could be King of England. Even me."

"The important part," said Phil, "is that the Badlaens came to Canada seeking to escape persecution. Seems a lot of Welsh and Brits felt the Badlaen claim to the throne was too legitimate for comfort."

"So what are you suggesting?" asked Jonas. "That it's the House of Windsor murdering Badlin boys and burning their houses?"

Phil shrugged. "I'm not drawing any conclusions. I'm just telling you what I found out."

"What you have found out," summarized Andy, "is that the Badlins have been victimized down through the centuries from Wales to Newfoundland to just down the street in Calgary, Alberta."

Phil looked at him. "Yeah. I guess that's about it."

"So why don't they move again?" asked Jonas. "There's a pattern of persecution followed by moving on."

"Why move?" asked Larry. "Sounds like it never helped in the past."

"Larry's right," said Andy. "There seems to be a lot more persecuting than moving. Moving seems a last resort."

"Trouble follows them wherever they go," said Larry. "That suggests they bring it with them. I should tell you about the pentagram and candles I found in their basement."

"You were in their basement?" asked Andy. He turned away from the window and slipped the goggles up onto his forehead.

Larry gave that look you see when people are mentally kicking themselves. Finally he said. "I won't go into details, but yes I was in the house, briefly, and saw evidence of devil worship." He then described everything he had earlier told Jonas.

"I'm astounded," said Phil. "The family is from Wales. Any cult they might belong to would be of the Earth Goddess. Pentagrams are from the Middle East."

"Maybe they picked it up in Newfoundland," suggested Larry.

Phil shook his head. "Eastern cults are even scarcer in Newfoundland. The region is mostly Welsh-Irish. The original Newfoundlanders left Great Britain to get away from invading cultural influences. Besides, the trouble started in Wales. I think it followed them all the way here."

"It can't be a claim to the throne," said Andy. "You said there's no evidence they've raised the issue in hundreds of years."

"True," agreed Phil, "but it could be related somehow."

Andy resumed his vigil at the window. "Your sister-in-law is wandering the street again. I think she's talking to herself."

· δ ·

DAY 6

House Painting For Dummies

By mid-morning Jonas was getting comfortable with the rhythm of painting. Short, quick rolls in the tray. Long, slow up and down motions applying paint to the wall. He found he could now spread the paint evenly without plastering it on and was optimistic he wouldn't run out before the job was done.

Jonas also found that he didn't have to focus on the actual effort of painting as much and could apply more of his concentration to other things, such as pondering the events of the past few days.

Was Dennis the killer? His behavior was textbook. Depressed ex-husbands want things back the way they were, and can lose all rationality trying to get it.

Were the Badlins cultists? Performing strange rituals in a candle-lit basement? If so, who knew? Or knew enough to want to do them harm? In sixty-plus years they had rarely stepped out of their house. How could they have offended anyone? Or were they lost royalty, biding their time before making another attempt at the throne? Was the English throne even worth pursuing these days? And if it was someone trying to extinguish the family line, how could they possibly succeed with two murders a hundred years apart? None of this made any sense.

And what about the fire? Were they really trying to kill the whole family? The relatively small amount of fire damage showed no commitment to burning down the house, never mind burn it down before the occupants could escape.

Then there was the daughter who wasn't. Priscilla. How could Ann be so certain just on Mrs. Luis' say so? And what about Ann? She'd been an absolute loon for four years. Yet since the murder, half the time she's been stranger than strange while the other half she almost made sense.

"Well, it looks better than I thought it would."

There was Ann, appearing out of nowhere with a large black and yellow book clutched in her arms. She was looking at the house and smiling. "There is something very satisfying about new paint," she said. "Like the smell of fresh coffee in the morning."

Jonas wondered if she might be having one of her lucid moments.

Ann turned to him and presented the book. "I got his for you," she said. "To help with your work."

Yes, thought Jonas, definitely lucid. She had read his mind that he wanted a book on house painting and had produced one out of the aether. He accepted the magical book and looked at the cover: Detectives for Dummies.

He looked up and Ann was already walking back into the house.

Sighing, Jonas sat down on the front porch and opened Ann's book. Leafing through the pages he decided that it really was for dummies. Jonas had no investigative training, but found he already knew most of what the book suggested. It was all basic, common sense observation and conclusion. It was only toward the end of the book that the more difficult issues were addressed.

On one page was a sketch of a villain who looked surprisingly like Dennis. The topic concerned psychopaths and their motives, motives that often made sense only to the villain.

Could Dennis be getting back at Susan by disrupting the neighborhood? The phone calls and drive-bys were obvious tactics. Were murdering a neighbor and setting fires just additional salvos in Dennis' psychological warfare?

Then another thought hit him. If that's how Dennis operated, what had that bastard done to Susan during three years of marriage?

As though invoking bad karma, Jonas looked up to see Dennis' rusted Honda coming up the street. Fumbling in one of his coverall's many pockets, he pulled out the small camera Andy had given him and aimed it at the car. By now Dennis was even with the house and, seeing the camera, roared off up the street. Jonas managed to snap off a shot of Dennis glaring out the side window at him.

Earlier that morning Andy had handed Jonas the pocket digital camera and installed a bug in Jonas' house phone. "Things will get worse with Dennis before they get better," he had said.

"How do you know?" Jonas asked him.

"They always do," was Andy's reply.

Jonas now wished he had asked Andy if he thought Dennis might be a psychopath.

Returning the camera to his pocket, he finished reading the section on how to identify psychopaths, which still didn't confirm Dennis one way or the other. Then he read the final section on unsolvable mysteries. It contained one sentence that was worth the price of the entire book: *When there appears to be no answer to the central problem, try solving peripheral questions first. Doing so may shed light on what at first appears unsolvable.*

· δ ·

Blind Justice

"I find it odd," said the judge.

Jonas was not happy with the judge. After lunch he had changed out of his overalls into his best suit and driven himself and Susan to the courthouse to get the restraining order against Dennis. After waiting in the hallway for an hour past their appointment, they finally got in to see *His Honour*.

The judge looked older than the Badlin place, with snow white hair — not a wig — and a face full of decrepit dead skin. The man was sour, and he appeared in no way inclined to grant the order.

"I find it odd," the judge repeated, "that your ex-husband should show up after a year of quiet and… harass you." He used the word harass with much reluctance. "Did you do something to provoke him?"

Susan sat next to Jonas like a fearful child. If the judge intimidated Jonas, he could only imagine the effect he had on Susan.

"Nothing," Susan said weakly, the latest in a line of one word answers.

"Humph," said the judge. He lifted some papers. "A few phone calls. One visit to the house. This doesn't look like harassment to me."

"The police arrested Dennis during that visit," Jonas said. "He was about to commit violence."

The judge peered at him. "So you say." He shifted to another piece of paper. "Ms. Smith. It says here someone recently gave your ex-husband a beating." His weasel eyes peered at both of them, bouncing back and forth. "Do you know anything about that?"

Jonas cleared his throat. "I'm sure Dennis has many enemies. He is not a pleasant man."

The judge harrumphed again and his eyes returned to the paper. "It says here, Mr. Smith, that you were present during the beating."

"I—" Jonas began.

The judge held up his hand. "It says you did nothing to help your ex-son-in-law and that you ran off after the beating was over."

"It happened so fast. I didn't know what to do. And I ran after the assailant to try to catch him."

"And did you catch him?" asked the judge.

"No," admitted Jonas. "He got away."

"And can you provide a description of this man?"

"He wore a ski mask. I've already answered these questions for the police. My statement is right in front of you."

"Yes," said the judge. "It is. And what it suggests is that I should issue a restraining order against you, Mr. Smith."

"But I haven't done anything!"

"And neither has your son-in-law. Yet here we are."

Jonas pulled the camera out of his pocket. "Dennis drove by the house again this morning. I took a photo."

The judge shook his head. "Driving down a public street is not a crime. Unless you can give me something more I am not going to limit the rights of an innocent man. Is there anything more?"

Jonas looked at Susan. "Is there more, honey?"

Jonas felt sure there was. Susan had not returned from the three year marriage the same carefree young woman who had entered it. And she refused to talk about it.

Susan shook her head.

The judge sighed. "Then we are done here. Good day."

Jonas ground his teeth. Dennis needed to be stopped, but he wasn't going to push Susan. If she did have more to say, Jonas would wait until she was ready to say it. "Thank you, judge," he said, begrudgingly.

As they shuffled from the court room, the judge called him back, leaving Susan out in the hallway.

"Mr. Smith," the judge said quietly. "I want to give you this card. It's for a very good trauma counselor I know."

Jonas looked blankly at the card.

"Mr. Smith, I've seen a lot of people in this courtroom. I can tell when people have been hurt or have the potential to hurt others. But the only power I have is to enforce the law and, as we both know, justice is blind. Make an appointment for your daughter to see my friend. She can help."

Jonas didn't know what to say. So he said: "Thanks. I will."

· δ ·

A Nation Of Criminals

"Typical," said Larry, after Jonas told his buddies about his meeting with the judge. "I'm surprised there's anyone locked up in jail at all."

"The jails are full," suggested Andy. "We are a nation of criminals where only the very worst are ever punished."

"Yeah," said Phil. "Punished with three meals a day and color TV. Our prisons provide a better lifestyle than that enjoyed by twenty percent of the free population."

"Have you ever been in jail?" Andy asked him.

"No," said Phil. "I'm not criminal enough."

"Then I wouldn't go around describing prison as a luxury resort."

"The point is," said Larry, "that if you want anything done you have to do it yourself." He looked at Jonas. "Do you own a baseball bat?"

"What? No!" said Jonas.

"We'll go out and buy one tomorrow."

"Look. I just want Dennis to leave Susan alone. I don't want to break his legs."

Larry squinted at him. "You sure?"

Andy pulled down his night vision goggles and looked out the window. "All quiet at the Badlin place. And the Henders."

"Maybe all the excitement is over," suggested Phil. "No more murders, or arson, or…" he looked at Larry. "No more break-ins."

"So what do you guys know about the family members?" Jonas asked.

"You mean the Badlins?" said Phil. "I'm not sure. In the twenty years I've lived here I've only seen a Badlin a couple dozen times. I may not have seen all of them."

"Individuals don't matter," said Larry. "Cults suppress individualism."

"Except for the leader," said Phil. "The leader always stands apart. The *group* worships him."

"I can't see Mr. Badlin as a cult leader," suggested Jonas. "I've met the man and he has zero charisma."

"Ah," said Larry. "But family cults are different. They don't use charisma. The patriarch controls his family through fear, grooming a son to take control when he dies. And they don't look for more followers outside the family, except through marriage. Neither do they let anyone inside the family leave."

"That *could* describe Badlin and his family," Jonas agreed. "You think William was murdered because he tried to leave? Then how do you explain the arson?"

Phil shook his head. "That theory doesn't pass muster. There aren't enough Badlins to maintain a dynasty. And certainly too few women. Cults of any stripe always have plenty of women to keep as chattel, and to do all the work."

"Phil has a good point," agreed Andy. "There's just the parents and two or three boys." He looked at Jonas. "That's what your sister-in-law told you, isn't it? A cult would have more women."

"Mrs. Luis provided this information to Ann," said Jonas. "But neither of them is very reliable. Mrs. Luis also claims there is a daughter, Priscilla. Badlin told me in no uncertain terms that there is not."

"You talked to Badlin!" asked Larry, sounding agitated.

"Just for a moment," said Jonas, "offering condolences on the murder of his son."

"Priscilla," said Phil. "I think Charles Badlin's wife was named Priscilla. Maybe that's who Mrs. Luis was thinking of."

Andy nodded. "Only someone as addled as Mrs. Luis would confuse a long deceased great-grandparent with a non-existent daughter."

FULL HOUSE

The conversation moved on from there, but Jonas couldn't stop thinking that the question of Priscilla was important.

· δ ·

DAY 7

If At First You Don't Succeed

The next morning Jonas was too caught up in trying to solve the murder to continue painting the house. He had lain awake half the night with possibilities churning through his head. Larry's suggestion that the Badlins were a cult got him considering the idea that one of the younger brothers murdered William in order to prevent him from becoming the next family head. Fratricide was as good a theory as any. But neither could he leave Dennis out of the equation. That Dennis should start harassing Susan just days before the murder couldn't be coincidence. Had Dennis somehow gotten it into his head that Susan was seeing the Badlin boy?

The uncertainty and lack of sleep had left him in a funk, unable to do much of anything. So instead of painting the house he found himself sitting in the attic room watching the street and waiting for Dennis to drive up or call the house. By eleven-thirty, Dennis had done neither.

Jonas didn't just watch the street in front of his house, of course. If Dennis had shot William Badlin or set the fire, he could be planning anything. Jonas' gaze panned up and down the street, tuned for trouble.

Despite his vigilance, Jonas didn't see the activity at the Badlin place until he heard the car door open. It was only then that he noticed all three Badlins getting into their car. Mr. Badlin and one of the boys climbed into the front while the other boy climbed into the back. All were dressed in black, which wasn't unusual, but Jonas still got the sense that they were dressed for a funeral. And perhaps they were. Today was likely the day they would lay William Badlin to rest. And not, apparently, in their back yard. There was no sign of a wife or daughter.

Jonas watched the car drive away, and then kept his gaze on the house. A knot in his stomach told him to expect something. He just wasn't sure what.

Minutes passed and Jonas began thinking that his stomach was just telling him it was hungry. Then something did happen. A man dressed in sweats and wearing a ski mask dashed out of Mrs. Luis' lilac bushes and ran up to the plywood sheeting on the fire-damaged side of the house. Larry.

Jonas couldn't believe it. Then he remembered Larry, after his first break-in, saying that they needed to wait until everyone left the house. Apparently he had been serious. Larry was going back to look around. Only this time he hadn't asked for assistance.

Jonas watched as Larry tore down the plywood and scuttled into the house. In broad daylight.

What to do. Call the police? Had someone else already called the police? Larry was going to get himself in deep trouble one of these days. Perhaps today. Or could Jonas use this to his advantage? Have Larry tell him what he found when, if, he got back.

Of course, Larry would probably tell him tales of pentagrams and candles, and human blood splashed on the walls.

Jonas couldn't believe what he was doing even as he found himself struggling into a dark sweater and pulling his paint-splattered painters cap down over his eyes. Feeling like a cat burglar in his own home, he crept down the stairs, past Ann's room filled with foul candle scent, to the main floor, then out the front door. The LeSabre was in the driveway, so the women weren't out, but he didn't see them as he left the house. He hoped they were all in the basement, perhaps packing up old clothes for the Salvation Army.

He crossed the street and then walked calmly down the sidewalk and up the Badlin's front step. He waited at the door a moment, and then walked around to the side of the house. The hole Larry had made in the burned wall was just large enough to squeeze through. Jonas went in headfirst and discovered a crawlspace maybe three feet tall.

He'd heard about crawlspaces in older houses, but had never seen one. They had something to do with insulation back before furnaces and air conditioning made insulation less important. The floor was rough planking covered with a century of dust, much of which floated in the air from Larry's recent passage. Jonas' movements stirred up more.

The crawlspace was dark. Jonas had not thought to bring a pen light like Larry's. But it was full daylight outside and enough light crept in to reveal a door in the ceiling closer to the center of the house. Scattered throughout the semi-darkness, like tombstones in a graveyard, cardboard boxes slumbered. Some had been ripped open, probably by Larry, to reveal packed clothes or old dishes.

Jonas ignored them and crawled toward the trapdoor in the ceiling. As he did he remembered another thing about old houses. They had no basements, another relatively recent innovation made possible by large earthmoving machines. Few such machines existed pre-1900. So much for Larry's tale of pentagrams and candles in the basement.

The trapdoor up into the house was open. Jonas sat beneath it and listened. Upstairs he could hear movement. Larry messing around. Quietly, he climbed up through the opening and sat on the main level floor, which creaked.

Jonas gritted his teeth and listened for Larry. His friend was still rummaging around, so he probably hadn't heard him. Jonas decided that the best approach was to slide himself across the floor. It would still make noise, but his distributed weight would put less pressure on squeaky nails. Slowly, he inched his way toward the noises Larry was making.

His path took him past the front door and the greeting room where he had sat with Mr. Badlin. The hallway continued on to the far exterior wall with two doorways on either side. Noise was coming from the first room on the left, where the door was open.

Jonas nosed his way up to the door, still lying flat on his stomach, and peered inside. It was a bedroom. Larry was inside going through a chest of drawers. Jonas looked around and saw that the bed had been moved and everything in the closet had been pulled out and thrown onto the floor. He looked back at Larry, who was sweating and muttering beneath his breath. He had pulled off his ski mask and Jonas could see fierce concentration in his eyes.

Jonas was about to reveal himself and ask Larry what the Hell he thought he was doing, when from outside came the sound of a car pulling up. The funeral service, apparently, had been a short one.

Before Jonas could even react, Larry was running toward him. He burst out the bedroom door and tripped over Jonas' legs lying prone across the hallway floor.

"Ouch," cried Jonas.

"What the Hell!" cried Larry. And then Larry was up again and running down the hallway.

Jonas pressed his hand against his thigh where Larry had kicked him, then climbed to his feet. No point being quiet. It was the Badlins he needed to hide from now, not Larry, who was noisily climbing back down into the crawlspace.

Jonas turned to go after him when he saw a lock of brown hair swaying from the door of the next room down. The door had been closed when he'd slid down the hallway. Now it was open and there was hair. The hair moved further into the hallway to reveal half a face, that of a twenty-something young woman.

Jonas paused to gawk, but the sound of shoes on the steps out front sent him running after Larry.

Larry had left the cellar door open, probably assuming Jonas would follow, which he did. Again on his knees, Jonas pulled down the cellar door and scuttled toward the broken wall. As he made his way toward outside he heard footsteps on the floorboards above him. He didn't stop to replace the plywood on the outside wall, but dashed away through the bushes, following the path he and Larry had taken during their first break and enter.

· δ ·

An Unexpected Ally

There was no sign of Larry further up the street. Jonas wasn't sure what he would say to him if there was. Jonas pulled off his painter's cap and sweater and rolled them up under his arm, then walked down the sidewalk toward his house. He dumped the sweater and cap into the laundry basket, pushing them to the bottom, then went up to the attic and got a beer.

By the time he finished the beer, the police were pulling up to the Badlin place.

Jonas sweated to the aroma of Ann's foul new candles rising up from below as he watched Detective Bradley and his silent partner speak with Mr. Badlin on the front steps and then walk around to the side of the house. Badlin seemed to be competing with the police as to who could be the least animated.

My God! thought Jonas. What have I done? I broke into my neighbors' house. And for what? To confirm he has a daughter? The stupidity of the situation overwhelmed him.

Jonas retrieved a second beer and sought desperately for an alibi. Painting the house? No sign of that. Out shopping? The car was in the front driveway. Sitting in the attic drinking beer?

No officer, I didn't see anyone break into the Badlin place. Yes, it is just out the window. I was busy staring at the wall.

Maybe the police wouldn't come over. Maybe they'd be just as useless as they had been for the past week.

The beer had just started to settle Jonas' nerves, flushing the adrenalin out of his system, when he saw Mrs. Luis come out of her house and go talk to the police. With her arm she pointed straight at Jonas' attic window. The police also looked up. Straight at him.

Jonas took a long swallow of beer. He knew they couldn't actually see inside. The sun shining on the window glass made that impossible. But it was obvious that Mrs. Luis had watched him go into the Badlin place. May also have seen him leaving by way of her neighbors' cherry bushes.

My God! What possible excuse can I give?

He took another long swallow of beer, and then looked at the aluminum can. If I drink fast enough, I can claim I was drunk when I entered the house. I can say I was looking for my cat.

No, I don't have a cat. I just thought I did when I was drunk.

Drunk people are never punished. Just pitied.

Jonas took another swallow as the police and Mrs. Luis walked toward his house. He finished the second can and was starting on his third when Ann appeared in the yard and intercepted the police. She spoke even louder with her hands than Mrs. Luis. In no time at all the police went back to their car and drove off.

Jonas sat there with his open can of beer as Ann's footsteps echoed on the attic stairs. Her eyes looked completely sane as she entered the room, grabbed Jonas' beer and took a swallow.

"You'd better think up a good story," she told him. "I just told the police that Dennis had come by and pulled you into his car. They're on their way to arrest him now."

· δ ·

Little White Lies

"I need your help."

Jonas stood on Larry's doorstep, the two men looking at each other like they hadn't both just committed a felony.

"Can't just now, little buddy," Larry said. "I'm busy hiding from the police."

"This'll help you too," Jonas told him. "I'm setting up Dennis to take the fall for today's break and enter."

Larry's expression widened into a grin. "Now you're talking."

In short order they were in Larry's truck heading to Dennis' apartment.

"Push the pedal down," Jonas suggested. "The police will already be there."

"This will never work," Larry said.

"It's better than the truth. And we may just get away with it."

"If we don't," said Larry. "I don't know anything. All I did was give you a ride."

"You're a good friend Larry." Jonas didn't know if he caught the sarcasm. "Are you sure you can pop the trunk?"

Larry grinned. "It's an old Honda. Anyone can pop the trunk. Even you."

Sure enough, when they arrived at Dennis' building a police car was parked out front. To Jonas' good fortune they had parked right beside Dennis' Honda and were nowhere in sight. They must be upstairs talking to Dennis.

Larry pulled into the lot and they both jumped out of the truck.

"Quick," said Jonas, "pop the trunk."

True to his word, Larry placed the tip of a screwdriver under the lid, tapped it once with his free hand, and the trunk popped open. The compartment looked much smaller than the LeSabre's. Jonas was thankful it was mostly empty, or his plan would fail right now.

"Now hit me," Jonas said.

"What?"

"Tap me on the chin. Be sure to leave a bruise."

"Are you sure?"

"We want to be convincing."

"Oh," said Larry. "If we want to be convincing...."

Jonas' head flew back as Larry gave him a hammer blow to the chin. He fell rather than sat into the trunk of Dennis' Honda. Larry helped him get his legs inside, and then closed the trunk lid after him. Jonas rubbed his jaw to the sound of Larry driving away. "I said a tap." Larry always was larger than life.

Jonas had no idea when the police would come back to their car, so he began shouting and pounding as soon as he felt Larry should be out of sight. It was tiring, banging around like that, and Jonas knew he would have to be convincing when the police did arrive. He called to mind the look on Dennis' face when he had come to the house, the pent up violence in his movements. And imagined the fear he would feel had Dennis actually hit him and thrown him into his trunk.

And it was at that moment that Jonas realized what Susan's life must have been like while living with Dennis. The helplessness and fear. Why it had taken three years to work up the courage for the divorce. And why Susan was so fragile and reluctant to talk about it now. That bastard! If Jonas wasn't locked in the trunk of Dennis' car, he'd be running up to the apartment to rip his lungs out.

When the police did hear him and opened the trunk, it was not a fearful kidnap victim they found, but an enraged captive ready to confront his captor. Fortunately it was just as convincing as the original plan. Despite everyone's claims of the uselessness of the police, Detective Bradley and his silent female companion did a more than adequate job of restraining Jonas and arresting Dennis. It was as if they had done it a thousand times before.

· δ ·

The Hatfields And The McCoys

"You look like shit."

Well, what else could Phil say? Jonas' jaw was several shades of blue and felt like oatmeal.

"Word from downtown," said Andy, "is that the police have Dennis dead to rights for breaking into the Badlin place today as well as assault and kidnapping when Jonas tried to stop him. They're also now looking at him for the murder and arson. But that's only by association. Nothing may come of it. Still, I don't think we'll be seeing Dennis again any time soon."

"It must have been quite the ordeal," said Phil. "Were you afraid?"

"I was too angry to be afraid," Jonas told him. "The more I think about it." He shook his head. The more he thought about it, the more he wished he had figured it out earlier. Four years earlier. It was so obvious now. How could he have been so stupid? Dennis wasn't just needy and controlling. He was abusive as well. Not a psychopath. A wife beater.

"Do you think it was him?" asked Phil. "Did Dennis kill William Badlin?"

All eyes were on Jonas now. Even Andy turned away from the window. As if whatever Jonas said would be the truth. Jonas almost laughed. He had told more lies today than the rest of his life combined. And committed more crimes. Some of them serious. And most of the story he had just told his friends was a lie. But he couldn't tell them the truth. The truth was too… ugly.

Had Dennis murdered William Badlin?

"No," Jonas said, and that was his honest opinion. Dennis was ten times a bastard, but Jonas didn't think he had murdered William Badlin. Dennis had nothing to do with the Badlins. Nor they with him. The Badlins were another story entirely.

"Well," said Larry. "I don't know who else it could be. Dennis seems the obvious choice."

Phil brightened. "What about enemies from Newfoundland? Tracked the Badlins down at last?"

"Could be," said Andy. "Some grudges never die. If the Badlins really were run out of town, there could be folks willing to chase after them."

"After a hundred years?" said Larry. "I think you're reaching."

"Could be a Hatfield and McCoy kind of thing," suggested Phil. "A family feud that spans the decades."

"And apparently the continent," said Larry. "Dennis is here and now. My bet's on him."

Jonas said nothing. All this talk was just going around in circles. That, and his jaw ached so much that speaking held no appeal. So while his friends dealt the cards and spun ever wilder theories, he just rehearsed the facts as he knew them in his mind. But by the time the game ended he was no closer than they to revealing the killer.

· δ ·

DAY 8

Priscilla

The next morning Jonas' jaw felt like God's own death, but he had work to do. He knew he should talk to Gwen about Susan. And then both of them should talk to Susan. But he wanted his jaw to heal up a bit first. Did Larry really have to hit him that hard?

There was painting to do as well, but that could wait.

What he really needed was to talk to Badlin.

Jonas put on his darkest clothes, hoping to put Badlin at ease, and then walked down the street. He could see additional police tape at the side of the Badlin place, cordoning off the entire area instead of just the wall. He still couldn't believe how stupid he had been yesterday. It was like he had been possessed by someone else, a different Jonas who had lost his mind.

Depending on how things went with Badlin, that might be his story. Temporary insanity.

Jonas was tempted to come clean with Badlin before someone shot holes in his story. Only, he had complemented the break-in with the kidnapping ploy and he didn't think that bell could be unrung as easily. It would give Dennis too much power over him. And he had to admit he found a certain pleasure in Dennis' arrest for the crime.

The door opened and Mr. Badlin stood in the threshold. He took one look at Jonas' jaw and said, "I understand you received that defending my house. I can only say thank you."

"It'll heal," Jonas told him. "Some things don't."

Badlin nodded and directed him to the couch where Jonas had sat during his earlier visit.

"I take it you'll fix that hole in your wall soon?" Jonas asked.

"Cement is arriving today. Thinking of getting one of those security systems as well. Don't care much for fancy electronics, but—"

Jonas interrupted: "I wanted to ask you something,"

"I don't know what that Dennis fellow wanted in my house."

That wasn't what Jonas was going to ask, but it did give him an idea. "I know why Dennis was here. He wanted to see Priscilla."

Badlin's nostrils flared. "Never heard of her."

"She's a young woman," Jonas told him. "Long brown hair. Green eyes."

Badlin stood. "I think it is time for you to leave."

Jonas knew that he had pushed too far. He stood and went to the door. He took one last look at Badlin. "Are you certain you've never heard of Priscilla?"

"Quite certain." Badlin shut the door.

· δ ·

Treasure Hunt

"What were you doing in the house?"

Larry had renewed his interest in painting and was helping Jonas set up the ladder. "I told you. Looking for a motive for the murder."

Jonas was wearing his painter overalls and had retrieved his cap from the laundry. "In a sock drawer?"

"That was William's room." When Jonas raised an eyebrow, he added: "I think."

"Did you find anything?"

"No. I'll have to go back."

"No you won't," said Jonas. "They just arrested Dennis for the break-in. If there's another one they will have to let him go."

Larry's jaw tightened. "But I have to."

"To look for clues?"

"Yes!"

Jonas shook his head. "Look, Larry. First you fed me that cock and bull about Satan worship in a non-existent basement, and now you're ready to go to jail for trying to find the killer of someone you neither knew nor liked. I'm not buying it. What are you really up to?"

Larry's jaw remained tight, and he paced around a three foot square of grass making a great show of wrestling with himself. "All right," he said. "But you have to swear to secrecy."

Jonas sighed, and then nodded. "All right. Secrecy. What's going on?"

"How long have I lived here?" Larry asked.

"I don't know. You were here when we moved in."

Larry waved at the duplex. "I was born in this house, Jonas. I grew from childhood with the Badlins as neighbors. My parents moved here when the street was built. Before that they lived less than a mile away."

"What are you saying?"

Larry sighed. "My family lived in Calgary back in 1900, when Charles Badlin showed up and began ruling the town like a dispossessed king, which is what he thought he was."

"You never said anything," Jonas said.

"How could I? You'd think *I* killed William Badlin."

"Why would I think that?"

"I don't know. To get even. Payback."

"Payback for what?"

"Charles Badlin was a charlatan. He robbed my great-great-grandfather. Just like he robbed anyone else with means in the area."

"But what were you looking for in the house?"

"Heirlooms," said Larry. "Jewelry. Watches. Snuff boxes. Several items that belonged to my family. I don't even know if the Badlins have them anymore. They may have sold them. I can't prove they took money from my family. But I do have detailed descriptions of several items the Badlins swindled from us."

Jonas shook his head. "I don't know, Larry. None of that sounds worth the trouble your asking for."

"No doubt you're right," said Larry. "But it shouldn't *be* any trouble. People break into other people's houses all the time. And with the fire damage providing easy access to the house.... How could I not go in?"

Jonas thought about that for a moment. "I suppose you've got a point. It was just bad luck the Badlins came home when they did."

"Story of my life," Larry agreed. "Bad luck."

"Well, I don't suggest trying it again," said Jonas. "Badlin is fixing the damage and installing an alarm system."

"Damn." Larry's expression soured, then brightened. "At least Dennis is getting what he deserves. At least some good has come out of this."

"Yeah." But inside Jonas knew that Dennis was getting off lightly. He deserved at lot more than a beating and kidnapping and break and enter charges.

· δ ·

After lunch, Ann cornered Jonas on the staircase and asked to know why he had broken into the Badlin house.

Jonas repeated the lie he had told the police when they rescued him from Dennis' trunk. "I saw someone snooping in the Badlin's yard," he said. "When he went in through the damaged side of the house, I went in after him to chase him out."

Ann stood patiently through Jonas' explanation, a frown on her face and her eyes as sane as he had ever seen them. Was this the same lunatic sister-in-law who had danced in the Badlin's back yard and wandered the street in the night?

"And I suppose," Ann suggested, "that you're going to tell me that it was Dennis you chased from the house?"

And here Jonas had to think fast. Dennis was Ann's idea. She would never go for such an unlikely coincidence. "I don't know who it was. He wore a jogging suit and a ski mask. I followed him down the street after flushing him out, but lost him right away. About all I can say is that he is fast on his feet."

"Uh, hum." Ann glared at him.

It was obvious that Ann wasn't falling for any of it. But what else could he say? That he and Larry were looking for stolen music boxes? Fortunately, and surprisingly, Ann changed the subject.

"Have you discovered who killed the Badlin boy yet?"

Jonas looked at her. He had the strangest feeling that no matter what he said, that Ann wouldn't believe him, that he had somehow become incapable of telling the truth and that Ann knew it. So he did the only thing he could think of. He told the truth. "No," he said.

Ann let out a huge sigh and disappointment filled her eyes. Then she was gone.

Jonas continued up the stairs into the attic and stood looking out the window. The street outside was quiet. The sun was out, but a wall of dark clouds lined the horizon. Indian summer was like that. Beautiful one moment, storming the next. Bad weather would put an end to his house painting.

But it wasn't the painting that worried him. As the clouds seemed to draw closer he felt that somewhere, just out of sight, a pot was boiling and would soon boil over. And when it did there would be more than just a dead boy in the street and a boarded up wall. Something bad was coming. Jonas could feel it in the depths of his bones. He couldn't explain it. Just as he couldn't explain who or why anyone would shoot William Badlin.

· δ ·

A Tale Of Camelot

Jonas watched as Phil stood and glanced out the window, then sat back down wearing a conspiratorial expression. "I found out something more about the Badlins."

"Let me guess," said Larry. "They're aliens from Venus."

No one laughed.

"Close," said Phil. "They lived in Wales a long, long time. Centuries. There are references to Badlin in Arthurian legend."

Larry sniggered. "Fiction!"

Andy shook his head. "Doesn't most fiction have roots in fact?"

"Exactly," said Phil, speaking in his teacher's voice. "Especially with historical fiction. In many cases, if it weren't for the romanticized fictional accounts passed down through the years we would have no idea of what actually happened in real history. In the case of King Arthur there is overwhelming evidence that when the Romans abandoned England, a Brit king did rise up to unite the southern tribes against Picts in the north and Saxons from the continent. There really was a King Arthur."

Larry's eyes turned oddly bright. "And some Badlin ancestor was his valet, I suppose."

Phil shrugged. "Unfortunately, the legends aren't that specific. There is, however reference to a Badlaen who married the daughter of one of Arthur's Knights, Sir Galahad. The same Galahad who was reported to be present at King Arthur's death. He is one of a dozen or so candidates for the unknown Knight who was charged by Arthur to protect Camelot until he returned."

Larry frowned. "That's all very vague."

"Ah," said Phil. "And now we see the downside of fictionalized history. The story of Arthur is so popular that we have an enormous body of material. So enormous that it is often contradictory and difficult to separate fact from fiction. And Arthur's Death was so romanticized that we have literally hundreds of variant versions, many of them quite mystical. Most all of them claim that Arthur was only injured and that he will someday return."

"Well," said Larry, "he hasn't returned yet."

"Which is what makes the Badlins interesting," said Phil. "If they are somehow tied up in the Arthur legends, they may still be waiting for him to return."

"So what you're saying," said Larry, "is that the Badlins really are a cult. A King Arthur cult. And that they do have some nefarious goal."

Phil looked troubled. "I don't know that nefarious is the right word. Arthur is supposed to return when England is in need of leadership. I don't think you can call that a bad thing."

"Most leaders who fill such a need," suggested Larry, "are called tyrants."

Andy stood up and shook a finger at Larry. "You and your cults! King Arthur stood for democracy and protecting the weak. He was a Christ figure, for God's sake!"

Larry leaned back into his chair, his arms out to his sides. "I was just saying.... Uhm. Anyone want a beer?"

"Actually," said Phil. "Most historians believe Arthur was a pagan. Most, if not all Arthurian Christianisms were added by later storytellers."

Andy sat back down. "We'll have to disagree on that point. My understanding is that the Romans had successfully converted southern England to Christianity before they left. I'll give you that they kept many of the older customs, but Arthur and his followers fought against the remaining pagans who were trying to reassert control."

"Some historians think that," Phil agreed. "Others think the Christian influence succeeded much later."

Larry still sat in his chair, exhibiting no evidence of the beer he had suggested. "But...," he ventured, "what about the Grail?"

The others all looked at him.

"Didn't Arthur send his knights in search of the Holy Grail? Christ's cup from the last supper?"

"That's the most popular interpretation," said Phil. "But scholars don't give much credence to it. Since it was Merlin, Arthur's pagan magician, who set the quest, the consensus is that the Grail is of pagan origin."

Andy was still frowning. "Everyone knows the Grail is Christ's cup."

Phil countered. "No one knows what the Grail is. It's the biggest mystery of the Arthur legends."

Larry seemed to recover his courage. "Poppycock," he said loudly. "A mystical mystery about a myth, and a waste of our good time."

"Speaking of pagans," said Andy, who had donned his goggles and was looking out the window, "I see Jonas' sister-in-law is out worshiping the moon again."

They all went to the window and Jonas looked down into the yard and saw Ann lighting candles in a circle in the front yard.

"At least she's taken them out of the house," said Phil.

· δ ·

DAY 9

Is There Such A Thing As Too Much Paint?

Run out of painters' tape and the whole world goes to Hell.

Jonas grudgingly drained his roller tray and resealed the open can of sky blue paint. Then he changed into clothes that weren't covered in wet paint and drove to Paint Heaven where he purchased $7.43 worth of tape. After a twenty minute absence he returned home to find a police car in his driveway and obscenities spray painted all over his new front exterior. He would have shouted his own obscenities, but felt he had better check on Gwen and Susan first. He could rant about the vandalism later.

"Jonas!" Gwen cried, rushing into his arms. "It was horrible. He tried to get into the house."

"I fought him off with a broom," Ann interjected. "He was no match for me." Gwen's sister cackled and waved her arms as though clutching a broom like a sword.

"Who?" Jonas demanded. "Who tried to get in?"

"It was Dennis," Gwen admitted. "He stood outside the door yelling. He said that Susan was his and he was going to take her away. When we wouldn't let him in, he got a spray can from his car and started writing on the walls. I'm sorry about your paint."

"Damn the paint," said Jonas. "Where's Susan?" He looked about the living room and saw only Gwen and Ann and two familiar police officers seated on the sofa.

"She's in her room," Gwen told him. "Resting. She's fine. Just shaken, like the rest of us."

Ann was still waving her invisible sword. Jonas looked back at the open door and saw that the lock bolt had been forced through the wooden mantle. The outside of the door showed the marks of boot kicks. The bastard had kicked the door in. And Ann had held him off with a broom?

"We locked the door," Gwen said, "then called the police. But he kicked the door open before they got here. I don't know what would have happened if the Badlins hadn't arrived."

"The Badlins?"

Gwen nodded. "Mr. Badlin and his sons — the two that are left — came quietly up the sidewalk and suggested to Dennis that he leave.

"And Dennis left?" Jonas was stunned.

Again Gwen nodded, her face flushed. "Mr. Badlin has a way of making suggestions. He spoke very clearly and politely, but in a way that suggested that his next suggestion would be anything but polite."

Jonas remembered his visit to Mr. Badlin and being asked to leave. He knew what Gwen meant.

"What about you?" he said to Detective Bradley. "What are you going to do about this?"

Bradley and his female partner rose from the couch together. The silent one was taking notes, had been since Jonas arrived. Bradley said, "We've taken statements from your family and Mr. Badlin, and we've taken pictures of your door and the front of your house. That, along with your son-in-law's recent entanglements with us should be enough to lock him up for a while. This time without bail."

"How long a while?" Jonas demanded.

"That's not for us to say, Mr. Smith. It's up to the judge."

Oh, great, Jonas thought, the same legal system that wouldn't grant a restraining order or lock Dennis up after kidnapping and breaking and entering. His anger was only mitigated by the fact that Dennis had committed neither of the latter felonies.

Detective Bradley left making vague promises that Dennis would be prosecuted to the fullest extent of the law.

· δ ·

An Awkward Thank-You

Before tending to the defacement of his house, Jonas felt obliged to visit the Badlins. For fifteen years he had lived on this street and not once had he seen the Badlins involve themselves in neighborhood events. Andy had lived in the area for sixty years and claimed the Badlins were as aloof as your most committed hermit. And Larry... well, Larry was born here and claimed the Badlin clan had always kept to themselves. But here they had come out and defended Jonas' family from a deranged madman. Jonas couldn't begin to express his gratitude, but he could give it a good try.

"Mr. Badlin," he began, once again sitting on the terse man's sofa, "you did me a great service today."

The older man stared at him with his hawk gaze. "You defended my home. I was only returning the favor."

Jonas almost winced. A reward for a lie. "Dennis," he said, "is not the easiest person to defend against."

A smile attempted to cross the older man's face, but failed. "I've fought worse," he said simply.

Worse? Jonas didn't know what to think. Maybe someone was after the Badlins. "If there is anything I can do for you—"

"Yes," Mr. Badlin answered even before he had finished speaking.

"There is?" Asking if there was anything he could do was just a pleasantry. It's what one said after such an event. No one ever expected to be called on it. "Of course," Jonas said. "Anything. I owe you."

Mr. Badlin ignored his words and leaned forward in his armchair. His voice, when he spoke, was low and hard as nails. "What I would like Mr. Smith, is for you to find out who murdered my William."

Jonas nearly gagged. Why did everyone think he could solve the murder? "But, the Henders boy. The police...."

Mr. Badlin cast a dismissive wave. "The police couldn't solve a crossword puzzle." He looked like he was going to spit. "Henders was drugged, or ensorcelled. Someone used him. I want you to find out who."

What Jonas wanted was to ask Badlin why in God's Heaven he thought Jonas could solve the murder. But he kept his mouth shut. He wasn't sure he even wanted to hear the answer.

Mr. Badlin rose from his chair, indicating the visit was over. Jonas followed him to the front door.

There was a creak of floorboards and he and Badlin both looked to the stairway and then up to find a young woman standing at the top of the stairs.

Badlin grunted, shook his head, then continued down the corridor into a room and closed the door.

The woman on the stairs walked down to the main floor and for the first time Jonas got a good look at the non-existent Priscilla. The long brown hair and green eyes were just as he remembered. She was shorter than Susan by a few inches, and younger by a few years if he was any judge. She could be either side of twenty. Her features were clear and sharp, like the cover of a fashion magazine. She was slim as well, but walked with a homey earthiness rather than Hollywood elegance. Her clothes were somewhat old-fashioned, but suited her.

She stared at him a moment, looking unsure of herself, then took on an air of splendid dignity. "I, too, wish to thank you for the support you have given our family since poor William was killed. Such support has been infrequent in our history, which is why my family maintains its aloofness and its suspicion of others."

Jonas didn't know what to say. Apart from breaking into their home and being caught by the very woman who now stood before him, he had done little else but accuse Mr. Badlin of being a liar. Why were these people being the least bit kind to him?

"Yet I fear," she continued, "that all your support will be for naught and there will be more deaths if you do not soon discover William's murderer."

Not another one! He wanted to scream: *I'm not a detective. I'm an unemployed oil man. And a redundant oil man at that. I can't even paint a house!*

But what he did say was, "I'll do my best."

She smiled. "I know you will. But do it soon, or all may be lost."

The door down the hall opened and the woman retreated back upstairs. Mr. Badlin said nothing as he opened the main door to see him out. He was obviously unhappy with what Priscilla had done.

· δ ·

A Big Bluff

Outside the attic the wind wailed.

"My sources tell me," said Andy, "that Dennis' bail has been revoked and that he will languish behind bars until his various hearings. Given the array of charges against him I don't think he'll be breaking down your door again any time soon."

"No," Jonas mumbled in agreement. But the words echoing in his head objected: *All may be lost.* And then there was Ann's growing anxiety that the worst was yet to come.

Jonas discarded a five and a seven and replaced them from the top of the deck. The resulting hand was worse than he had started with— a knight high nothing. He forced, and then covered, a quick smile in an attempt to bluff, but looking around the table could see that no one bought it. His friends knew he had nothing. He was such an awful liar. Still, he'd continue to feign a better hand and fold at the last second. It was how the game was played.

Larry replaced one card, his face expressionless the entire time. "With Dennis behind bars, the neighborhood should be a lot safer."

Jonas nodded. *All may be lost.* The words twisted through him. For the first time in his life, Jonas knew real fear.

Andy and Phil both stood pat, leaving Jonas to bid or fold. He put on a show of indecision, then folded, to the surprise of no one.

"I bid a dollar," said Larry, then took the pot as Andy and Phil quickly folded. Nothing in their hands either.

Jonas wondered briefly if Larry might also be holding an unwinnable hand, but was just a better bluffer. *All may be lost.*

"You know," said Larry, "With Dennis' grocery list of violations — threats, break and enter, kidnapping, defacement of property, and those are only the things we know about — maybe he's an arsonist and a murderer too." He paused while the others looked at him. "I mean, if Ricky Henders didn't do it, as the police are now saying, perhaps Dennis did."

"And why," asked Andy, "would Dennis kill William Badlin?"

"Why would anyone kill William Badlin?" Larry returned. "He's been hiding in a house all his life."

All may be lost.

"What I mean," said Andy, "is that Dennis is obsessed with Jonas' daughter. Apart from entering the Badlin house, which I still don't understand, all of his anger has been at Jonas' family."

Larry shrugged. "Who knows what goes on in a madman's head? Perhaps he believed the Badlin boy had intentions on Susan."

"That's a good theory," said Phil. "I've been asking myself since this whole thing started what the connection was between this house and the Badlin place. I mean, everything that has happened has been either there or here, but I could see no relationship. Now if, as Larry suggests, Dennis is solely responsible for everything and is suffering from some kind of delusional paranoia, well, that is the simplest explanation."

"But," said Andy, "I still don't understand how Dennis got Ricky Henders to confess. How does a deluded maniac get a smoking gun in the boy's hand when he's been so sloppy about everything else?"

"It's obvious," said Larry. "The boy was on drugs and picked up the gun Dennis dropped fleeing the scene. Or, Ricky was on drugs and really did shoot the Badlin boy. Maybe the police are wrong and they hand the killer all along."

Andy shook his head. "As straight-forward as we all see this coming down to a jilted ex-husband, the police see holes everywhere. About the only thing that is cut-and dried is this morning's attack on Jonas' house. That was undeniably Dennis. They have multiple witnesses, the spray can in his car, and a confession. I heard that Dennis admitted to the attack. But he denies all the other charges. This isn't over yet."

A third time, Priscilla's words echoed in Jonas' mind. *All may be lost.*

"Is it true," asked Phil, "that the Badlins chased Dennis away?"

Before Jonas could answer, Larry jumped in. "Of course it's true. Jonas chased Dennis away from the Badlin place. In return, the Badlin's chased Dennis away from Jonas' place."

"Unthinkable," said Andy. "Getting involved just isn't something the Badlins do." He looked at Jonas. "Are you sure there is no relationship between your family and theirs? Something that might explain why they helped, and why Dennis might go after them?"

Jonas shook his head, dumbfounded. "The Badlins are strangers to me. I'm as mystified as you." And this, at least, was true.

They accepted that and Andy dealt the next hand.

Autumn winds continued to hammer at the window. *All may be lost.*

· δ ·

DAY 10

Family Matters

It was the hardest thing Jonas had ever done. He considered asking Gwen to help, but decided not to. If he did that, he knew that she would take the lead and he would just sit there. Gwen would fix things. She was good at that. But Gwen fixing things wasn't what he wanted. Jonas had to take a stand. He had to act the father. He had been walking on eggshells around the issue for far too long.

"Are you sure you're ready to talk about this?" he asked Susan.

It was midmorning and they were sitting on the sofa in the living room across from the repaired front door. First thing after breakfast Jonas had braved the chill winds left by the night's storm and painted over Dennis' vandalism of the day before. He had then applied wood filler and a coat of pale blue paint to the damaged door, after which he had visited a hardware store and installed a heavy-duty bolt lock. The door looked good as new. Better. He had even bought a can of plastic cement and filled in and smoothed the crack in the concrete porch. His success in repairing the damage to the house had given Jonas the confidence to discuss Dennis with his daughter after four long years.

"I think I know," he told her, "how Dennis was during your marriage."

Susan's eyes were fluid with held back tears. She was twenty-five years old, but she was still Jonas' little girl.

Susan nodded, a quick slight motion of her chin. "You were right daddy. You and mom never liked Dennis. I was an idiot. I think part of me wanted to marry him just because you didn't like him. I was such a fool."

Jonas reached an arm around her shoulder and Susan collapsed into his chest. Tears broke loose and Jonas could feel as well as hear the muffled sobs.

"He hit you," Jonas said, knowing that was easier than waiting for Susan to say it. Her head rocked up and down against his chest.

"You could have come to us. Your mother and I."

"He wouldn't let me." Susan's voice was cracked and the tears continued, but Jonas knew they were good tears. They were tears that had built up over months and years and his daughter had been drowning in them. They needed to be released, and at last Jonas was father enough to let her release them.

"Dennis was... controlling. The more I went against his wishes, did anything he didn't want, the angrier he was. The more violent."

Jonas held his daughter tight as the whole sordid tale came out. The horrors his daughter had lived through during three long years of marriage followed by months of painful reflection and nightmares. Even after leaving him she couldn't truly leave him. The memories lingered.

"It's my fault," Jonas said as Susan fell silent. "I should have seen the signs. I should have seen what was happening and taken action. I must have been too wrapped up in my work. I—"

Susan pressed a finger against his lips. "No. It's Dennis' fault. He fooled us all."

Dennis. Any guilt Jonas had harbored for framing Dennis for the break-in and the kidnapping vanished. He should go to jail forever for how he had treated his daughter. In fact, Dennis was safer behind bars. If he showed his face around here again, Jonas wasn't sure what he would do.

"But I don't understand," he said. "Why did Dennis come back? He was gone for a year after the divorce. It was over."

Susan pulled away and looked at him with red-stained eyes. "That's the part I don't get. When he phoned that first time, and I answered, he said that someone had called him and told him that I still loved him, that I was playing a game of catch-me-if you-can."

"What! Who?" Jonas demanded.

"I don't know!" she cried. "Who would do such a thing? And when I told Dennis it was a lie, he claimed that was part of the game. That *no* didn't mean *no*."

Susan hugged him again and Jonas knew that she would be stronger going forward, that he would be stronger too, partly because they had finally had this talk, and partly because she now knew that she was less alone, that her father would be there whenever she needed him.

"We need to talk about this with your mother," Jonas said.

The shuddering against his chest began anew and Jonas feared Susan had begun crying again. Then he realized it was laughter. Susan pulled away and her face was filled with teary-eyed smiles. "Mother and I had this talk a year ago. We were just waiting for you to be ready."

Jonas laughed, and his own eyes began to water. "Of course you did. I'm a fool!" And then he hugged his daughter, seeking her comfort and protection. They were a family again.

· δ ·

By midday the last of the winds died down and Jonas resumed painting. What's more, he found he was truly enjoying himself. His brush strokes were sure and efficient and he finished an entire wall in record time. He couldn't remember when he had last been happier.

After his talk with Susan he'd sat down with Gwen in their bedroom and again the tears flowed, for both of them. He couldn't believe how patient his wife and daughter had been with him, letting him walk on eggshells all this time while they had worked things out long ago. They knew he hadn't been ready to face the reality of Susan's marriage. All this time it was he who was the fragile one, not Susan. Susan was tough as nails. She had to be after what she'd gone through.

Jonas had never felt so stupid, but at the same time he felt relieved. A dark chapter in the life of his family was behind them. They were ready — he was ready — to move forward into the next chapter. And he was eager to see where it would lead.

As he folded away the ladder he realized that he hadn't worked things out with quite his entire family. There was still Ann.

And there she was, Gwen's sister, walking around the side of the house and admiring his handiwork. "Nice. Maybe you should consider house painting as a career. You've developed a talent for it."

Jonas smiled. He had expected her to say something loony, like the blue paint was too bright a shade of pink, or that elephants had escaped from the basement again. That she was entirely lucid was no longer a surprise. It was possible that the new aromatherapy was working wonders or that her dementia simply came and went, but Jonas didn't think that was it. The dementia's coming and going was entirely too convenient. He suspected she faked much if not all of it, that she was saner than anyone. He just didn't know why she acted the loon.

"What do you know about the Holy Grail?" he asked her. Why not go for the hard questions?

Ann frowned. "That it's a topic you shouldn't concern yourself with."

"I've met Priscilla," he told her.

Ann's face brightened. "I'm not surprised. Pricilla knows who she can trust. But you're barking up the wrong tree. Mordred's descendants lost interest in their cause centuries ago. I doubt that any of them even remember what they once were."

"Mordred's descendants?" At any other time Jonas would believe Ann was speaking nonsense, but not with what Phil had told them regarding the Badlin's history. "You mean the people who chased the Badlaens out of Wales?"

Ann nodded, looking surprised. "So you have been doing your homework. The Mordrites have pursued the Grail since before Mordred wounded Arthur, but there has been no sign of them in generations. It must be someone else. Someone who fears what they don't understand."

"But why me?" Jonas demanded. "Why do you insist that *I* be the one who finds this someone?"

Ann looked him up and down, and then sighed. "It shouldn't fall to you. It should be me, or Gwen, or Susan. But Gwen has shunned her obligation, Susan is just learning hers, and I... you may have noticed that I am not entirely well."

Jonas had no idea what she was talking about. Perhaps he had jumped to soon to declare her sane. "What do you mean Gwen shunned her obligation! She's the kindest, most giving person—"

"—Yes, yes," Ann agreed. She put a hand to her forehead. "And she is my sister and I love her. But just as the Mordrites have forgotten who they are, so too has our Gwen forgotten. She doesn't believe in her responsibility, so you must assume it."

Ann swayed on her feet and Jonas reached out a hand to steady her. "I must get back to my candles," she said. She looked at him then, and Jonas saw the fate of the world lined in the tiredness around her eyes. "I would solve this mystery if I could, but I fear it is beyond me. The aroma from the candles allow me moments of lucidity, but at great cost." She shook her head. "You are the only one left. If you fail, all is lost. Be true, Jonas."

And with that Ann fled into the house.

· δ ·

A Quest For The Grail

Jonas sat at the attic window gazing down the street at the Badlin place. Storm clouds had returned with the declining sun and now brooded over the city. The temperature had dropped and when the clouds opened they could bring rain or snow. He hoped the afternoon's paint would be dry enough to weather the storm.

He didn't know what to make of his last encounter with Ann. During dinner Gwen claimed Ann was ill in her room. Jonas could smell the candles, apparently Ann's only medication. Whatever the illness, Jonas no longer thought Ann crazy. He couldn't explain it, but he believed her. Something bad was coming and, apparently, he was the only one who could see and do something about it.

He reflected back on his admission to Susan, that he should have seen and done something to get her away from Dennis. He felt the same way now. Something was wrong in the neighborhood and he couldn't just sit idly by. He had to take action. But what?

Taking out a sheet of paper he wrote down the names of everyone in the neighborhood, including Dennis, Detective Bradley, and his silent female partner. Then, one by one, he crossed out everyone who couldn't possibly have reason to hurt the Badlins. He crossed out Ricky Henders and Dennis as well. If it was either of them the police would have found something.

When he was done only three names remained: Andy, Phil, and Larry. His poker buddies. His name would be there as well, he knew, if someone else was making the list. There were, of course, other neighbors whose names he could have left, but he didn't think any of them had spent five minutes thinking about the Badlins. But here he and his friends sat every evening talking about the Badlins and spying on them with night vision goggles. How could they not be suspect?

He couldn't imagine any of his buddies as a killer, even Andy with his secretive military past. But as he thought this he recalled various movies and TV shows about Special Ops units performing feats of near magic. And how did Ricky Henders end up on his front porch with a gun in his hand, not remembering anything of his recent past? But no, not even Andy. He'd never suspect any of them, but they were the only ones left. It had to be one of them, didn't it?

As the minutes ticked away toward eight PM, Jonas pondered thoughts he didn't really want to consider. Outside, thunder rumbled. Then, at ten minutes to eight, he called the Badlins and then Detective Bradley.

· δ ·

When all three friends arrived for their regular poker night, Andy went over to the window and slipped on his night vision goggles, just as Jonas knew he would.

Jonas had had very little time to think things through, and felt he'd been almost incoherent when he spoke on the phone. But that was how life happened. No dress rehearsal. You learned to play it by ear or you died trying. Jonas greatly hoped that no one would die trying tonight.

"We have activity," Andy said.

"What's happening?" said Phil.

"Looks like the Badlins are taking a road trip. They're loading some luggage into their car. And a small wooden crate."

"Let me see!" Larry demanded, throwing down his cards. His voice was sharper than Jonas ever recalled hearing it.

"They're going back in the house," Andy reported, offering the goggles to Larry.

Larry stared at the night vision goggles for a moment, then turned and bounded down the stairs.

"We'd better go too," Jonas said. Andy and Phil shrugged and grabbed their jackets.

The street was empty as the four men raced along the sidewalk then across the street and into the gravel driveway at the side of the Badlin place, Larry in the lead. Thunder boomed overhead. The sun had set but a splash of blood red twilight still warmed the sky. Jonas arrived to find Larry with his face pressed against a glass rear window of the Edsel. No Badlins were in sight.

The other two arrived moments later, Andy wheezing and clutching his knees. "I'm not sure," he puffed. "That this. Is a good. Idea."

Phil said nothing, but looked around to see if they had attracted any attention, which they hadn't.

Jonas was tempted to speak, but didn't. If this was going to work at all he'd have to just let it play out. See where the cards fell.

He didn't have to wait long. Larry tried the car doors, which were locked, then lifted a fist-sized rock from beside the house and smashed it against a rear side window like a hammer.

Jonas thought the rock would just bounce, but the window must pre-date safety glass. The glass shattered and Larry dropped the rock. He pulled his hand away bloody where shards had torn into his skin.

"Larry!" shouted Phil. "What do you think you're doing?"

Larry ignored them all, but reached into the back seat and pulled out the wooden crate Andy had described being loaded into the car. The lid was held by a single brass latch that Larry flipped open. He then pulled back the wooden lid.

All four men peered into an empty box.

After a moment's silence Andy asked, "What did you expect to find?"

Larry said nothing. He just continued to stare at the box.

It was Jonas who spoke. "The Holy Grail," he said. "It was Larry all along, searching for the Holy Grail."

"Are you nuts?" Phil began to say to Jonas, but stopped short when Larry reached down and pulled a gun from an ankle holster. He waved it briefly at all three men then settled on Jonas. "Where is it?" he demanded.

"Geez Larry," said Andy. "You've got to be kidding."

"It's mine!" Larry cried. He flicked the gun on Andy, then Phil, then back to Jonas. He was letting them know that he was willing to shoot any of them. "For fifteen hundred years it's been mine, my family's. The Badlins stole it. They can't even use it. They just keep it from us. All these years. And now I'm so close. I knew that killing the boy would bring it out of hiding. And now it's almost mine."

"Really?" said Phil. "The Holy Grail. It exists?"

Andy scrunched his face. "*You* killed the Badlin boy?"

Jonas could hear sirens in the distance. Whether from his message to Detective Bradley, or the Badlins calling the police after the car was broken into, Jonas didn't know. But it would soon be over.

Larry was again waving the gun at Jonas. "I don't know how you found out. Or how you magicked the Grail out of the box. But I will have it. Tell me where it is! Or die."

The sirens were coming closer. Jonas wasn't sure how Larry would react. He thought he knew Larry, but it turned out he didn't know him at all. "The Grail was never in the box," he told his neighbor of fifteen years. "It never could be. Should I assume it was your great-great-grandfather who committed murder here a hundred years ago?"

"I told you," Larry snarled, "the Grail belongs to us."

Jonas continued talking as the sirens grew louder. "Your ancestor looked in the house safe, so he wouldn't have found it either. He couldn't have."

"Why not?" Larry demanded. "What is it you know?"

"I can't be sure," Jonas said slowly. "I can only guess. But if I'm right, the Grail can't be put in a box. Even if it is here, which it may not be."

"What are you babbling about?" Larry cried. He cocked an ear toward the approaching sirens.

Jonas kept speaking, stalling until the police could arrive. "Your family has been chasing after the Grail for fifteen hundred years, but in that time you've forgotten what it is you're after. The Grail isn't a golden cup or anything else you can put in a box."

"The Grail is the key," Larry blurted. "The key to the kingdom. He who possesses the Grail possesses the kingdom!"

"But only if it is possessed by Arthur," Phil guessed. "Or a direct descendant of Arthur. Which is why the Badlins can't use it."

"That's right," said Larry.

The sirens were almost on them now, but Larry showed no sign that he would flee. Apparently he was willing to be captured if it meant bringing him closer to his prize.

"Larry is a descendant of King Arthur," Jonas said.

"Yes, that's right," said Larry. "Through Mordred."

"Arthur's patricide," added Andy. The retired military intelligence man was slowly moving sideways to get into a position where he could jump Larry.

Larry moved his gun toward Andy then back toward Jonas. "The Grail is mine," he repeated. "Only my family can use it. Where is it?"

And at that moment two police cars pulled up in front of the house and four officers with drawn guns tumbled out. Among them were Detective Bradley and his female partner.

Andy used the distraction to get further in position, but couldn't move on Larry while he kept his gun aimed at Jonas' heart.

Larry's voice was cold. "Tell me where it is."

"I will," said Jonas. "When you put down that gun."

Larry stared into Jonas' eyes, oblivious to the calls from the police to drop his weapon. Then, slowly, he lowered the gun as if to put it down, but then changed his mind and began raising it again.

Andy and Phil hit him from opposite sides at almost the same time as the gun went off. Phil slammed Larry's large gut with his elbow while Andy grabbed Larry's gun hand with both of his, forcing the gun to point toward the ground. Andy then slammed the top of his skull into Larry's chin.

"Good one!" Phil crowed as Larry let go of the gun and slumped to the ground.

"They did teach me a few things in the military," Andy admitted.

Then his friends looked at Jonas and their eyes went wide. Jonas followed their gaze and saw a dark stain expanding on his left sleeve. Only then did his arm begin to sting.

Three of the police lifted Larry off the ground and handcuffed his wrists behind his back while Detective Bradley secured the handgun.

Larry lifted soulful eyes and looked at Jonas. "Tell me, please."

Jonas looked away from his wound and shook his head. "After all these years of playing poker, Larry, you finally bought my bluff. I have no idea what or where the Grail is."

Larry screamed with rage as the police hauled him away. Andy called out over his cries: "He killed William Badlin. He admitted it to us."

The police pushed Larry into the back of one of the squad cars and chained him to a railing inside. Then the car pulled away, taking Larry, still screaming, with it.

· δ ·

The Grail Is Found

Detective Bradley took statements from Andy and Phil and Mr. Badlin for what seemed hours while Jonas stood in the gravel driveway, his arm stinging and blood dripping slowly to the ground. Then an EMS truck arrived and a young woman committed triage on Jonas' arm, declaring his injury a simple flesh wound. Bradley and his partner finished with the others and came over to where Jonas sat on the truck's tailgate admiring the white bandages and enjoying the kick of the painkillers.

Despite what had happened, Jonas felt very much at peace. He didn't think about Larry, though he knew he would have to re-evaluate the friendship they had shared in light of who Larry was. There would be time for that later. Instead he thought about Priscilla and Ann, and the trust they had put in him. He hadn't let them down. And he thought of Gwen and Susan who stood just outside the police tape, anxiously watching him. Detective Bradley had said he could join them after giving his statement. All the wonderful women in his life. Then there was Andy and Phil tackling Larry. Friends. Real friends. Jonas had just been shot by his best friend, but somehow life had never been better.

"Your statement?" Detective Bradley reminded him.

"Right," said Jonas, pulled from his thoughts. "I hope you have a lot of paper."

Jonas felt even better as he unburdened his soul, coming clean of all the lies he had told since the Badlin murder. Bradley was clearly unhappy, especially about the fake kidnapping, while his lie detector partner smiled the entire time, even during the more ludicrous parts of Jonas' story.

When Jonas finished, Bradley shook his head and went to his car to call in his report. His silent partner stayed, however, and spoke for the first time. "Don't worry," she said. "Things will work themselves out. I doubt Mr. Badlin will raise any charges against you, and any lawsuit Dennis tries to file will be quashed by his credibility." She paused. "You may want to claim that you misled to the police as part of setting your trap for the killer. Just a suggestion. Now go home and take care of your family."

Before Jonas could go home, however, Mr. Badlin invited him into the house. "I want to thank you," the older man said solemnly, "for finding William's killer. And for preventing him from doing further harm."

"And I want to thank you," Jonas returned, "for keeping the Grail safe despite the huge cost to you and your family."

Mr. Badlin stared at him for a moment. "Then you believe in the Grail?"

"Not before today. Not even yesterday, when I met her."

A movement and Priscilla entered the sitting room and sat beside him on the sofa. "How did you know?"

"I didn't. I just thought that the killer could be one of my poker buddies, so I baited a trap. Larry took the bait and revealed himself."

Priscilla smiled. "I meant, how did you know that I am the Grail?"

Jonas felt his face going red. "That was the easy part. With all the denials and confusion surrounding who you were, you had to be important. The Badlins have been hiding the Grail for centuries, but the only thing I saw them hiding was you."

"Some believe," said Mr. Badlin, "that the Grail holds the secret of health and longevity. But that is a misunderstanding."

"The Grail *is*," suggested Jonas, "someone with health and a long life."

"More to the point," said Badlin, "the Grail will be King Arthur's wife."

Priscilla spoke. "After Guinevere was sent away to the monastery because of her adultery, Arthur was to remarry."

"A daughter of the Sidhe," continued Badlin. "Magical. Merlin's daughter, in fact."

"Together," said Priscilla, "we would have completed Arthur's dream of universal democracy. We would have ended the war between the old faith and the new."

Jonas interrupted. "But Arthur's bastard son, Mordred, wounded Arthur near to death."

"And so I wait," said Priscilla, "for Arthur to heal. Only then we may complete the dream."

"It's been 1500 years," said Jonas.

Priscilla sighed. "But the time is not yet. Arthur convalesces. I wait. Until the appointed day."

"Your secret is safe with me," said Jonas.

Mr. Badlin smiled. "We know. You are of the clan, Jonas Smith, tasked to protect the Grail."

Jonas sat straighter. "I am?"

Priscilla also smiled. "Through your wife, Gwen. And her sister Ann. Both have Sidhe blood, as does your daughter, Susan."

"But—" said Jonas.

Priscilla continued. "—Ann guided Gwen in choosing your home on this street."

Jonas shook his head as the last card fell in place.

· δ ·

Poker Knight

"I'm sorry about your arm," suggested Phil. "When I tackle students with knives they are usually pretty slow. Larry was slippery as an eel."

Jonas sat at the round table with his arm in a sling. "I don't really need this," he admitted. "But it makes Gwen and Susan happy." I'll be good as new in no time.

Andy dealt out the cards. "I still can't believe it about Larry. My contacts in the police agree that he drugged Ricky and shot William himself. After they arrested him they searched Larry's house and found various drugs and weapons. Lot's of old news clips about the Badlins as well. And some old documents belonging to a Welsh cult called Mordrites."

Jonas remained quiet. There was much he could say, but maybe it was better if people just forgot about Mordrites and the Grail. And the Badlins.

"But why now?" asked Phil. "Larry has lived next to the Badlins his entire life. Why did he move now?"

Andy smiled. "That one's easy. It seems that Larry made some bad investments in the stock market and stood to lose everything. It was now or never."

Phil turned to Jonas. "Is it true that Mrs. Luis hired you to paint her house?"

Before Jonas could answer Ann, the game's new fourth, spread her cards out on the table. "Believe it because it's true. Jonas has found his new career. And I have three kings and two jacks. Is that good?"

· δ ·

MERLIN'S SILVER

FRIDAY

Eight Pieces Of Silver

The silver tea service rattled on the passenger seat of the Austin Mini, its polished gleam casting midday rainbows against the windshield. Joan's nervous gaze flicked between the service, the windshield, and the road ahead.

And the day had begun so innocently.

Joan had gone to the estate auction out of simple curiosity, with no intention of buying anything. The estate was that of Sir Samuel Reginald Halifax who, until cancer had claimed him, had been Calgary's wealthiest and most mysterious resident, a recluse with more rumor than fact surrounding him. Who knew what strange and marvelous items would appear on the auction block?

The auction itself was in the BMO Center on the Stampede and Exhibition Grounds, just southeast of the city's seediest neighborhood, the Beltline. How the City Fathers ever thought it a good idea to locate food banks and homeless shelters just five minute's walk from Calgary's greatest tourist attraction was as mysterious as the late Sir Halifax. But the parking lot and grounds boasted decent security, so Joan hadn't had to deal with transients. Joan detested transients.

On her own merit, Joan never would have been allowed into the auction. The staff had been instructed to keep out anyone who even hinted of riffraff. Fortunately, Joan's husband Patrick was a junior partner at Calgary's most prestigious law firm: *Hinckley, Manners, and Tate*. A flash of embossed lettering on a business card got her through the door.

The auction hall was enormous, with a giant projection screen and a camera that zoomed in on each item as it went up for offer. Joan sat open-mouthed as a procession of elegant furniture, priceless paintings, brass statuettes, and thick, dusty books appeared on the big screen and sold for unimaginable amounts of money. Joan had always believed that she and Patrick had money but, here, she was definitely outclassed.

"And now," called the auctioneer, "we have an eight-piece silver tea service. Included is a lidded tea pot, kettle with spirit light, sugar bowl with tongs, creamer, slop bowl, tea strainer, and portable serving tray with filigreed handles, all in pristine condition. This set is unique in that it contains no craftsman's mark. It is thought to be a one of a kind set, likely dating from the late eighteenth century. Since the entire service is sterling silver, the starting bid is $5,000. Do I hear $5,000?"

Joan noticed that, unlike the earlier items, few bid cards went up. She assumed this was because the provenance was unknown. Half the joy of antiques was bragging about the craftsman who had created the piece and the chain of ownership since that creation. All that was known about the tea set was its most recent owner: Sir Samuel Reginald Halifax. Still, surely that would count for something.

"Do I hear $6,000?" called the auctioneer, at which all but two cards fell. "$7,000. Going once."

Joan saw that only one card remained aloft, belonging to a middle-aged man wearing an expensive business suit. The buyer was getting a bargain. On impulse, she stuck her card in the air.

"We have another bid," said the auctioneer. "Do I hear $8,000?"

Joan watched the other card remain firmly in place. $9,000 was still a bargain.

"$10,000," cried the auctioneer. "$10,000, going once."

The price had jumped from five to ten thousand so quickly that Joan had scarcely breathed, but the other card had wavered lower and the auctioneer called, "Going twice."

"Sold for $10,000 to bidder number 274," called the auctioneer as his gavel hit the stump with an echoing finality.

A woman with a clipboard appeared as if by magic at Joan's side, taking her information and verifying that Joan's check was good by calling her bank on a cell phone. Joan hated cell phones. The woman then handed Joan an embossed paper of authentication and a yellow receipt.

"Use this receipt to claim your purchase at gate four when you leave," the woman told her, and then she was gone.

Joan sat a while longer as other items were sold, again at prices that turned Joan's stomach. When a ten inch marble statue of a tall, bearded man in flowing robes, called *Merlin* by the auctioneer came up, also without provenance, the man who had bid on the tea service bought it for $2,000.

She watched the same clip-boarded woman descend upon him and was somewhat shocked to see him pay her with cash. When the woman left, he pulled out a cell phone and had an animated discussion with someone on the other end.

Cell phones. People claimed they were the marvel of the century, but to Joan they seemed like the world's greatest nuisance. You could be interrupted any where at any time in the middle of any thing, usually by someone trying to sell you a second cell phone. A month ago Joan had turned off her phone and put it in a drawer. She hadn't missed it since.

The man kept looking in her direction, then glancing away when she looked back, and somehow Joan felt it was she who was the topic of discussion on the phone and not the statue. Grabbing her purse, she stood and walked quickly toward gate four.

"Give us a moment to find an appropriate box," the clerk told her after she had shown him her receipt and he had returned with the tea service.

Joan looked around and saw the well-dressed man coming toward her.

"That's okay," she said, lifting up the silver tray with its contents. "I'll take it as-is."

The clerk stared at her, aghast, as she ducked away from the counter and made her way toward the exit.

A voice called behind her, "Madam! Madam!" but it didn't sound like the clerk's. As she reached her car in the parking lot, the owner of the voice caught up to her.

"Please," said the man in the expensive suit. "You purchased the tea service fair and square. I'll give you that. It was my error to cease bidding too soon. I'm hoping we can come to an agreement. I'll offer you $11,000 for it now. That's a thousand dollars profit in the space of an hour. Not bad by any standard." He paused to catch his breath.

Joan set the service carefully on the roof of her Austin Mini and positioned herself between it and the waiting man. She couldn't help but notice how few people were nearby.

When she didn't answer, the man said, "$12,000, but that's as high as I can go."

Joan remembered him paying cash for the statue. Was he going to pull ten dozen hundred dollar bills out of his pocket? Even if she wanted to sell the service, she wasn't going to do it like this, cash from a stranger in a parking lot.

A Ford Mustang rolled through the lot and pulled into a stall two spaces away. The man turned as the driver and two passengers got out, his expression oddly nervous. But when he saw they were a mother and two children, his face relaxed.

While he was distracted, Joan opened her car door and pushed the tea service onto the passenger seat. The man whipped around to stare at her, but didn't move as the mother and children walked past. Joan hurriedly slid into the driver's seat and shut and locked the door. The man waved and tried to block her Austin Mini as she pulled out, and she nearly knocked him down. As Joan drove toward the exit, she cast glances in the rear-view mirror and saw his tie flailing in the breeze as he continued to wave his hands. And then she was through the park gate and racing toward Macleod Trail; she had made her escape.

On her way home, Joan turned into Willow Park Village and pulled in front of Royalty Jewelers. Having spent $10,000 she was damn well going to find out what the tea service was actually worth, especially seeing as how the well-dressed man was so interested in it. She still wondered if she shouldn't have just taken his money. The next time someone offered her a wad of hundreds in a parking lot, she'd try to be more clear-headed.

"This is in very good condition," said the appraiser. He stood bent over the service, squinting through a magnifying glass, moving it from piece to piece. He lifted the lid from the tea pot and peered inside. "I'd swear this has never been used. It could have been made yesterday."

"It's supposed to be eighteenth century," Joan told him.

The appraiser turned over several of the pieces and waved his magnifying glass. "Strange. There are no craftsman marks. There's no way to date this."

"How much is the silver worth?"

The appraiser put down his glass and retrieved a large scale from underneath the counter. "I'd have to run tests to verify the purity and ensure it isn't merely plating, but it appears to be solid Sterling."

He set the entire service on the scale and began sliding weights back and forth. "Yes," he muttered. "Yes, yes." He picked up a solar-powered calculator and punched some buttons. "At current silver prices we are looking at a little under $3,000. But I don't advise selling it as metal. The craftsmanship is superb. This belongs in a collection. Pity there is no provenance."

"It used to belong to Sir Reginald Halifax," Joan suggested.

The appraiser raised an eyebrow. "That could be worth something. You have documentation?"

Joan showed him the embossed paper the clipboard lady had given her.

The appraiser picked up his magnifying glass and examined the document. "Yes," he muttered. "Incontestably genuine. This is worth a bit. You shouldn't sell the service with paperwork for a penny under $4,000." When he saw Joan's expression he added. "It will appreciate in time, of course. In a decade or two you may be looking as $5,000."

Joan thanked him and left the store.

As she turned the Austin Mini into Canyon Meadows Drive, Joan had no idea how she was going to explain her bargain hunting to her husband. Yes, dear, I found this exquisite tea service and paid only triple what it is worth. But look on the bright side, someday when we are both dead and buried, it will be worth exactly what I paid for it. Tea, dear?

All thoughts fled, however, as she turned into her street to find the road blocked by a fire engine. Several men in bright yellow coats and hardhats guided hoses while the truck's engine pumped water from a hydrant. A house was on fire. Her house. The firemen seemed perplexed, however. No matter how much water they poured onto her house, the fire would not go out. Not until there was nothing left to burn.

When the firemen finally shut off the pumps, all that remained of her and Patrick's home was a muddy hole in the ground.

· δ ·

Starbuck Sally

"A Double Double Mocha-Cap," said Joan. "If you have any whisky, throw that in too."

The Starbucks server dropped his jaw and pinched his forehead. "Uhm, I don't think we can do that."

Joan sighed and threw a five dollar bill on the counter. "It was a joke. I could use a good laugh right now."

The server continued to appear flustered and walked over to the furthest machine to prepare her coffee. Joan accepted a paper cup that was both too hot and too strong, and joined Sally at a table.

"I hate Starbucks," Sally told her. "I'm a Timmy's girl." She took a deep slurp of her coffee, and then grimaced. "Why did you ask to meet here?"

"Patrick's coming," Joan told her. "He likes Starbucks."

"Patrick? In the middle of a work day? What's the occasion?"

Joan lifted the lid of her cup and blew on the contents to try to cool it. She soon gave up. "To celebrate the occasion of our being homeless." She went on to explain that an unquenchable fire had just destroyed her and Patrick's home of fifteen years.

When she was done Sally said, "Wow." And took a sip of her coffee. "You seem very... calm."

Joan shuddered a laugh. "You should have seen me half an hour ago. I went through a whole box of Kleenex. And I think I left permanent impressions of my fists on the dashboard of my car. The firemen thought I was having a seizure."

"But you're... okay now?"

"It is amazing," Joan told her, "how shock can go around masquerading as calm. Please don't ask if I'm *okay*. You won't like the answer."

Sally sat there as Joan watched her search for something safe to say. Finally she landed on, "Good thing no one was in the house."

Joan nodded. "When Patrick and I decided not to have children or pets... well, something like this happening was never the reason."

"Why your house?" Sally asked.

"Why my house what?"

"Why would someone burn down your house?"

Joan looked at her. "What makes you think it was arson? I assume it was a gas leak or something. That might explain why the fire was so hard to put out. The gas kept feeding it."

Sally's face reddened and she gave an uncomfortable laugh. "I watch too many cop shows. My mind just automatically leapt to arson. What do I know about fires?"

"Probably more than I do," said Joan. "I'll wait for the reports from the Fire Department and my insurance company before I try to guess what happened. Truth is I'm not really concerned about the house. It was just a building. But everything Patrick and I own was in there. It'll take years to replace." She let out a nervous laugh. "All I have left are the clothes on my back and a tea service in my car."

"You have a tea service in your car? Most people settle for a cup holder."

Joan explained the estate auction and her impulsive purchase. "I suppose the auction saved my life. If I hadn't gone, I would have been home when the fire broke out."

Sally's reaction was not what Joan expected. "Sir Samuel Reginald Halifax is dead?"

Joan nodded. Well, Sally did have an interest in celebrity doings.

"And you have his tea service?"

Joan nodded again and Sally was silent for a moment. Then, "I have a friend who is in Europe for a month. You can stay at her place while you figure out where you and Patrick are going to live."

A fortyish man with wavy black hair appeared at Sally's shoulder. "May I join you ladies?" He sat down and Joan pushed her untouched coffee toward him.

"Just how you like it," she said.

"Thanks," said Patrick. "But I may need something stronger. I went by the house on the way here. You weren't kidding when you described it over the phone. There's not a scrap left. The basement walls appear to have melted — I didn't know concrete could melt — and I couldn't find a single burned brick from the fireplace. It's as if the house never existed. Whose phone did you use, by the way?"

"One of the firemen's," Joan murmured, and then louder, "Sally says she knows of a house where we can stay for a few weeks while we sort things out."

"Thank you, Sally," said Patrick, "but my office has already made arrangements. A Regency Suite at the Hyatt. Best I could do. Calgary has the most pathetic hotels on the continent."

"The Hyatt will be fine," said Joan, then she gritted her teeth. "Though I hate downtown." Before Patrick could suggest changing hotels, she raised a hand and added, "But I'll survive for a few weeks." Patrick worked downtown and it would be nice if he could walk to his office until they found a new place to live.

MERLIN'S SILVER

"This house I know of is very nice," said Sally. "It's in Signal Hill. You'll love it there."

Patrick looked at Sally. "We appreciate the offer but we'll be fine at the Hyatt."

"Yes," Joan added, "It will be nice to be pampered by the staff."

"Well," said Sally. "At least let me store your belongings. No sense cramming them into a tiny hotel room."

"Belongings?" said Joan. "They all burned. All we have are two cars and a tea service."

"A tea service?" Patrick asked.

Oh well, thought Joan, compared to one's house burning down, what's a little shopping spree?

· δ ·

Welcome To The Hyatt Regency

It was a nice hotel. The underground parking was only slightly better than none at all, but the hotel itself was an art museum, its walls decorated with mountain and prairie settings inhabited by cowboys and Indians. Originals, not prints. Its most distinguishing feature was the ceiling above the front desk lobby, which was designed as a giant upside-down canoe.

The staff were amiable, but turned apprehensive when they discovered that Mr. and Mrs. Longmeyer had no luggage. "You wish to stay how long?" a receptionist asked. "With no luggage?" Eyebrows rose further when they saw the silver tea service in Joan's hands. Joan could almost read the questions in their eyes: What *were* these people going to do in their hotel room?

When Patrick explained that theirs was the house that had burned to the ground that afternoon, the staff quickly regained their practiced cordiality.

An elevator took them to the eighth floor where a middle-aged bellhop placed the tea service with great care on the lone table in what Joan discovered was a rather small hotel room— the Calgary Hyatt, apparently, only had small rooms. His demeanor suggested that Joan's luggage was hardly the most unusual he had carried in his many years in the hotel industry.

The bellhop had scarcely left when a twenty-something woman in a blue uniform arrived with several shirts and other items luggage-less patrons might require. Everything was still in its original packaging. This really was a full service hotel. Patrick tipped the woman and then the Longmeyers were alone in their temporary home.

Since leaving Starbucks Patrick hadn't said a word about the tea service except that it was very shiny. He did not mention the $10,000 Joan had spent, even though Joan had never spent $10,000 on anything in her life. Silence was the worst. She hoped it was just the loss of the house and all their worldly possessions that was distracting him and that he would have a more reasonable reaction later. Joan supposed she could always sell the service if he was too upset. Perhaps that man with the hundred dollar bills was still roaming around the Stampede grounds.

After a few minutes, Patrick put on his *all business* expression and Joan thought: here it comes.

"Look," he said, "I don't know how to say this so I'll just say it. I have to go to Toronto for a few days to see an important client."

Ok. Not what she had expected. Toronto? She supposed it made sense. *Hinckley, Manners, and Tate* had clients everywhere. "When do you have to leave?" she asked.

"Tomorrow morning."

Joan stared. "Tomorrow! But our house just burned down! How can you possibly leave at a time like this?"

"I asked the office to send someone else." Patrick wagged his head. "But our client won't see anyone but me. I'm the only one familiar with his case."

"But, tomorrow?"

"It's probably for the best." A boyish smile crinkled the sides of Patrick's mouth. "I hired a house-hunting firm to shortlist some decent properties on the market. It will take them a few days. By the time I get back they'll be ready to show us what they've come up with. Until then it's just a waiting game."

That was Patrick. All logic. Never an impulsive act. Joan could only hope that when Patrick did decide to react to her reckless spending, he would surprise her.

· δ ·

Sleepless In Calgary

After a very nice dinner in the hotel restaurant they walked along an outdoor mall to a theatre and watched a movie. She suspected there would be a lot of movie outings in the near future. The film — *Harry Potter Goes to College* — had none of the charm of the earlier books and movies and Joan feared that an attempt to salvage the franchise would result in Harry becoming a space pirate or a gigolo. Neil Young was right when he said it was *better to burn out than to fade away.*

Returning to the hotel they enjoyed a nightcap in the lounge and then rode the elevator up to their room.

The bed was very soft, the pillows down-filled. Joan fell asleep almost immediately. Her dreams were filled with smoke and fire. She was in the house while it burned, the image jarring her awake. The loss of the house hit her again. Everything. Gone.

She reached for the comfort of Patrick's shoulder and touched a cool pillow instead. He was sitting in an armchair by the table in the dark, his gaze fixed on the tea service. Its polished silver cast dull, fiery reflections of the bedside clock's red LEDs.

"Did you dream of the house fire as well?" she murmured.

Patrick turned to look at her. "What? No. I couldn't sleep. So I got up." He sighed and then crawled into bed beside her. "Guess I should give it another try."

Joan rolled to face him and slipped her arm across his shoulder. Patrick rarely had trouble sleeping. Perhaps the fire was bothering him more than he was letting on. "Are you sure you can't postpone your trip?"

Patrick shook his head. "Not without causing problems at work. But I'll see if I can't cut it short."

Joan lay in the darkness for a long time listening to Patrick breathe.

She had never put much value in material things. CDs, DVDs, books, pewter, clothing. Neither had Patrick. They owned a few favorite movies and books, and an encyclopedia set that had never been used. Old letters tucked in a drawer. A copper dog. There was nothing that had been lost in the fire that could not be replaced.

Perhaps Patrick felt differently. Perhaps there was sentimental value in some of the souvenirs he had purchased or gifts he had received. Some quirk of character that she didn't know. Joan felt a little thrill.

· δ ·

SATURDAY

A Necessary Shopping Spree

Joan kissed Patrick goodbye in the hotel lobby then watched through the main glass doors as he climbed aboard a Hyatt shuttle van. Just as the van pulled away for the airport, Sally walked in.

"There you are," Sally said with a smile, and then glanced around the lobby. "Nice digs."

It seemed to Joan that Sally was paying more attention to the people than the place.

Turning her attention back to Joan, Sally said, "Are you ready?"

"For what?"

Sally rolled her eyes. "For the mall, girl! We gotta get you a new wardrobe. What *is* that you're wearing?"

"A shirt the hotel brought up last night," Joan answered. Solid beige linen with long sleeves, square white buttons, starched lapels, and a complete absence of taste. Though nice enough in a *don't notice me* kind of way, it wasn't something Joan would ever buy.

"Shopping would be lovely," Joan said. "And it will take my mind off things."

"Where's your car?" Sally asked. "I took the LRT because parking's impossible. No wonder no one shops downtown."

"You haven't seen the hotel," Joan said, "until you've seen the parking area. Let me show you the dungeon."

Sally turned her head. "Dungeon?"

Several minutes later they drove up the ramp to street level. "So what do you do if your car is bigger than an Austin Mini?" asked Sally. "That was the absolute *closet* of parkades."

Joan smiled. "I'm told there is an outdoor lot a couple blocks away for oversized vehicles, oversized meaning almost everything. I love my Mini."

By the time they had navigated several one way streets and were heading south on Macleod Trail, Joan remembered something. "Shouldn't you be at work?"

"And let you go shopping alone? Perish the thought. I swapped shifts."

Sally was single and a hair dresser. Joan couldn't remember when they had first met. It seemed Sally had always just been there; maybe Joan had gone to her salon to get her hair done.

Anyway, they had become best friends. Sally was everything Patrick wasn't. She planned for nothing and lived life a minute at a time. Hanging out with Sally let off the steam that Patrick's detailed plans built up. It was a triangle that worked.

Joan glanced at Sally as they drove past the Mustard Seed Street Ministry. A line of the homeless cluttered the sidewalk. Transients looking for work, food, rest, or all three. They all had long, greasy dark hair and greasy dark clothes and shared dark looks. Some wore dark gray baseball caps pulled low over their eyes. They seemed to Joan as gypsies who had lost their colors and their songs, and sadness shuddered down her back.

In contrast, Sally's blond hair lit up the vehicle. Today it was puffed out like a giant light bulb. It had probably taken two cans of mousse. Sally changed her hair style even faster than she changed her mind.

Joan glanced at herself in the rear-view mirror. She hadn't changed her own hair in years. It was coal black and short at the sides, reminiscent of Lisa Minnelli, though Joan herself looked nothing like the actress. Patrick liked it this way so she never even thought about changing it. She also noticed thin lines around her eyes and the corners of her mouth. When had she gotten old? Sally was about the same age as Joan, but looked a decade younger. Apparently fast living paid off.

"Oh," said Sally as they drove past the Stampede Grounds. "Isn't that where your auction was yesterday?"

"Yup. It's a lot quieter now than it will be in July"

Sally shrugged. "Never been to the Stampede. Rodeos ain't my *thing*. At least, not yet."

As they continued toward South Centre Mall, Sally talked about what was her current *thing*: karaoke. "I never knew entertaining drunks could be so much fun," she said. "And they always buy me drinks. Sometimes even the bar buys me drinks. They say my singing keeps people in the bar."

Joan glanced from Sally's wild hair to her low-neck top to her tight jean shorts. "I think it's your outfits that keep people in the bar."

Sally tapped her chin and smiled. "That too."

On an impulse Joan drove past the Mall and into Canyon Meadows to show Sally the hole in the ground where her and Patrick's house used to be. Someone had erected one of those rent-a-fences around the property and had wrapped it in a mile of police tape. A man with a notebook stood near the fence shaking his head. An insurance appraiser.

"Never seen anything like it," he said. "This was caused by a house fire?"

"What did the fire department say?" Joan asked.

The man shrugged. "No sign of accelerants, if that's what you're asking. No sign of anything. Everything, and I mean everything, was incinerated, including bricks, plumbing, metal appliances, and most of the concrete. We're trying to find an expert who can tell us what could cause this. If they come up empty," — it sounded like a certainty — "we'll contact the military."

"The military!"

The appraiser looked at her. "I'm grasping at straws here. Perhaps some sort of weapon caused this. Terrorists maybe."

"Why would terrorists incinerate my home?" demanded Joan. The man really was grasping at straws.

Sally chirped in. "A demonstration! They were testing the weapon. Maybe they'll rob a bank next. Or knock off a brewery."

The appraiser chuckled. "Young lady, I think you've watched too many movies."

Young lady? Joan shook her head. She couldn't remember the last time anyone had called *her* a young lady. She really was going to have to ask Sally about her secret of eternal youth. Perhaps she sold it at her salon.

They left the appraiser and the hole in the ground and went to South Centre Mall, a shopping wonderland where you could find just about any store you could want. Joan shopped here at least once a week.

They parked the Austin Mini outside The Bay and walked through the mall toward Le Chateau, Sally's favorite clothing store, and Talbots, Joan's source of daily apparel.

As they walked past the Sony Store, the TV screens caught Joan's eye. There was a news report about a house fire. At first Joan thought it was a rebroadcast about her and Patrick's house; the blaze was furious and seemingly immune to the rivers of water being thrown at it by the Fire Department. But then the camera pulled back and turned on a reporter standing next to a soot-covered man. "This is the second fire of this type in as many days," the reporter told the camera with canned sincerity. "Mr. Cushing, do have any idea why someone would target your home?"

The soot-covered man shook his head as tears ran down his cheek. "None. I've got no enemies. I'm just an investment banker."

Sally laughed. "An investment banker with no enemies. Yeah, right. Though I can't imagine disgruntled investors blowing up his house."

Joan hardly heard her. "I know that man," she said. "He bid against me for the tea service at the auction."

"You're kidding," said Sally. "How's that for coincidence?"

"It can't be coincidence," Joan said. "We both bid on the same item and within a day both our houses are holes in the ground."

"That's pretty out there," Sally suggested. "But you're right. That's about as far from coincidence as you can get. What are the odds?" She was silent for a moment. "You know, it's probably nothing, but maybe you should get rid of that tea service. I'm sure I could find you a buyer."

"No," said Joan. "I'm sure you're right. This is real life, not the movies. Who would demolish a person's house just for bidding on some silverware? There has to be another explanation."

Though try as she might, Joan couldn't think of one.

· δ ·

Odds Bodkins

Joan dropped Sally off at her house in Lake Bonavista before heading back to the Hyatt. She found a bellhop to deliver her bags to her room, and then headed for the bar.

It was still early afternoon, but after seeing that news report she *really* needed a drink. Joan walked through the hotel's main level admiring the daylight streaming in from the high windows, how it brightened the marble flooring, vaulted ceiling, and ornate support pillars. She could almost forget that just outside those walls were the traffic, smog, and soot-covered cement of downtown. And two burnt-out holes in the ground.

"Mrs. Longmeyer?"

The man who addressed her sat in a deep cushioned chair holding a newspaper. His face was round and his hair was a tangle of wiry blond, almost white, with a bald spot in the middle. He had no eyebrows and was wearing John Lennon glasses— small rounded lenses with a near invisible wire frame.

"Yes, I'm Joan Longmeyer," she admitted. "You are?"

The man stood, yet appeared to be still sitting. He couldn't have been more than four feet tall, despite not showing characteristics of dwarfism. He was simply short. He folded the newspaper and held it under the wing of his arm.

"Odds Bodkins is the name. I am pleased to make your acquaintance."

"You're kidding!"

The little man frowned. "No. I am being perfectly honest. I have anticipated meeting you ever since I heard of you."

"I meant your name."

Again a frown. "What about my name?"

"It's, well, isn't that the name of Don Quixote's horse?"

"Is it?" asked the little man. "I cannot say I have ever met this Quixote fellow, so I do not think he named his horse after me."

"Never mind," said Joan. "How do you know who I am?"

He cocked his head. "You *are* the fine woman who bought a silver tea service at auction yesterday?"

"Y-e-s-s."

"I wish to buy it from you."

And here was the second person in as many hours suggesting she sell the tea service. "I've only owned it for a day," she told him.

"And frankly," said Odds Bodkins, "I am surprised that you still have it in your possession. The fact that you do speaks volumes to your strong character. I understand you lost a house yesterday."

"What do you know about that?"

"I know who did it. Well, not specifically who did it, but I know their character. Unlike yours, it is not strong. It is, however, quite determined. The sooner you rid yourself of the tea service, the better off you will be."

"You're saying that my house was destroyed because I bought a tea service at auction?"

"It's somewhat more complicated than that. Actually, it is vastly more complicated than that. But in simple terms, yes, your house was destroyed because you purchased a tea service. Since you cannot unpurchase it, the next best thing is to get as far away from it as possible."

"And you're here to help me with that?"

"Quite," said Bodkins. "Turn the tea service over to me and you will never see me or it again." Then he frowned. "You have not served tea with it, I hope?"

Joan shook her head.

"Good. That would be a very bad idea. It was never meant to serve tea."

"What else would it be for?"

"Looks can be deceiving." The little man waggled his eyebrows, as if hinting at a deeper meaning. "At one time it was a tea service. But that was long ago. It has not been a tea service for centuries."

"Look," said Joan, "Why should I believe a word you're saying?"

Bodkins grinned. "Because I can do this!"

With lightning speed he drew the newspaper from under his arm and folded it into a large origami bird, possibly a pigeon.

"Um, that's quite a talent."

"But you have not yet seen the best part."

Odds Bodkins threw the bird up into the air where, instead of falling back to Earth, it flew south towards the bar, then, finding no way out of the building, turned back and whizzed over Joan's head, flashing the classified section on the bottom of its wings at her. When it reached the north end of the lobby it circled in the hollow space of the upside-down canoe in the ceiling. When the large glass door slid open to admit someone from the street, the paper pigeon made its escape.

"Ah," said Odds Bodkins, "I have always loved pigeons. So sad that the homing variety is no more."

"How did you do that?" Joan demanded.

The little man shrugged. "It is merely a trick." Then his eyes grew dark and serious. "These determined men who desire the tea service can also do tricks. Their tricks, however, are much less amusing than mine. Incinerating houses for example. You would be wise to be rid of the silver."

He pulled a thick stack of hundred dollar bills from an inside coat pocket. "I believe you paid $10,000 for it. There is at least that much here. Take it and these men will have no further cause to bother you."

Joan stared at the money and at the little man's guileless, round face. Possibly she was overwhelmed, but her mind couldn't help but think of the cartoon tycoon from the Monopoly game. But in this game instead of building houses, houses were destroyed. "I have to think about this," she said.

Odds Bodkins stuffed the cash back into his pocket. "Of course you do. That is your character. You gather information, analyze it, think things through, make a plan. Then you act on that plan."

To Joan's astonishment, the little man had just described Patrick. He went on, "Do not take too long to decide. I have my tricks, but those who would do you harm may still get past me."

He sat back down in his chair, unfolded a newspaper, and began to read. His earlier newspaper had flown out the door so Joan wasn't sure where this one had come from.

"What are you doing?" she asked.

"Standing guard," he said, not looking up.

"Sitting guard," she corrected.

"If you prefer."

Joan turned toward the elevator — the bar no longer seemed a good idea — then stopped. "Tell me," she asked Odds Bodkins. "Why didn't you or these desperate men just buy the damn thing at yesterday's auction?"

"Stupidity," he said. "Mostly mine. The Halifax family has been hiding the service for generations. The desperate men did not know where it was until their agent spotted it at the auction. As for myself, I thought Sir Reginald had the good sense to *pass it on* before he himself passed on. I was looking forward to not knowing where the *damn thing*, as you say, was. That it sold at auction caught everyone by surprise."

"But my house," said Joan, "was destroyed, possibly after being searched, not one hour after I bought it."

"More of my stupidity," said the little man. "One, or perhaps more than one, of these desperate men must be sending agents to every estate auction."

"In Calgary?"

Odds looked at her. "In the world. The desperate men have become even more desperate than I imagined. The odds of the tea service going to auction are almost zero."

"And yet, according to you, it did."

The little man clenched a small fist. "Which is exactly why I should have expected it! Stupid. Stupid. Stupid. Stupid. Now leave me. I must think about your defenses." He busied himself with his paper.

Joan stared at the little man. "Odds" was an appropriate name. She took the elevator to her room and, instead of unpackaging her purchases, she sat on the bed, thinking. If only she was less like Patrick and more like Sally, she would have taken Bodkins' money and been done with it. The realization galled her.

· 8 ·

Strangers In The Night

After Odds Bodkins' talk of desperate men, Joan hid in the safety of her room. She ordered Buccatini Pasta with coffee from room service and then sat on the bed and stared at the silver tea service while waiting for Patrick to call.

She tried to imagine herself preparing tea and biscuits and serving them to Patrick and Sally — and Odds Bodkins of all people — and failed utterly. She couldn't remember ever serving tea in her life. Didn't everyone drink coffee these days? And didn't they just go to Tim Horton's or Starbucks rather than serve it themselves?

It was difficult to make sense of much of what the strange little man had told her. It *used* to be a tea service? So what was it now? And why did desperate men want it? That stock broker whose house had been destroyed, was he the agent who had been sent to the auction? Was his home destroyed because he had failed to buy the tea service for them? Or was he just an innocent bystander, like her? Did these desperate men even exist? Perhaps it was Bodkins who had destroyed her and the broker's homes in order to soften her up before spinning his fanciful yarn and offering money? Odds Bodkins obviously wasn't his real name, but why would he use such an unlikely alias?

The alarm clock by the bed displayed ever later red numbers and when they reached nine o'clock Joan began worrying in earnest about Patrick. Why hadn't he called? By ten o'clock her worry pre-empted any other thought and she dialed 4-1-1 and asked for the Toronto hotel where Patrick was staying. It took forever to route the call, and another chunk of time insisting she didn't want to write down any numbers, please just put the call through, before she reached the hotel.

"We have no guest here by that name," replied a heavily accented voice. "Wait. Here it is. Mr. Longmeyer has a reservation, but he hasn't arrived. It is past midnight so we may have to give his room away."

Joan hung up. She had forgotten about time zones. Even if Patrick had met with his client before checking into the hotel, surely he would be there before now.

Patrick had a cell phone, of course; his office insisted he carry a corporate phone. It was a job requirement to be at the beck and call of clients and coworkers twenty-four hours a day. Unfortunately, his cell number was stored in the speed dial list in Joan's cell phone, which had been in a drawer in her house when the house had burned down. She seriously doubted that Patrick's phone would ring if she pressed '1' on the room phone. Grudgingly she admitted that perhaps cell phones did have their uses.

She dialed 4-1-1 again and this time was quickly connected with Air Canada reservations, only to be put on hold for fifteen minutes. When someone did finally talk to her they made her jump through hoops to prove she was Patrick's wife. Due to privacy concerns they could not give out Patrick's flight information, but they had no qualms about collecting *her* personal information; enough to write a book.

"I can confirm that Patrick Longmeyer was booked on a flight to Toronto this morning," her inquisitor finally admitted. "Oh. It looks like his reservation was cancelled. I'm afraid a cancellation fee was applied—"

Again Joan hung up. Cancelled? Where was he? She called room service and ordered a bottle of Pinot Noir, then drank until she was semi-sedated and fell asleep.

· δ ·

Joan awakened to a dark room and the sound of breaking glass and muffled shouts coming from next door.

Half asleep and wine-muddled, Joan exercised the poor judgment of cracking open her door and poking her head into the corridor. The hallway was empty except for a chair in which sat a small man reading a newspaper. Odds Bodkins looked up at her and winked. From the next room came the sound of moving furniture and muscles being bruised.

Folding his newspaper, Bodkins cocked his head. "Menace averted. I misdirected the malcontents to the room next door, whose unimpressed occupant is none other than Manny 'The Meat-Hammer' O'Riley, the current world heavyweight champion. I understand he is sensitive about his beauty rest. The goons sent to steal the tea service are discovering just how sensitive."

Joan blinked. Somehow finding Bodkins in her hallway wasn't half the shock she thought it should be. "Are these goons your desperate men?"

Bodkins laughed. "Oh, no. Just ordinary hired goons. If they were the desperate men, Manny would not stand a chance. Are you ready to sell the tea service yet?"

Joan ducked back in her room and closed the door. The sounds next door were winding down. She considered calling the front desk, but decided finishing off the wine was a superior option. She didn't remember going back to sleep.

· δ ·

SUNDAY

A Little Distracted

With the sun fully risen and Joan freshly washed and dressed in one of the outfits she had bought yesterday with Sally, she stepped into the corridor and found an empty chair. No sign of Odds Bodkins. Then the door to the next room opened and from it emerged the largest man Joan had ever seen. He spoke in a surprisingly soft voice.

"I hope the noise last night didn't disturb you. Can you believe it? Some burglars broke into my room." He grinned. "They found more than they bargained for. The police hauled them away a little worse for wear."

"You didn't change rooms?" Joan asked.

The Meat-Hammer shrugged. "The hotel will move me today. They wanted to last night, but changing rooms in the middle of the night would have been more troublesome than dealing with burglars."

"Of course," Joan agreed. She supposed that for someone like The Meat-Hammer this was probably true. "You have a match today?"

"Naw. We're making a movie. I play a librarian."

"Good luck with that," Joan told him.

His grin widened. "It's a comedy."

Joan cast him her most serious expression. "Beating people to a pulp is easy. Comedy is hard."

The Meat-Hammer lost his smile and worry lines formed around his eyes.

"I'm sure you'll be wonderful," she told him.

He nodded and they rode down the elevator in silence.

Odds Bodkins was in his usual cushioned chair in the lobby reading his newspaper. "It'll get worse," he murmured, not looking up. "Now that their thugs have failed, the desperate men will come in person." Without putting down his paper he pulled the wad of hundreds from his inside pocket and set it on the small table next to the chair. Switching the newspaper to his other hand he pulled a similar stack of bills from the other side of his coat and added it to the first.

Joan studied the tabletop. There was enough money there to choke a horse. Literally.

"You're not concerned that these desperate men will come after you?" she asked.

The little man laughed. "Odds Bodkins can take care of himself. The bird you witnessed yesterday is the least of my skills."

"Is that so?"

"Oh, yes. I also do card tricks." He raised an empty hand, rotated his wrist, and out of nowhere a deck of fifty-two appeared in his hand. "Pick a card. Any card."

"Mr. Bodkins—"

"Please," said the little man. "Call me Odds."

Joan sighed. "Odds, you are quickly becoming a living cliché."

The little man put down his newspaper and looked at her closely. "Is that good?"

"Not really," Joan told him.

Odds muttered something and opened his hand. The cards turned into butterflies and fluttered away. Joan was certain she saw the Ace of Spades on the wings of several of the creatures.

"Does this mean you have not yet decided to sell the tea service?"

Joan wrestled with her thoughts. "I haven't been able to think about it. My husband appears to be missing so I'm a little distracted."

Bodkins snapped his fingers and the stacks of cash on the table disappeared. "I am certain that he will show up. The desperate men will have no interest in him."

"I wish I had your confidence."

"Very well. In the hope of giving you some of my confidence, I will ask around for you."

Joan looked at the little man's face. His expression said he was serious. "I appreciate that."

Bodkins stood up and again reached into an inside pocket. This time his hand emerged with a black business card. "As for the tea service, if you will not do the wise thing, I encourage you to do the next wisest thing."

"And that would be...?"

"Get some protection." The business card vanished from his hand and Joan found it in her own fingers. She read the card: *Madame Elona's Curiosity Emporium*. It showed an address just south of downtown. Near the homeless shelter.

"Tell Elona that Odds Bodkins sent you and she will give you some real magic instead of tourist trickery."

"And what will you be doing?"

"I shall remain here and guard the tea service."

Joan let out a deep breath. "If last night is any indication, you have your work cut out for you."

Odds grinned at her. "My lady, I assure you that Odds Bodkins is up to the task." Then the little man sat down and resumed reading his newspaper.

· δ ·

Joan left the hotel on foot, intent on walking to Patrick's office to demand to know where Patrick was. Or at a minimum get his cell phone number from a workmate. Halfway there she realized that it was Sunday and the office would be empty. Damn!

Balling her fists with anemic anger she turned south and walked two blocks before realizing where she was going. Bodkins' curiosity shop. It wasn't far. The Beltline district sat just south of the downtown core, smack dab between the city's highest rent office buildings and the Stampede and Exhibition Grounds. Someday developers would plough the whole Beltline under and populate it with million dollar condos, but until then it was the roughest part of the city, filled with transients, hookers and drug addicts. Joan avoided driving there whenever possible, and here she was walking toward it. She must be out of her mind.

· δ ·

A Little Protection

At 10:00 a.m. on a Sunday morning in June, the Beltline actually didn't seem so bad. Most of the shops, restaurants and nightclubs were closed and the streets were virtually deserted. Further east toward Macleod Trail, a good number of the city's transients would soon emerge from the Mustard Seed Mission, unlock stolen bicycle locks from stolen grocery carts, and begin scavenging the alleyways for beer bottles, pop cans, and anything else that might turn a small profit or bear a passing resemblance to food. Walking past an alley, Joan saw one of the grimy, bearded fellows already at work. Maybe they started their day earlier than 10:00 a.m.

Checking the black business card, Joan read the designated address and soon found the shop. She was relieved that Madame Elona's Curiosity Emporium was one of the few businesses open on a Sunday morning. A bell above the door jingled as she went inside.

For an emporium it was rather small. Even for a Starbucks it would have been small. Every inch of wall and counter space was used. Unnamable objects hung like bats from the ceiling. Curiosities. Toward the back of the store a beaded curtain parted and a gypsy slash tramp slash thief made an entrance. The proprietor.

"Velcome," she said expansively with an eastern European drawl. Madame Elona's exuberance suggested she hadn't seen a customer in years.

"Madame Elona, I presume."

The woman smiled, exposing missing teeth. "In ze flesh. How may I zerve you thiz day?"

Good question. Joan wasn't certain what to ask for or even if it would make the slightest difference. A wreath of garlic might keep vampires away, but it wasn't going to prevent burglars from breaking into her hotel room.

"I need protection—"

"I have just ze thing!!!" the gypsy exclaimed, using two too many exclamation marks. She huddled over a counter and came up with a copper ring with a blue gemstone. "Zis ring vas vorn by the Princez Halibella of Uzbekistan. It protected her from poizon, azzazins, and ze clap!"

"I don't think so," said Joan. She was pretty certain Uzbekistan had only existed since the fall of the Soviet Union and had never had royalty.

The gypsy tossed the ring onto the counter and scuttled to a small table. She extracted a silver bracelet from the flotsam. It had arcane symbols engraved from end to end. "Ze circlet of Kazar!" she whispered. "Vorn by the sorceress Iona, making her impervious to attack by jealous peerz. It iz a bit more expenzive than Halibella's ring, but I zee you are a voman of taste."

"I am also a woman who recognizes fake silver when she sees it," said Joan. "Here's the deal: Odds Bodkins sent me."

The gypsy let out a noisy breath and threw the bracelet back onto the table.

"Why didn't you say so?" she said, dropping the fake accent. "Or did you just want a taste of my shtick?"

"And a very entertaining shtick it is," Joan suggested. "But Odds feels I need some protection and he sent me to you."

The woman nodded. "Odds knows what's what and he's a good man, unlike most of my customers. If he says you need protection, you need protection. Wait here." The woman scuttled through the beading to the back room.

While she waited, Joan perused various curiosities that didn't amount to much more than shiny rubbish. What the gypsy returned with also looked like rubbish, but it wasn't shiny.

"This will do the trick," said Madame Elona, pushing a small pouch the size, shape and color of a shriveled apple into Joan's hands.

Joan looked at it. Turned it sideways. Shook it. Listened to it. Smelled it. Considered tasting it, but decided not to. She looked at the grinning gypsy. "A bag of dirt?"

"You are very perceptive. No wonder Odds likes you."

"This will protect me?"

"Of course! It is not just any dirt. It is dirt from the grave of a Faerie King." She leaned in to whisper. "From the land of Faerie. Very difficult to procure. Just conceal it about your person and it will lend you the protections of a Faerie King."

"I see," said Joan. The gypsy's manic grin did not inspire confidence. "By *difficult to procure* you mean expensive."

The gypsy blew out a breath. "Expensive? What I have given you is priceless! It cannot be sold, only given."

Joan returned her gaze to the bag of dirt. It weighed less than half a pound. "So you're not going to charge me for it?"

The woman frowned. "What part of priceless do you fail to understand? All I ask is that once you no longer require it that you pass it on to someone who is worthy. Two people come to mind. Odds Bodkins or myself. This is a great gift."

Joan slipped the bag into her jacket pocket. "Then I thank you." What else could she say?

· δ ·

A Transient Encounter

Joan stepped out onto the sidewalk and winced against the sudden sunlight. She hadn't realized just how dark it had been inside the curiosity shop. She looked at her watch to find it was almost 11 a.m. When she returned to the hotel she would have brunch.

"Give it over!"

Joan turned to find herself face to face with a lanky teenager. He wore a dirty army surplus shirt over a dirtier white T-shirt. His hair was long, stringy, and unwashed. The rough skin of his face was sun-darkened, a deep tan most women would kill for. He stood swaying, his eyes burning feverishly. In his fist he clutched a hunting knife. The knife was the only part of him that looked respectable. My God, thought Joan. I'm being robbed by a transient.

"Money!" mumbled the transient. "Now!"

Joan peered closer and wondered if this really was a teenager. He could be in his twenties, his scrawniness making him look younger.

"You deaf?" the transient demanded. He waved his knife inexpertly.

"I'm not deaf," Joan told him. "What I am is broke." Patrick had once told her to tell beggars she didn't have anything if they approached her. He said they'd nod politely and go find someone else to hit up. Enough people gave them money that they didn't pester those who didn't. Patrick never understood her fear of transients. Now, here she was, being accosted. Joan measured her nerves and decided she was holding up well.

The transient waved his knife at Madame Elona's Curiosity Shop. "You just came out of a store. You must have money."

"No," said Joan. "If I just came out of a bank, I must have money. If I just came out of a store, I must have less money. Right now I have no money. Run along and accost someone else. You'll have better luck." She attempted a friendly smile.

The transient stared at her and began to shake. Well, shake more than he had been shaking. Then he shouted "Eaygh!" and lunged at her with the knife.

Joan was so shocked that she only had time to think *That's not supposed to happen* before the knife stopped suddenly just short of her chest and melted around the transient's fist. Her next thought was *That's not supposed to happen*, but with a completely different *that*.

The transient's "Eaygh!" rose to a blood-curdling scream and before Joan could get a good look at the lump of bone, flesh, and metal that used to be the transient's hand he was running down the sidewalk. Joan doubted he had a destination in mind. Running just seemed the appropriate thing to do.

"Vell," said Madam Elona from the shop's doorway, her gypsy accent returned, "I am zurprised you needed proteczion zo zoon."

Joan looked at her. "I didn't think transients used knives when they begged."

The gypsy turned her head. "Zhat vas no beggar. Zhat vas a jumped-up drug addict."

"Oh," said Joan, her heart starting to hammer in her chest. "At least now we know your bag of dirt works."

· δ ·

Façade Of The Mundane

By the time Joan finished walking back to the hotel her pounding heart had returned to normal. Almost. It was also nearly noon and she was starving.

In the lobby she encountered a disturbance. Two people were yelling and stabbing fingers in the air. Patrons of the hotel were giving the couple a wide birth. Joan would have done the same except that one of them was Sally and the other was Odds Bodkins.

Joan walked straight up to them. "I'm not interrupting anything, am I?"

Odds turned to smile at her. "A good day to you, Mrs. Longmeyer."

"Lunch?" Sally suggested through gritted teeth.

The little man turned back to the hair stylist. "Go wait for your friend in the restaurant. We have some business to discuss. It will not take long."

"I don't think so," Sally said.

"Or," suggested Odds Bodkins, "we could continue discussing our differences in public."

Sally glared at him then stormed off.

"You two know each other?" Joan asked.

"We just met," Odds said. "That one is trouble. I would stay away from her if I were you. She is not to be trusted."

"We've been best friends for years," Joan told him.

Odds wagged his head. "Her kind has no friends."

Joan was about to ask what he meant by that when Odds sat down in his usual cushion chair and picked up his newspaper. "I see you received some protection from Elona. Good."

Joan tapped the pocket of her jacket with the flat of her hand. "How did you know?"

"I can feel it of course. It is no small magic."

"I was attacked by a jumped-up, drug-crazed wacko when I left the curiosity shop," Joan said, partly because it was a cool story, but mostly because she wanted to see Odds' reaction.

Odds turned a page of his paper. "Good fortune it was on the way out and not on the way in. Is he still alive?"

"Yes," said Joan. "When he comes off his high he may wish he wasn't."

"Lost causes, all of them," murmured Odds. "Of course, they do not exist in my world."

"Your world?" echoed Joan. She sat down in the chair opposite the little man. That seemed to make him happy as he put down his newspaper and smiled at her.

Odds waved his hand. "This hotel, your downtown, your Mustard Seed, the big building where you bought the tea service. All is just a façade draped over the real world. None of it is important in the grand scheme of things. Beneath that façade is the real world, a world rarely seen by those, like you, who dwell in the façade."

Odds seemed greatly impressed by his oration. Joan not so much. "So this real world. It contains the tea service, and I'm assuming *you*. What else?"

The little man opened his mouth to speak, and then slowly closed it. "No. The less you know the better. There was a time long ago when the two worlds grew close together. Things turned out badly, for both worlds. Efforts have been made since then to keep things at a distance. Everyone has been happier for it."

He looked at Joan, his small eyes penetrating. "That is another reason you should give up the tea service. It does not belong in your world. The longer you have it the more trouble it will cause. Sell it to me and you can go back to your ordinary existence and not be troubled by the world that lies beneath."

Odds Bodkins' words scared Joan for reasons she couldn't put her finger on. Despite not understanding any of it, she felt she should do as he suggested. Get rid of the tea service and get on with her life. But it still didn't feel right. Something was missing. Then she remembered.

"My husband, Patrick, is still missing," she said.

Joan was certain she saw real concern in the little man's eyes. "Yes. The good news is that my inquiries have not yet turned up anything."

"How is that good news?" Joan asked.

Odds raised an eyebrow. "It means the desperate men probably do not have him. His absence likely stems from a more mundane source. I will look into more ordinary causes." With great urgency, Odds Bodkins stuck his nose into his newspaper.

· δ ·

A Suitable Response

Lunch with Sally consisted of the best pork medallion with Caesar salad Joan had ever tasted, accompanied by repeated offers from Sally to find a buyer for the tea service. Perhaps it was just Odds Bodkins' words lying heavy on her mind, but Sally sounded just a bit too eager to help Joan get rid of the silver.

"Really, Sally," Joan told her. "It's just a tea service. Right now I have bigger problems to deal with. A hole in the ground where my house used to be. A missing husband...."

"Ok," said Sally, clearly disappointed. "But as you say, you do have a lot on your plate right now. How about I hide the tea service for you? Out of sight, out of mind." Joan couldn't remember ever seeing Sally's eyes wider.

"Let me think about it," Joan said, hoping that would be enough to satisfy her. She had never seen Sally like this. Sally, without a care in the world, suddenly keenly interested in something. Then there were Odds Bodkins' words: "She is not to be trusted." Joan had known Sally for years and the strange little man for less than two days, but right now she did not fully trust her friend.

Though Sally didn't say so, Joan could tell she didn't like Odds Bodkins any better than he liked her. In fact, Sally's lack of interest in the odd little man was a little out of character. Odd people like Odds and odd stories like the tale he was selling were natural fodder for Sally's wild imagination. But she wasn't biting. Instead she seemed fixated on the tea service.

"I need to get up to my room and check for messages from Patrick," Joan said. She had already checked with the front desk before lunch but that was forty minutes ago.

"I'll come with you, if you like," suggested Sally.

"No, no. I'm sure you have better things to do than watch me fret."

Joan charged the meal to her room and left the restaurant before Sally could think of a good reason why she should join her. Joan didn't feel like company just now.

In the lobby Odds still had his nose stuck in his newspaper. Joan didn't stop, but instead took the elevator up to her room. She was actually trembling with trepidation at the prospect there would be no message waiting and that she would spend the rest of the day by the phone growing increasingly worried. So it was almost surreal when she discovered a recorded message from Patrick on the hotel phone service.

"Horribly sorry I didn't call last night," Patrick began. "My plans changed suddenly and by the time I thought to call, the hour was late and I didn't want to wake you. I've only just now managed to find a free minute and of course you are out. I hope to be back in Calgary tomorrow. I'll tell you all about it then. Love you. Oh, and I hope you are enjoying your vacation at the Hyatt. Bye now."

Patrick had sounded rushed and there was a lot of noise in the background. Still, he had finally called and everything was all right. All that worry for nothing. But... where did he call from? He had cancelled his Toronto flight. Had he booked a different one? Or gone somewhere else?

As she sat pondering what it all meant, Joan noticed that the message light was still blinking. She had a second message.

Hoping it was Patrick with more information, such as the name of his hotel or even his cell phone number, Joan pressed the message button and listened.

"Mrs. Longmeyer. Sorry to have missed you. My name is Mr. Smith and I represent certain interests who were unable to attend the Halifax estate auction on Friday. These interests would dearly love to obtain the silver tea service you were fortunate enough to have acquired and are willing to offer you a sum significantly above that which you paid. Please call me back at your earliest convenience."

The message ended with a local phone number that Joan purposefully did not write down. Though the words were just as congenial as Odds Bodkins' offer, she found the message disturbing. How did Mr. Smith know where she was staying? Since there was no mention of desperate men, the offer likely came from the desperate men. Or, for all she knew, there were no desperate men and it was Odds Bodkins who burned down her house. Mr. Smith could represent desperate men, Odds Bodkins, or someone else entirely. Maybe even Sally. It was all so confusing.

The only thing Joan knew for sure was that she wouldn't sell the tea service to anyone until her husband was safely returned. That and that this whole business scared her to death.

After pacing the room for a few minutes, Joan decided to journey downstairs and inform Odds Bodkins of the messages and her decision not to do anything without Patrick. When she arrived in the lobby, however, she discovered the little man missing. Even more disconcerting, there was an abandoned newspaper in his chair.

Joan had the chilling conviction that the stakes had just been raised. Very quietly and composing herself as best she could, she returned to her room where she sat on the edge of the bed and tried to think of what to do.

At last she reached a decision and called the front desk. "This is Mrs. Longmeyer in room 812. I have some silverware that I have very foolishly been keeping in my room. I would like to have it transferred to the hotel safe. Yes, thank you. I would also like to switch rooms. Preferably to a different floor. No, there is nothing wrong with this room. I just require a change of scenery."

· δ ·

Beds Are Burning

Her new room, four floors up from where she'd spent the two previous nights, was identical to the old one with the exception of the art hanging on the wall and a slightly different view of downtown office buildings. Neither room had a balcony.

Joan waited by the phone all evening, but it never rang. She called the operator twice asking if her room change may have resulted in her missing a call, but the woman on the phone reassured her that callers were connected to people not room numbers. To protect the privacy of guests, room numbers were not given out.

Eventually she gave up waiting for Patrick to call and concluded that he had been kidnapped by the desperate men, Odds Bodkins, or perhaps even Sally since Joan had refused to allow her friend to sell or hide the tea service. She recalled a poster from an old TV series she used to watch that said *Trust No One*. She hadn't really understood the poster or the TV series, until now.

At this point she wasn't even sure she trusted Patrick. What if he hadn't been kidnapped? Perhaps he was in Vegas gambling, or kept a mistress across town. Could he be using the destruction of their home as an excuse to indulge his inner child? Joan let out a nervous laugh. Is this what hysteria felt like? Patrick had called and said he was fine. She had to trust him.

Joan realized she was getting a headache. In the past three days she had been forced to ask herself more questions than she had asked herself in the preceding three years. She didn't know what to think and just wanted it all to go away. She laughed out loud as she recalled Odds telling her just that. Get rid of the tea service and return to the façade Joan knew as ordinary life.

She crawled into bed telling herself that if she felt the same way in the morning she would go ahead and sell the tea service to Odds Bodkins, and then hope that everything would go back to normal.

· δ ·

During the night she awoke to the sound of fire engines and the smell of smoke. The desk clock said exactly three a.m. Joan figured she must be dreaming about her house fire again and closed her eyes. Then an alarm went off, so loud that only the dead could sleep through it. By the time she climbed into her robe a knock came at the door. Joan opened it and a young man in a hotel uniform informed her that there was a fire on the eighth floor and that the hotel must be evacuated.

Joan put on her shoes and pulled her jacket with the protection in the pocket over her robe. She then stuck her head back into the hallway. The alarm was still ringing, but the staff member had moved on to other doors. The sense of urgency waned so she went back in her room and got dressed in clothes she had bought Saturday morning.

When she stepped back into the hallway she found people from other rooms on her floor moving toward the stairs at the end of the corridor. Apparently the elevator had been shut down.

Most of them had also taken the time to get properly dressed. Joan followed the herd into the stairwell and shuffled down the steps, but when she reached the eighth floor she left the stairs and poked her head through the doorway into the corridor.

Room 812 was in flames. Firemen had just arrived up the opposite stairwell and were rushing forward with hoses and axes. Wow. Firemen really did use axes. Near room 812 a small man sat slumped in a chair with his face in a newspaper. Odds Bodkins did not look like he was sleeping.

Joan fled back into the stairwell and made her way to the lobby. Bodkins dead! At least now she had some answers. The desperate men, apparently, were real. Odds was right that she was in danger. She should have gotten rid of the tea service long ago. She needed to get rid of it now. But was it too late. She should have written down Mr. Smith's phone number.

In the lobby Joan went to the registration desk. Just because she had deleted the message didn't mean that the hotel wouldn't still have a copy. But there was no one there. Everyone was being directed out the lobby entrance and into the street. Joan allowed herself to be herded with them.

· δ ·

Safe House

On the other side of the door, someone grabbed her elbow. Joan swung her head around, and then looked down into the worried eyes of Odds Bodkins.

"Good," he whispered. "You are still alive."

"I would like to be able to say the same about you," Joan said.

The little man frowned, and then grinned. "Ah. That was just a doppelganger. An animated puppet. It will take more than a sorcerer-assassin to put down Odds Bodkins."

"A sorcerer-assassin? So it wasn't a simple arsonist setting fire to my old room?"

Odds shook his head. "No. When the assassin found neither you nor the tea service, he realized that the handsome man sitting guard in the hallway was not really me. That he had fallen for a red herring. Out of peevishness he blasted the room and disabled my doppelganger. Good fortune you left your new room before he could find it." The little man looked about. "He may be watching out here. We should go."

"Go where?" Joan asked.

"Someplace safe." He pulled her by the elbow into the night shadows of a growing number of EMS vehicles.

Joan stopped. "Wait! We need to get the tea service."

"You will find no one to open the hotel safe now. It will be undisturbed there for a while."

"You knew I put it in the safe?"

"And switched rooms. What kind of a guardian would Odds Bodkins be if he did not know these things?"

"But you left the lobby this afternoon. I thought they'd taken you."

"Taken me? The great Odds Bodkins! Oh ye of little faith. I left my station in the lobby because it had served its purpose. The time of agents of desperate men lurking about the hotel had ended and the time of making my defenses a little more imaginative had begun."

"The doppelganger?" Joan asked.

"Among other things," Odds agreed. "Sitting in plain sight was no longer a deterrent. As I said, these men are desperate." He frowned. "And impatient. I had not expected an attack on my life so soon." He put a finger to his lips. "But the time for talk must be suspended. Now is the time for stealth."

Leaving the shadows of the EMS vehicles, Odds spoke not a word and his shoes made not a sound. Joan tried her best to emulate him. He led Joan south through alleys and parkades toward the Beltline district. The Beltline district. At night. Odds had a strange notion of *safe*.

When they reached Tenth Avenue, Joan expected Odds to turn east toward Madame Elona's Curiosity Shop. Joan wouldn't be the least surprised to learn the gypsy kept the store open through the night as well as on Sundays, but Odds surprised her by turning west. After two blocks he brought them to a stop in front of the old Y.W.C.A. building.

Huge Y-M-C-A letters were stilled etched in the stonework above the wooden doorway, but it hadn't been used as such for years, not since the new and vastly larger building had been opened a dozen blocks to the north in the much newer and pleasanter district of Eau Claire. As far as Joan knew the old building was rented out to various clubs and organizations for weekly and monthly meetings. She suspected that transients regularly snuck in at night before the doors were locked.

Odds Bodkins produced a key from somewhere and unlocked the door. They stepped inside and he locked it again. The building was very dark, with the light of streetlamps seeping through small soot-darkened windows providing the only illumination. Joan listened for the sounds of transients, but found only silence.

Still moving quietly, Odds led her down a wide hallway to the back of the building and then stepped through a door into what, in the almost full darkness, appeared to be a kitchen. He opened a narrow door and removed from it a broom, a mop, and a bucket. He then entered the closet and disappeared.

Joan stared into the empty closet and wondered if she should put the cleaning implements back in. Then Odds' head appeared, mounted on the back wall like a hunting trophy, and asked her if she was coming.

"Sure," whispered Joan. The night couldn't get any crazier. "Why not?" She stepped into the closet and touched the back wall. Her hand went right through and she found herself staring at her wrist attached to the wall. She felt another hand grab hers and pull her forward and through the back of the closet. She blinked as sudden light blinded her.

"Sit here," Odds said, leading her to a soft chair. The little man then disappeared through a narrow doorway and returned a moment later.

"It was needed that I put the closet back in order," he explained. "People use it during the day."

"Of course," Joan said. She looked around and now that her eyes had adjusted she discovered that the room wasn't nearly as brightly lit as she'd thought. There were dozens of small tables of various design and material upon which sat an equal variety of lamps, all of which were turned on. No two of the tables or lamps were the same. Arranged between the tables were all manner of furniture: sofas, recliners, hard back chairs, bar stools, even a futon. The place looked like a badly organized furniture store.

Odds must have noticed her interest.

"I have a chair for every mood," he said.

"I never suspected," Joan told him, "that you were such a moody fellow."

"Odds Bodkins is a very complicated man," he agreed.

"So what do we do now?" Joan asked.

Odds sat in a hard chair across from Joan and said, "After sunrise we shall return to your hotel where you will remove the tea service from the safe. You will sell it to me and take the money I give you and check into a hotel as far from downtown as you can and lie low." He paused. "It will probably take me two days to fully get word out that you no longer have the tea service and that anyone still interested in it can come see me, if they dare."

"Won't that put you in danger?" Joan asked.

"From the desperate men?" asked Odds. "I have nothing to fear from them. The tea service itself, however, is another matter. I am not certain that it is not itself a danger to me."

Joan was going to ask the little man what he meant, but she suddenly remembered Patrick. Joan still had no idea where he was. And now that she had fled the Hyatt, he would have no way to find her.

"What about Patrick?" she said, assuming Odds would know what she meant.

The little man grinned. "I tracked him down."

"You did?"

"Of course. You did not believe that a mere mundane could hide from Odds Bodkins, did you?"

Odds had used that word before — mundane — but Joan had no idea what it meant. "Where is he?"

Odds pulled a timepiece on a chain out of thin air, glanced at its face, and then dropped it. Watch and chain vanished. "Right now your husband is 4000 feet above Greenland."

"What?"

"Instead of going to Toronto as he had planned, your Patrick acted upon a sudden impulse and boarded a plane for England."

"England? Wait! Patrick acted on a sudden impulse?"

"Yes, I know," said Odds. "Such behavior is totally out of character for him, but not really surprising considering his house was demolished not hours after his wife spent $10,000 on a tea service. Such events can knock a man out of the rut in which he has been treading, even if he has been treading it for years."

Joan opened her mouth, not certain what she would say. What she ended up saying was, "I'm so proud."

Odds looked at her, startled. "Are you? Well, and you should be. Patrick's expedition was a complete success."

"He had an expedition?"

"Of course. He is a very observant man. He suspected there was something unusual about the tea service and took a picture of it with that fancy mobile phone camera of his. His nature prevented him from acting on so little information, of course, so at the airport he made a difficult decision and flew to England instead or Toronto in order to find out more about the tea service. He spoke to the right people, went to the right museums and antiquities dealers. He is now returning to you to tell you exactly what the tea service is and why you should leave it in the nearest ditch and run like hell."

Odds frowned and let out a sigh. "Oh. I have upset you. I suspect I have given you too much information at once."

Joan didn't feel upset. In fact, she was feeling pretty good. Patrick hadn't been kidnapped by desperate men. He was safe and coming home. And he had acted on an impulse. Joan had been waiting years for Patrick to act on an impulse. She hoped this was just a beginning.

Odds still looked worried. "Rest here a while. Your husband's plane arrives in 5 hours. We will take a taxi to the airport and collect him."

Joan began to say, "I'm not tired," but the little man, like his pocket watch, had vanished into thin air.

· δ ·

MONDAY

Early Checkout

Joan didn't sleep, but instead pondered everything that had happened, trying to decide if she understood any of it. As she examined her thoughts she wandered among the strange little man's collection of furniture, sitting on different chairs and turning lamps off and on. They all seemed like plain old living room furniture, nothing special or exotic. Nothing magical. She found no other doors to the room, just hard walls of faded white paint. The closet door she had entered by was closed and had no handle. She suspected she had not entered in the normal way, but had come through the door itself rather than through an open door. She rapped on the door and her knuckles struck wood. Joan shook her head and returned to one of the chairs. By the time Bodkins returned she was no closer to understanding anything and hoped that Patrick would offer more clues.

"We must return to the Hyatt," Odds told her, "and reclaim the tea service from the hotel safe. The staff have resumed accommodating guests, mostly to help them check out, and dark agents are again on the prowl. It will not be long before they investigate the safe."

"But if these dark agents are in the hotel, won't they be watching for us?"

"Of course, which is why they shall not find us. We will hide in plain sight."

"Somehow, I'm not comforted."

"I shall throw a glamour or two," said Odds. "We shall be hidden long enough."

Outside on the street, Joan was surprised to see bustling traffic, on foot and vehicular. The Beltline was an entirely different place during the morning commute. It took only a moment to hail a taxi and minutes to arrive at the Hyatt.

The hotel was a mess. From the street you could see broken windows and smoke-blackened walls on the eighth floor. The curb-side entrance was littered with ash while the lobby stank of smoke. A flock of appraisers chased an angry older gentleman to and fro, while he waved at ruined works of art. Anything not damaged by fire had been ruined by smoke. And anything not ruined by smoke had been wrecked by water. Joan could not recall ever seeing anyone so livid.

Odds wasted no time dragging Joan to the front desk where she asked if she could check out.

"Of course," said the desk clerk. He looked her up in the computer and his face fell. "I'm afraid your room on the eighth floor was completely destroyed." He frowned. "Apparently, that's where the fire started."

"My room is on the twelfth floor," she informed him.

After a few mouse clicks he said. "Yes. You moved to a new room yesterday afternoon." He cast her a speculative stare.

"Call it woman's intuition," she suggested.

He looked back at the screen and continued clicking his mouse. "Looks like your twelfth floor room was also destroyed. Some lunatic went in there with what we think was an axe and hacked everything to bits."

"Thank God that was after I had been evacuated from my room," Joan said.

"Y-e-s. I see you spent three nights with us."

"Loved every minute," she told him. "I'm recommending your establishment to my friends. After the repairs, of course."

The clerk grunted. "Because of the inconvenience of the fire and the loss of your belongings I'm at liberty to waive your bill."

Joan smiled. "I would expect nothing less of the Hyatt."

"It says here you have something in our safe."

"Yes. If you could put it in a box that would be marvelous."

The clerk made a brief phone call and a few minutes later a young woman in hotel livery emerged from a door behind the reception desk. She carried an appropriate size white and brown box displaying the Hyatt logo. Joan peeked inside and was relieved to see the silver tea service packed in bubble wrap.

"Thank you," she told both clerks and turned to make her way to the elevator that went down to the dungeon.

Odds clutched her elbow. "Leave your car. It will be watched."

"But—," Joan began.

"Taxi is always the most discreet form of travel." Odds led her outside to a waiting taxi and ten minutes later the tea service was stowed in Bodkins' YMCA safe house.

They immediately returned to the street where Odds had asked the taxi to wait. "Take us to the airport," he told the driver. "There's a good man."

· δ ·

Merlin In A Tea Cup

Joan had never seen such a look of surprise on Patrick's face as when he found her waiting for him at the airport.

"I can explain—" he began.

"—Odds has already explained," she told him.

Patrick scrutinized the little man who had been standing with Joan at Arrivals. "You must be Odds Bodkins."

Odds grinned. "I am pleased they still remember me back home."

"Oh," said Patrick, "You left quite an impression."

"I do aim to impress," he said.

Patrick turned back to Joan. "Do you still have the tea service?"

"Yes, I—"

Patrick cut her off. "—Get rid of it. Now. That tea service is quite possibly the most dangerous thing in the world today."

"That it is," agreed Odds. "Look, there is a Tim Horton's upstairs. Let us go quaff a coffee and discuss how you two may extricate yourselves from this predicament in a calm, orderly fashion."

Patrick's gaze turned inward, the way it usually did when he was thinking deep thoughts, and Joan was afraid he'd want more time to think things through before engaging in discussion, but he surprised her by saying, "Okay, but we'll go to Starbucks." Well, he couldn't leave the entire rut behind at once, could he?

Over coffee Joan recounted meeting Odds Bodkins and the various break-ins and arsons that had occurred at the Hyatt over the weekend. She also mentioned Mr. Smith, who Odds confirmed was a broker for the desperate men.

"Mr. Smith," said Odds, as if it were somehow scandalous, "is not his real name, of course."

Patrick said nothing. He just listened and drank his coffee without seeming to taste it while his eyes bulged at appropriate moments.

When Joan's story ended with the taxi to the airport, she asked Patrick to tell his tale.

"I'm sure Odds Bodkins could tell it better," Patrick said.

"Oh no," said Odds. "You did good work in London. I am keen to hear your perspective."

"Very well. After showing a photo of the tea service to several antiquities dealers, they directed me to a place called, and I'm not kidding, The Museum of Unnatural Sciences."

Joan interrupted. "Didn't any of the antiquities dealers want to buy the tea service?"

"None of them would touch it," Patrick told her. "They claimed the tea service is cursed."

"Cretins," said Odds. "The tea service is anything but cursed, They were either too afraid to give you the real story or too lazy to have learned it themselves."

"I got the real story at the museum," Patrick continued. "It seems that in the eighteenth century a fellow calling himself Merlin started up a school of magicians in the heart of London."

Joan let out a small laugh, and then drew her lips together when neither Patrick nor Odds joined her.

"Apparently this was a school of real magic. And this Merlin fellow was supposed to be the same Merlin of Arthurian Legend."

"And where had this Merlin character been hiding for 1200 years?" Joan asked.

"He was busy," Odds said quickly and in a tone that brooked no discussion. "Remember what I said about this mundane world and the world underneath. Just because mundanes do not see someone for centuries does not mean he is not occupied elsewhere."

"The point," said Patrick, "Is that this school caused no end of trouble, not the least of which was the creation of a silver tea service magicians could use to focus energies and work even greater magic."

"Now that is unfair," cried Bodkins. "The school did much wonderful work. Especially in the early days. It was only near the end, when Merlin's students grew prideful and rejected his guidance that things began to go awry."

Patrick sipped his coffee and nodded. "The museum said that was one theory, but after 200 years no one is sure of what really happened."

"I told them what happened!" Odds insisted.

"Oh, they remember you," said Patrick. "You're the one who had a spitting match with the curators and told them the tea service they had on display was a fake."

"Well, it was. The real tea service was here. Hidden away in a locked vault at the Halifax estate."

"You didn't tell them that."

"Of course I didn't tell them. The fewer who knew the tea service's location, the better."

"They said you melted down their display tea service."

"Of course I did. To show them it was a fake. No one can destroy the real tea service."

"But," said Joan, "if it was a fake, why not just leave it be?"

Odds Bodkins blew out a gust of breath. "Because real or fake, such a claim would have caused the same damage there as has happened here. There are those who would kill just on the rumor of the tea service's discovery."

"Okay, okay," said Joan. "The real question is why? What makes this tea service so valuable, so dangerous, that houses and hotels are being demolished over it?"

Odds folded his arms and glowered, so Patrick picked up the story. "The museum said that when this magic school made a nuisance of itself, Merlin shut it down. But the London aristocracy still weren't happy. They asked: What is to stop this from happening again?"

Merlin responded by creating the tea service. He told the Londoners that he had poured half his ability into the silver so that he would be less of a threat to them.

Joan frowned. "How did they respond to that?"

"They ran him out of town."

"Not surprising," said Joan.

"Stupid, stupid, stupid." Odds Bodkins was banging his forehead against the table. "There are times," he said, "when you should *not* act upon spur-of-the moment decisions. In this case it was an ill-fated double-whammy."

"How's that?" asked Patrick.

"First," said Odds, "Merlin was not the problem. It was his students who were unscrupulous. Reducing himself in power not only did not solve the problem, but made it worse by limiting what he could do about it."

"And the second whammy?" asked Joan.

"He did not think through the ramifications of creating the tea service."

Patrick halted his cup in mid sip. "And what are those ramifications?"

Odds looked at him. "You must understand that magic is impossible to destroy. It is like water. It just changes state. If you melt ice it becomes water. If you heat water it becomes vapor. If temperatures fall, the vapor becomes ice again. Knowing this, Merlin hoped that the silver in the tea service would serve as a vessel, a container for magic, that it would sit there, unused, forever."

"But that's not what happened," suggested Joan

"Unfortunately, no. While silver is terrific for storing magic, which is why so many rings and amulets are made of silver, it is also a great conductor. You would never be able to use a ring of power if you could not draw the magic out of it."

"Merlin would have known this," said Patrick.

"Of course he did. Which is why he sealed the tea service after filling it with power. But he failed to think things through. At full power he could have sealed it permanently. At half power that seal would wear down."

"How long would it take this seal to wear down," asked Joan.

"So that magicians could use it? About 200 years."

"I see."

"Wait another hundred years and even mundanes will be able to use it."

"This is a pickle," said Joan.

"So now," said Odds, "you know why it is important that I possess the tea service and not these black magicians who would use it for no good."

"Black magicians?" asked Joan. "That would be your desperate men."

Odds Bodkins nodded.

"Why should we believe you?" Patrick asked. "For all we know *you* could be one of these black magicians."

Odds Bodkins cast him a freezing look. "If that were the case I would have recovered the tea service three days ago and you would both be dead."

· δ ·

Every Good Magician Deserves Furniture

Leaving the Airport Starbucks, the three took a taxi back downtown. The driver assumed they had all just gotten off an airplane and excitedly told them about last night's fire. "I hope you did not book the Hyatt," he concluded.

When Odds told them they were not going to a hotel, but wished to be dropped off at the old YMCA building, the driver lost his exuberance. Apparently Joan wasn't the only one with an aversion to the Beltline.

Patrick appeared greatly bemused by the kitchen closet entrance to Odds Bodkins' furniture warehouse. "What do you do when people are in the building?" he asked.

Odds laughed. "I need no entrance. I can come and go as I please. We only go this way to accommodate you two."

Taking in the vast array of tables, chairs, and lamps, Patrick said, "Some of these are quite old. And they are all in mint condition. You could probably sell them for a small fortune."

"I have no need of money," Odds answered. He pulled from his inside coat pockets the two stacks of hundred dollar bills Joan had seen earlier, and set them on one of the small tables. "But I do love my furniture. I would not trade any of it for the world."

While Patrick stared at the money, Joan broached a subject she had been thinking about during the taxi ride.

"Odds, you said earlier that you didn't fear these black magicians, but you did seem concerned about the tea service. You said it might be dangerous to you."

The little man cast her a serious look. "Yes. Any magician who possesses the tea service will have almost unlimited magical power. To my knowledge I am the only magician who can be trusted with it. Even so, a wise man once said: power corrupts; absolute power corrupts absolutely."

"Machiavelli?" suggested Joan.

Bodkins' eyes went wide. "What? No. It was Merlin. Prince Machiavelli merely quoted him. Where was I? Oh yes. I am afraid that once I have the power, I may be tempted to use it. Still, I see no other option."

"Why don't you destroy it," said Patrick, at last pulling his gaze away from the money.

"As I said at the airport. Magic cannot be destroyed."

"Not the magic," Joan clarified. "Patrick means the tea service. Can't you unseal the silver and let the magic out?"

Bodkins looked thoughtful. "An intriguing idea. I never considered it before because such a thing was quite impossible."

"If it's impossible...." said Joan.

"But do you not see?" said Odds, waving his hands with excitement. "Time has weakened the seal! What was once impossible is now merely difficult."

"So you can break the seal?"

"I? No. But that is not the point."

"What is the point?"

"The point is that the seal can be broken."

Patrick looked around the spacious room. "Where is the tea service, anyway?"

Odds calmed his excitement and waved a hand. "It is in a box over there. I need a moment to think this through. How to break the seal?"

"I don't see anything," said Patrick.

Another wave. "On that table. Do not bother me just now."

"The only thing on that table is a lamp."

Bodkins let out a groan of annoyance. "It is right— Gods and fishes! It is gone!"

"I thought you said this place was protected!" said Joan.

Odds had jumped up, moving faster than his short legs should allow, and was inspecting the table. "It is. It would take a magician a month to break through my defenses."

"Then it wasn't a magician," said Patrick. "Could it have been someone renting the space upstairs?"

"Or a transient?" Joan added.

"It would take a mundane much longer than a month."

"Then who?"

Odds rubbed his jaw. "There are those who are more or less immune to magic. They would not even notice a protection never mind be restrained by one."

"Who?"

"The Fey."

"The what?" asked Joan.

The little man's expression grew even more annoyed. "Have you people forgotten everything in your history? The Fey. Fairies. The people from under the Hill."

"I thought Fairies were magical," said Joan.

"Of course they are," said Odds. "They are born of magic. They eat, drink, and sleep magic. When they die, even the dirt they are buried in becomes magic." He gave Joan a steady look. "Something you have recently learned."

"Then how could a Fairy just walk in here?" demanded Patrick.

Odds wagged his head. "This is not their realm. Under the Hill they use magic as easily as they draw breath. They have great wars where they blast and defend against each other with whooping scads of magic. But here, in this world, they can neither cast it or be affected by it. Which is why so many come here as refugees. To get away from the wars back home. Ironically, people native to this realm can use Fairy magic with ease. Which is why that protection of yours works," he added, glancing at Joan. "But it will not protect you from the Fey. If that drug addict you encountered yesterday had been Fey, his knife would have killed you just as surely as if you had no protection."

"Knife?" exclaimed Patrick. "Drug addict!"

"It was nothing," Joan told him, knowing they would have a long talk about it later. She had left the incident out of her narrative at the airport hoping to avoid just such a discussion. Then to Odds she said, "But if Fairies can't use the tea service, why would they want it?"

Odds tapped his chin with a finger. "The Fey have an obsession."

"Like you and your furniture?" suggested Patrick.

The little man cast him a sharp look. "No. Much stronger. The Fey love all things gold. They are like magpies stealing shiny objects."

"But the tea service is silver."

"That tea service can be traded for a mountain of gold, though I suspect any black magician she does business with will simply kill her instead."

"Her?" asked Joan.

Odds Bodkins shook his head and sighed. "Where is your friend Sally?"

· δ ·

Hair-A-Go-Go

"Sally is a Fairy?" asked Joan.

"I've always had my suspicions," said Patrick. "Not that she was a Fairy. Such a thing would never occur to me. But I always suspected there was something different about her. She's so... flighty."

"And she never ages," suggested Joan.

"She came here relatively recently," said Odds. "Perhaps two hundred years ago."

When Joan looked at him he added, "The Fey don't die a natural death. They live until they are killed. That is one reason for the wars under the Hill. It is the only way to keep the population down."

"And you think Sally took the tea service?"

The little man looked at her with wide eyes. "Of course Sally took the tea service. She knew about it. She has been hounding you to get it into her greedy little hands. She must have been watching you and followed us here. I would not have been able to detect a Fey following us."

"That's hardly conclusive," said Joan, defending her friend.

"Occam's Razor," said Odds.

"What?"

"The simplest explanation is almost always the right one. There are relatively few Fey in this world and even fewer in this city. The desperate men would have as much difficulty finding one as I would and none of the Fey would trust the black magicians enough to work for them. The chances of our Fey not being Sally are absurdly small."

"Oh."

"Taxi's on its way," said Patrick, putting away his cell phone.

"Gods and fishes," said Odds. "I hear people upstairs. Hopefully there are none in the kitchen." He stepped part way through the closet door and looked back at them. "Is everyone coming?"

There was someone in the kitchen. A gray-haired woman in her sixties preparing a potato salad. When she saw three people walk out of the cleaning cupboard, she fainted dead away.

"She will remember nothing," said Odds, waving a hand quickly over her face.

They walked down the hallway and out the front door under the curious gaze of several other older women. Their taxi arrived a few minutes later.

It was a long, silent ride to Sally's house in Lake Bonavista. When they pulled up in front of the house, Odds asked the taxi driver to wait as they wouldn't be long.

Joan stood on the sidewalk looking at her best friend's house in a whole different way. For the neighborhood it was a small house. Sky blue with white trim. Flowers, many of them in bloom, lined the sidewalk and the front of the house. Today — though the house looked no different than usual — it conveyed a Fairyland appearance. Joan knew that was just her mind applying Odds' description of the Fey.

She hurried to catch up as she noticed Odds and Patrick marching up the sidewalk. When no one answered the buzzer, Joan tried the door and discovered it was unlocked.

"Broken," said Patrick demonstrating that the lock and bolt were both engaged, and that the wood frame was damaged where the bolt had been ripped from its socket.

"Sally!" Joan called as she walked into the living room, a living room where every square inch of the walls and tabletops were covered in gold trinkets or coins. "These were never here before."

Odds looked around, touching several of the gold pieces with gentle fingers. "The Fey do not show their treasure to others. They bask in its company but hide it when they entertain."

"Whoever broke the door obviously wasn't a burglar," said Patrick.

"A black magician must have her," Odds said grimly. "And the tea service."

"Why do you say that?" asked Joan.

"Because there is a house where a hole in the ground should be." Returning to the taxi, Joan said she wasn't ready to give up and directed the driver to the nearby strip mall where Sally worked, and led Patrick and Odds into the Hair-A-Go-Go Salon.

"Is Sally in?" Joan asked.

"Not today," said Cathy, one of Sally's co-workers. But as she spoke she flicked her head toward the curtained doorway at the back. The curtain looked surprising similar to Madam Elona's back room entrance and Joan briefly wondered if the curiosity shop used to be a hair salon. She could easily picture Madame Elona curling people's hair.

Odds stumped his way into the back room and emerged tugging Sally by the ear. "Ow," she cried, but otherwise offered no resistance. Under his free arm Odds carried the brown and white box from the Hyatt.

"Occam is once again proven correct," Odds cheerfully said to Joan. He turned to Sally. "Now, young lady, you are going to tell us what you have been up to."

"Sally," said Joan. "I can't believe it was *you* who stole my tea service."

"You were too indecisive," Sally said. "Every minute you kept Merlin's silver was a minute where you could get yourself killed. Since you wouldn't act, I had to act for you. I'm going to auction the tea service to the highest bidder and give the money to you. I mean, I was going to do that." She glared at Odds. "I guess now I'm selling it to him."

"Actually," said Joan. "I've already sold it to Odds. It was his property you stole."

"Oops," said Sally.

"I assume you have already made some of the calls," said Odds. "From your house. And one of the magicians you called tracked you there."

"Can you believe it?" said Sally. "If you can't trust a magician, who can you trust?"

Odds shook his head. "Magicians are thieves and renegades. There is only one you can trust."

Sally looked at him closely. "Which one is that?"

"Odds Bodkins," said the little man.

"Right," said Sally. "Then I guess it's a good thing that you ended up with the tea service."

"I don't want it."

"What?"

Odds nodded his head. "Your auction must proceed as planned. We are going to return to your house—"

"It's still there?"

"—Yes. And there you will finish making your phone calls."

"I will?"

"And in case you don't have ALL the black magicians on speed dial, here are their numbers." Odds handed her a sheaf of paper he pulled out of thin air.

Sally ran her eyes down the list of numbers. "Wow."

"We need as many magicians as we can get under one roof." said Odds.

"You have a plan?" Joan asked.

The little man looked at her. "Odds Bodkins always has a plan."

As they left the salon, Sally's co-worker Cathy wished them luck. Apparently the scene she had witnessed was not unusual for Sally's hair salon.

They paid the taxi driver and took Sally's Volkswagen Beetle back to her house. Joan and Patrick sat in Sally's gold-encrusted living room over her protestations — she wanted to put the gold away — while Odds set Sally up in the kitchen with his list of black magicians and a cell phone.

"This phone is untraceable," he explained. "We won't have any more black magicians showing up at the door. It also makes international calls at no change. This list is of every magician in the world."

"Can I get one of those phones?" Patrick called into the kitchen.

Odds called back, "No."

"Yeah" said Patrick, his voice quiet. "Of course not. We should go," he said to Joan.

"Go?"

"Well, Bodkins has his tea service. He and Sally have a plan. And we have our money back. They don't need us."

"Are you forgetting that we lost everything we own when our home was destroyed?"

Patrick sighed heavily. "That would be hard to forget."

"Well," said Joan, raising her right hand and clenching it into a fist. "I want to see the bastard who demolished our home and give him a piece of my mind."

"That doesn't strike me as a good idea." Patrick took her fist into his two hands and Joan unclenched her fingers. "Do I have to explain why?"

"Well, maybe I won't give him a piece of mind. But I do want to watch Odds kick his—"

"—Kick who?" Odds interrupted, hearing his name as he joined them from the kitchen.

"The black magicians," said Joan.

"Oh. While I do hope to greatly disappoint the magicians, I am uncertain about kicking them. Unlike the Fey in the land under the Hill, magicians do not kill each other. We have words. And sometimes a punch or two is thrown, but mostly we are quite civilized."

"But you destroy homes in fits of peevishness!" cried Joan.

"Odds Bodkins avoids such behavior whenever possible," said Odds. "The black magicians, however, are considerably less civil."

Sally joined them from the kitchen. "We should go. I've finished making the calls and the auction will begin in an hour. And there is always the possibility that someone from my earlier round of calls will show up to demolish the house. We shouldn't be here if they do."

· δ ·

Dark Clichés

Sally drove them a short distance to an obscure, heavily forested arm of Fish Creek Park. The parking lot was very small. Sally's Beetle was the only vehicle. A three minute walk into the trees brought them to a large glade surrounding a circle of tall standing stones.

"I didn't know this was here," said Sally.

"Thirty seconds ago it was not," said Odds. "The fire pit you selected would never have accommodated the host I hope will arrive."

"My phone list was shorter than yours," Sally remarked.

Odds marched up to a low, flat stone in the center of the circle and opened the box from the Hyatt. Removing each piece from its careful packaging of bubble wrap he assembled the tea service on the stone. When he was done he waved his arms once and walked back to join the others.

"What did you do?" Joan asked. Such hand or arm waving in the past had usually accompanied magic.

"I bound the service to the stone. It will not be impossible for someone to run off with the silver, but it will be difficult. They would have to take the stones and half the glade with them."

He motioned toward the trees. "I suggest we move to a safer distance. One or more of my fellow magicians will surely arrive early and attempt some mischief."

No sooner had they moved back into the trees when a black-bearded man, dressed in black, appeared out of thin air and peered about the clearing, his dark gaze finally resting upon the tea service.

"Look at that," whispered Sally. "Could a black magician possibly be more cliché?"

"I heard that," said the man in a deep, cavernous voice. "I came first. The cliché came after."

"Silly me," said Sally.

Ignoring her, the magician approached the tea service, looked around it, possibly for trip wires and the like, then attempted to lift the silver setting off the stone. Failing in this, he stood up straight and boomed, "Odds Bodkins!"

"At your service," said Odds, stepping out from the trees after cautioning the others to remain hidden.

"It's been a while since we last met," said the magician in black.

"A couple hundred years," Odds suggested. "Hardly long enough."

The magician in black harrumphed. "You beat me here. Why didn't you just kill the Fairy and take the tea service?"

"Because unlike you," replied Odds, "I have honor and a conscience. Rumor has it that you also once had those attributes."

The black magician let out a villainous laugh. "Such attributes are for the weak. I have surpassed such needs."

From the trees Sally said, "More source material for that cliché."

Anger overtook the black magician's face, but Odds quickly diffused the moment. "We are going to play this auction fair and square," he said. "The tea service goes to the highest bidder and the rest of us go home."

The black magician stared at him. "Are you mad?"

"That has been suggested on occasion," Odds admitted. "But I do feel quite sane."

One by one, additional magicians appeared about the glade, eying each other warily and exchanging barbs. Odds rejoined his friends in the trees as the new arrivals attempted to walk off with the tea service and continued bickering with each other. Joan was surprised to see that not all of them looked like villains.

"It is about time the others began showing up," Odds told her. "Any longer and Bart and I would have been duking it out."

"Black Bart?" said Sally, suppressing a giggle.

"I'm the original!" Bart shouted from the growing hubbub of black magicians.

"Should we start the auction?" Joan asked. "It's turning into a mob out there." Indeed, about twenty magicians now stood among the standing stones. Shouting at each other and waving fists.

"A few more need to arrive," said Odds. "Until they do, I shall go out there and keep things cordial." The little man left the trees and worked his way to the center of the standing stones. He put one foot on the edge of the stone that held the tea service hostage and said in a loud voice, "I have not seen this many rats since the black plague hit London."

The shouting stopped. Then a man dressed all in green and with a scar down his cheek laughed. Soon they were all laughing.

"I should have known you'd be at the bottom of this, Bodkins," said the magician in green. "None of the rest of us would be so stupid as to gather so many of us in one place."

"Is that flattery I hear?" asked Odds.

"No," said the man in green.

Odds shook his head. "'Tis a sad thing. Now, on to business. I think most of us are here."

"I thought this was the Fey's auction?" Bart demanded.

"Yeah," called others among the magicians. "Bring out the Fey!"

"Very well," said Odds. "This is Sally's auction. But let me warn you, if anything should happen to the young lady, I will be very, very angry."

"No problem," said the magician in green. "None of us will hurt her during the auction."

He said nothing about *after* the auction, Joan noticed.

Hesitantly, Sally moved out of the trees and stood near one of the outermost standing stones. "Do—do I hear one pot?" she asked.

"One *pot*?" asked Bart.

"Of gold," said Odds. "She is Fey."

Bart sighed. "Fine. I bid ten pots of gold."

· 8 ·

Tempest In A Tea Cup

The bids escalated rapidly as one magician after another called out: "Twenty pots", "Thirty", "Thirty-one." This last bid from a skinny magician who hadn't quite figured out the lay of the land. "Forty pots."

Joan wanted to ask Patrick if he thought the magicians could conjure gold out of thin air, but didn't want to speak since Black Bart, at least, could hear whispers.

Her question was answered when the magician in green said, "What are you up to, Odds? All of us here can pull gold out of thin air. This bidding will go on forever."

"Not forever," said Odds. "Just how much energy are you willing to expend summoning your gold? Even magic is finite. By the way I bid fifty pots."

"But we all have roughly equal magic," said Bart. "Sixty pots."

"And how much magic will you have left after conjuring up Fort Knox," responded Odds. "One hundred pots."

The bidding rose more cautiously after that.

When the bidding reach 500 Joan noticed that the tea service appeared to be glowing. Perhaps it was the declining sun reflecting into her eyes, but it didn't seem that way. Patrick touched her shoulder and tipped his head toward the silver tray. He had noticed too.

One by one the magicians also seemed to notice, but instead of interfering with the bidding, the bids intensified. When a thousand pots of gold was reached, a lightning bolt struck the glade. The bidding stopped and was replaced by more lightning.

From the middle of the fray, Odds came running, grabbed Sally by the elbow, and dove into the trees near Joan and Patrick.

"I thought magicians were too civilized for this sort of thing?" Joan said to the little man.

"Everyone has their breaking point," admitted Odds.

"The glowing tea service," suggested Joan. "The magic is leaking?"

"The magicians are drawing upon it," said Odds.

"All the magicians?"

"Well, except me."

"Will they be able to hurt each other?" Joan asked.

"Tricking them into hurting each other was not my plan."

"What is your plan?"

"Would you be so kind as to give me your protection?" Odds asked.

"If you feel you need it." Joan dug the little bag of dirt out of her jacket and handed it to the magician.

Odds immediately ran out into the clearing and positioned himself behind one of the standing stones. Lightning flew all around him gouging great holes in the earth. Each blast was accompanied by a sound not unlike the clash of cymbals. The magicians flitted about the clearing to avoid the lightning, but some strikes came close, with a few actually hitting one or more of the dark men. Instead of being incinerated as Joan expected, the magicians merely shouted angrily and called down more lightning. It was madness.

Suddenly Odds slipped from behind the standing stone, lobbed the bag of dirt like a hand grenade, and ducked back behind the tall stone.

The resulting explosion blinded Joan and left her ears ringing. When she could see again, the lightning war had ended and most of the magicians were lying on the scorched earth, groaning. The tea service was a slag of black metal.

Odds slipped out from behind the stone again and inspected the tea service's remains. "Well," he said, "This has turned out nicely."

Black Bart climbed to his feet. "Do you have any idea what you've done?"

"I?" said Odds. "I have done nothing. All of you, now, have destroyed the most powerful source of magic in the world."

"I think you helped," said the magician in green from where he sat on the ground slapping his left ear.

"Helped? I think he set the whole thing up," said another of the magicians.

Then one of them said, worriedly, "Merlin is sure to notice. He'll come out of retirement to find who's responsible."

"Then I suggest you start running," said Odds. "Now."

En masse, the magicians began popping out of the clearing. Bart was the last to leave. "This isn't the end," he warned.

"I look forward to seeing you again, Bart. Perhaps in another couple of hundred years?"

Bart shook his fist and vanished.

"A cliché to the end," observed Sally.

"I think Odds is becoming something of a cliché himself," said Joan. "Now that his plan has succeeded, he'll tell us how clever he is. It would have been nice to know the plan beforehand."

Odds Bodkins tossed his head sheepishly. "I was not certain that it would work. I also did not want to get your hopes up in case things went badly."

"Fine," said Joan. "So what did you do that might have gone badly?"

"I needed them all to draw upon the tea service," Odds said. "One magician, or even ten, would never get enough of its magic flowing at once."

"That explains the glowing silver," said Joan. "Why did it explode when you tossed the Fairy dirt at it?"

"Fairy dirt!" cried Sally. She glared at Odds. "You're nothing but a grave robber."

"I," said Odds, "have never been under the Hill. The Fey earth was here already. I merely used it."

"Can we move on to the explosion?" Joan asked.

"It is simple," said Odds. "When the protection came in contact with the silver, it cut off the flow of magic. But by then the flow had risen to a flood. The magic hit a wall and bounced inwards. Imagine all those lightning bolts going off inside a teacup? The weakening silver couldn't contain all that magical energy in motion and it exploded."

"So the magic is gone?" asked Patrick.

"*You* could say that," said Odds. "But as *I* keep saying, you cannot destroy magic. You can only change its state. However, the magic is no longer in the silver and the tea service is now worthless."

"So where did the magic go?" asked Joan.

Odds raised his arms and turned in a circle. "It is all around us. Cast to the four winds. Eventually it will permeate everything and everyone." He smiled. "Things may even get interesting.

"The important thing is that we magicians no longer have a source of magic to draw upon. We shall have to make do with what we can draw from within ourselves."

"Aren't you afraid of Merlin?" asked Sally.

Odds looked at her. "What do you mean?"

"The other magicians all fled. They seemed concerned that Merlin might find them and blame them for destroying the tea service."

"And well they should be afraid," said Odds. "Merlin is the great magician who taught them how to be magicians. They have always been afraid that Merlin may undo them."

"But you're not?"

The little man slumped his shoulders. "They all knew Merlin from before he poured much of his magic into the tea service. They have no idea that Merlin is now no more powerful than they themselves." He frowned. "You should keep that tidbit to yourselves, by the way. Things could get dodgy if the black magicians ever find out."

"So how do you know this?" asked Patrick.

"Odds Bodkins knows many things," said Odds.

"You are not Odds Bodkins," said Joan.

Odds looked at her, startled. "What do you mean I am not Odds Bodkins? I should know who I am."

"You are Merlin," accused Joan. "You look different, and are shorter than the Merlin they knew," she said, remembering the marble Merlin statue from the auction. "But you are so unlike the other magicians that you must be him. And you seem to know Merlin as only Merlin could."

Odds ground his teeth and clenched his fists. "200 years!" he cried. "200 hundred years I have kept my secret, and now here I am, exposed. Gods and fishes!"

"Your secret is safe with us," Patrick said.

"It is not you I am worried about." He looked pointedly at Sally.

"What? Me? I didn't hear anything. My ears are still ringing from the explosion." Sally stuck fingers in her ears. "La la la la la...."

"A pot of gold a year," grumbled Merlin. "To keep my secret."

"Now *that* I heard," said Sally. "Deal."

"But why?" asked Joan. "Why did you start the magic school in the first place?"

"Why does anyone do anything?" Merlin demanded. "For companionship. For hundreds of years I was the only magician in the world. A fellow gets lonely. And here all these people were walking around with the potential to be great magicians if only they knew how. How could I not teach them? Then there would be others like me." He lowered his face. "I had hoped to find a friend."

"I'll be your friend," said Sally.

Merlin wagged his head. "The last Fey I befriended left me trapped in a cave for 300 years."

"How did a Fey manage that?" asked Joan, since earlier Merlin had told her the Fey were mostly powerless in this world.

Merlin's face reddened. "I was younger then. And the world was more complicated."

"Hey," said Sally. "I style hair and sing karaoke. Trapping people inside caves isn't my thing."

Merlin appraised Sally, as if seeing her for the first time. Then he wrapped his arm around her shoulder, which was no mean trick considering Sally stood a foot and a half taller than the magician. "Tell me," he said "about this... Kar-a-oke. It sounds most intriguing."

· δ ·

A New Room With A New View

The house Joan and Patrick settled on turned out not to be a house, but a condominium. Neither of them had ever lived in an apartment and both looked forward to the adventure of adjusting their life style.

"Are you still okay with the location?" Patrick asked as they stood on the balcony looking out over the city.

The apartment was on the top floor of a new tower that had been built on Macleod Trail just south of downtown. All of the apartments had been sold pre-construction but, through his office, Patrick had managed to snap up a defaulted contract.

"Of course I'm okay with the location," said Joan. "What's not to like?"

The view, she had to admit was beautiful. Unlike the Hyatt, it did not look out over downtown, but instead looked south toward the Stampede and Exhibition grounds where Joan could see the tops of Ferris wheels that in a few weeks would be lighted and turning as the Calgary Stampede got under way. The balcony also looked west toward the Rocky Mountains, where several peaks were still tipped with snow despite the advent of summer. Below the mountains stretched the Beltline district where Joan could see transients lined up outside the Mustard Seed Mission waiting for handouts and employers seeking day laborers.

"I like this location because I can walk to work," Patrick said. "But what's the attraction for you? You hate downtown."

Joan turned to face her husband. "I don't *hate* downtown. I have lived in fear of downtown. That's an entirely different thing. And I'm looking forward to confronting those fears."

"If you're sure…"

"Patrick, I have never been more sure of anything. Of course, I reserve the right to change my mind."

Patrick chuckled. "Nothing wrong with a change of mind. But what are you going to do with yourself without a yard to tend?"

"I was thinking," she said, turning to look out over the Beltline, "of volunteering some hours at the Mustard Seed."

"More fear-fighting?" asked Patrick, smiling.

"For now," said Joan. "I may feel different tomorrow."

Patrick took her hand and led Joan indoors. "And what do you feel like for dinner. Pizza? We haven't sent out for pizza in years."

"That would be nice," said Joan. "But I thought we might go to a pub."

"A pub?" said Patrick, doubtfully. "I go to pubs all the time with clients. I thought we were going to try different things."

"This is a special pub," said Joan. "It's Sally's karaoke pub. She's taking Odds there tonight and he has promised to sing."

"That's… different," Patrick agreed. "She's not… you're not… expecting *me* to sing, are you?"

Joan smiled. "Baby steps, darling. Baby steps."

· δ ·

Our titles are available at major book stores
and local independent resellers who support
Science Fiction and Fantasy readers like you.

EDGE Science Fiction
and Fantasy Publishing

www.edgewebsite.com

Our titles are available at major book stores and local independent resellers who support Science Fiction and Fantasy readers like you.

Alphanauts by J. Brian Clarke (tp) - ISBN: 978-1-894063-14-2
Apparition Trail, The by Lisa Smedman (tp) - ISBN: 978-1-894063-22-7
As Fate Decrees by Denysé Bridger (tp) - ISBN: 978-1-894063-41-8

Black Chalice, The by Marie Jakober (hb) - ISBN: 978-1-894063-00-7
Blue Apes by Phyllis Gotlieb (pb) - ISBN: 978-1-895836-13-4
Blue Apes by Phyllis Gotlieb (hb) - ISBN: 978-1-895836-14-1
Braided Path, The by Donna Glee Williams (tp) - ISBN: 978-1-77053-058-4

Captives by Barbara Galler-Smith and Josh Langston (tp)
   - ISBN: 978-1-894063-53-1
Children of Atwar, The by Heather Spears (pb) - ISBN: 978-0-88878-335-6
Chilling Tales: Evil Did I Dwell; Lewd I Did Live edited by Michael Kelly (tp)
   - ISBN: 978-1-894063-52-4
Chilling Tales: In Words, Alas, Drown I edited by Michael Kelly (tp)
   - ISBN: 978-1-77053-024-9
Cinco de Mayo by Michael J. Martineck (tp) - ISBN: 978-1-894063-39-5
Cinkarion - The Heart of Fire (Part Two of The Chronicles of the Karionin)
   by J. A. Cullum - (tp) - ISBN: 978-1-894063-21-0
Circle Tide by Rebecca K. Rowe (tp) - ISBN: 978-1-894063-59-3
Clan of the Dung-Sniffers by Lee Danielle Hubbard (tp) - ISBN: 978-1-894063-05-0
Claus Effect, The by David Nickle & Karl Schroeder (pb) - ISBN: 978-1-895836-34-9
Claus Effect, The by David Nickle & Karl Schroeder (hb) - ISBN: 978-1-895836-35-6
Clockwork Heart by Dru Pagliassotti (tp) - ISBN: 978-1-77053-026-3
Clockwork Lies: Iron Wind by Dru Pagliassotti (tp) - ISBN: 978-1-77053-050-8
Clockwork Secrets: Heavy Fire by Dru Pagliassotti (tp) - ISBN: 978-1-77053-054-6

Danse Macabre: Close Encounters With the Reaper edited by Nancy Kilpatrick (tp)
   - ISBN: 978-1-894063-96-8
Dark Earth Dreams by Candas Dorsey & Roger Deegan (Audio CD with Booklet)
   - ISBN: 978-1-895836-05-9
Darkness of the God (Children of the Panther Part Two)
   by Amber Hayward (tp) - ISBN: 978-1-894063-44-9
Demon Left Behind, The by Marie Jakober (tp) - ISBN: 978-1-894063-49-4
Distant Signals by Andrew Weiner (tp) - ISBN: 978-0-88878-284-7
Dreams of an Unseen Planet by Teresa Plowright (tp) - ISBN: 978-0-88878-282-3
Dreams of the Sea (Part 1 of Tyranaël) by Élisabeth Vonarburg (tp)
   - ISBN: 978-1-895836-96-7
Dreams of the Sea (Part 1 of Tyranaël) by Élisabeth Vonarburg (hb)
   - ISBN: 978-1-895836-98-1
Druids by Barbara Galler-Smith and Josh Langston (tp)
   - ISBN: 978-1-894063-29-6

Eclipse by K. A. Bedford (tp) - ISBN: 978-1-894063-30-2
Elements by Suzanne Church (tp) - ISBN: 978-1-77053-042-3
Even The Stones by Marie Jakober (tp) - ISBN: 978-1-894063-18-0
Evolve: Vampire Stories of the New Undead edited by Nancy Kilpatrick (tp)
   - ISBN: 978-1-894063-33-3

Evolve Two: Vampire Stories of the Future Undead edited by Nancy Kilpatrick (tp)
 -ISBN: 978-1-894063-62-3
Expiration Date edited by Nancy Kilpatrick (tp) - ISBN: 978-1-77053-062-1

Fires of the Kindred by Robin Skelton (tp) - ISBN: 978-0-88878-271-7
Forbidden Cargo by Rebecca Rowe (tp) - ISBN: 978-1-894063-16-6

Game of Perfection, A (Part 2 of Tyranaël) by Élisabeth Vonarburg (tp)
 - ISBN: 978-1-894063-32-6
Gaslight Arcanum: Uncanny Tales of Sherlock Holmes
 edited by Jeff Campbell & Charles Prepolec (tp)
 - ISBN: 978-1-8964063-60-9
Gaslight Grimoire: Fantastic Tales of Sherlock Holmes
 edited by Jeff Campbell & Charles Prepolec (tp)
 - ISBN: 978-1-8964063-17-3
Gaslight Grotesque: Nightmare Tales of Sherlock Holmes
 edited by Jeff Campbell & Charles Prepolec (tp)
 - ISBN: 978-1-8964063-31-9

Green Music by Ursula Pflug (tp) - ISBN: 978-1-895836-75-2
Green Music by Ursula Pflug (hb) - ISBN: 978-1-895836-77-6

Healer, The (Children of the Panther Part One) by Amber Hayward (tp)
 - ISBN: 978-1-895836-89-9
Healer, The (Children of the Panther Part One) by Amber Hayward (hb)
 - ISBN: 978-1-895836-91-2
Hell Can Wait by Theodore Judson (tp) - ISBN: 978-1-978-1-894063-23-4
Hounds of Ash and other tales of Fool Wolf, The by Greg Keyes (tp)
 - ISBN: 978-1-894063-09-8
Hydrogen Steel by K. A. Bedford (tp) - ISBN: 978-1-894063-20-3

i-ROBOT Poetry by Jason Christie (tp) - ISBN: 978-1-894063-24-1
Immortal Quest by Alexandra MacKenzie (tp) - ISBN: 978-1-894063-46-3

Jackal Bird by Michael Barley (pb) - ISBN: 978-1-895836-07-3
Jackal Bird by Michael Barley (hb) - ISBN: 978-1-895836-11-0
JEMMA7729 by Phoebe Wray (tp) - ISBN: 978-1-894063-40-1

Keaen by Till Noever (tp) - ISBN: 978-1-894063-08-1
Keeper's Child by Leslie Davis (tp) - ISBN: 978-1-894063-01-2

Land/Space edited by Candas Jane Dorsey and Judy McCrosky (tp)
 - ISBN: 978-1-895836-90-5
Land/Space edited by Candas Jane Dorsey and Judy McCrosky (hb)
 - ISBN: 978-1-895836-92-9
Lyskarion: The Song of the Wind (Part One of The Chronicles of the Karionin)
 by J.A. Cullum (tp) - ISBN: 978-1-894063-02-9

Machine Sex and other stories by Candas Jane Dorsey (tp)
 - ISBN: 978-0-88878-278-6
Maërlande Chronicles, The by Élisabeth Vonarburg (pb)
 - ISBN: 978-0-88878-294-6
Milkman, The by Michael J. Martineck (tp) - ISBN: 978-0-77053-060-7
Moonfall by Heather Spears (pb) - ISBN: 978-0-88878-306-6

Necromancer Candle, The by Randy McCharles (tp) - ISBN: 978-1-77053-066-9

Of Wind and Sand by Sylvie Bérard (translated by Sheryl Curtis) (tp)
- ISBN: 978-1-894063-19-7
On Spec: The First Five Years edited by On Spec (pb)
- ISBN: 978-1-895836-08-0
On Spec: The First Five Years edited by On Spec (hb)
- ISBN: 978-1-895836-12-7
Orbital Burn by K. A. Bedford (tp) - ISBN: 978-1-894063-10-4
Orbital Burn by K. A. Bedford (hb) - ISBN: 978-1-894063-12-8

Pallahaxi Tide by Michael Coney (pb) - ISBN: 978-0-88878-293-9
Paradox Resolution by K. A. Bedford (tp) - ISBN:978-1-894063-88-3
Passion Play by Sean Stewart (pb) - ISBN: 978-0-88878-314-1
Petrified World (Determine Your Destiny #1) by Piotr Brynczka (pb)
- ISBN: 978-1-894063-11-1
Plague Saint, The by Rita Donovan (tp) - ISBN: 978-1-895836-28-8
Plague Saint, The by Rita Donovan (hb) - ISBN: 978-1-895836-29-5
Pock's World by Dave Duncan (tp) - ISBN: 978-1-894063-47-0
Puzzle Box, The by Randy McCharles, Billie Millholland, Eileen Bell, and Ryan McFadden (tp) - ISBN: 978-1-77053-040-9

Reluctant Voyagers by Élisabeth Vonarburg (pb) - ISBN: 978-1-895836-09-7
Reluctant Voyagers by Élisabeth Vonarburg (hb) - ISBN: 978-1-895836-15-8
Resisting Adonis by Timothy J. Anderson (tp) - ISBN: 978-1-895836-84-4
Resisting Adonis by Timothy J. Anderson (hb) - ISBN: 978-1-895836-83-7
Rigor Amortis edited by Jaym Gates and Erika Holt (tp)
- ISBN: 978-1-894063-63-0

Shadow Academy, The by Adrian Cole (tp) - ISBN: 978-1-77053-064-5
Silent City, The by Élisabeth Vonarburg (tp) - ISBN: 978-1-894063-07-4
Slow Engines of Time, The by Élisabeth Vonarburg (tp)
- ISBN: 978-1-895836-30-1
Slow Engines of Time, The by Élisabeth Vonarburg (hb)
- ISBN: 978-1-895836-31-8
Stealing Magic by Tanya Huff (tp) - ISBN: 978-1-894063-34-0
Stolen Children (Children of the Panther Part Three)
by Amber Hayward (tp) - ISBN: 978-1-894063-66-1
Strange Attractors by Tom Henighan (pb) - ISBN: 978-0-88878-312-7

Taming, The by Heather Spears (pb) - ISBN: 978-1-895836-23-3
Taming, The by Heather Spears (hb) - ISBN: 978-1-895836-24-0
Technicolor Ultra Mall by Ryan Oakley (tp) - ISBN: 978-1-894063-54-8
Ten Monkeys, Ten Minutes by Peter Watts (tp) - ISBN: 978-1-895836-74-5
Ten Monkeys, Ten Minutes by Peter Watts (hb) - ISBN: 978-1-895836-76-9
Tesseracts 1 edited by Judith Merril (pb) - ISBN: 978-0-88878-279-3
Tesseracts 2 edited by Phyllis Gotlieb & Douglas Barbour (pb)
- ISBN: 978-0-88878-270-0
Tesseracts 3 edited by Candas Jane Dorsey & Gerry Truscott (pb)
- ISBN: 978-0-88878-290-8
Tesseracts 4 edited by Lorna Toolis & Michael Skeet (pb)
- ISBN: 978-0-88878-322-6
Tesseracts 5 edited by Robert Runté & Yves Maynard (pb)
- ISBN: 978-1-895836-25-7

Tesseracts 5 edited by Robert Runté & Yves Maynard (hb)
- ISBN: 978-1-895836-26-4
Tesseracts 6 edited by Robert J. Sawyer & Carolyn Clink (pb)
- ISBN: 978-1-895836-32-5
Tesseracts 6 edited by Robert J. Sawyer & Carolyn Clink (hb)
- ISBN: 978-1-895836-33-2
Tesseracts 7 edited by Paula Johanson & Jean-Louis Trudel (tp)
- ISBN: 978-1-895836-58-5
Tesseracts 7 edited by Paula Johanson & Jean-Louis Trudel (hb)
- ISBN: 978-1-895836-59-2
Tesseracts 8 edited by John Clute & Candas Jane Dorsey (tp)
- ISBN: 978-1-895836-61-5
Tesseracts 8 edited by John Clute & Candas Jane Dorsey (hb)
- ISBN: 978-1-895836-62-2
Tesseracts Nine edited by Nalo Hopkinson and Geoff Ryman (tp)
- ISBN: 978-1-894063-26-5
Tesseracts Ten: A Celebration of New Canadian Specuative Fiction
edited by Robert Charles Wilson and Edo van Belkom (tp)
- ISBN: 978-1-894063-36-4
Tesseracts Eleven: Amazing Canadian Speulative Fiction
edited by Cory Doctorow and Holly Phillips (tp)
- ISBN: 978-1-894063-03-6
Tesseracts Twelve: New Novellas of Canadian Fantastic Fiction
edited by Claude Lalumière (tp)
- ISBN: 978-1-894063-15-9
Tesseracts Thirteen: Chilling Tales from the Great White North
edited by Nancy Kilpatrick and David Morrell (tp)
- ISBN: 978-1-894063-25-8
Tesseracts 14: Strange Canadian Stories
edited by John Robert Colombo and Brett Alexander Savory (tp)
- ISBN: 978-1-894063-37-1
Tesseracts Fifteen: A Case of Quite Curious Tales
edited by Julie Czerneda and Susan MacGregor (tp)
- ISBN: 978-1-894063-58-6
Tesseracts Sixteen: Parnassus Unbound edited by Mark Leslie (tp)
- ISBN: 978-1-894063-92-0
Tesseracts Seventeen: Speculating Canada from Coast to Coast to Coast
edited by Colleen Anderson and Steve Vernon (tp) -ISBN: 978-1-77053-044-7
Tesseracts Eighteen: Wrestling With Gods
edited by Liana K and Jerome Stueart (tp) - ISBN: 978-1-77053-068-3
Tesseracts Q edited by Élisabeth Vonarburg and Jane Brierley (pb)
- ISBN: 978-1-895836-21-9
Tesseracts Q edited by Élisabeth Vonarburg and Jane Brierley (hb)
- ISBN: 978-1-895836-22-6
Those Who Fight Monsters: Tales of Occult Detectives
edited by Justin Gustainis (pb) - ISBN: 978-1-894063-48-7
Time Machines Repaired Whie-U-Wait by K. A. Bedford (tp)
- ISBN: 978-1-894063-42-5
Trillionist, The by Sagan Jeffries (tp) -ISBN: 978-1-894063-98-2

Vampyric Variations by Nancy Kilpatrick (tp)- ISBN: 978-1-894063-94-4
Vyrkarion: The Talisman of Anor (Part Three of The Chronicles of the Karionin)
by J. A. Cullum (tp) ISBN: 978-1-77053-028-7

Urban Green Man edited by Adria Laycraft and Janice Blaine (tp)
-ISBN: 978-1-77053-038-6

Warriors by Barbara Galler-Smith and Josh Langston (tp)
-ISBN: 978-1-77053-030-0
Wildcatter by Dave Duncan (tp) - ISBN: 978-1-894063-90-6